For Mum and Dad

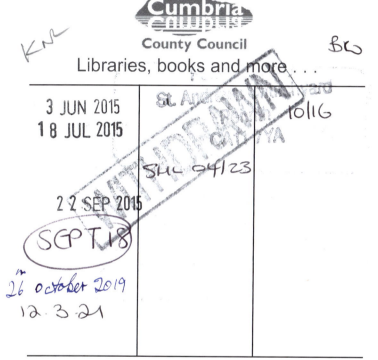

First edition published 2012
2QT Limited (Publishing)
Burton In Kendal
Cumbria LA6 1NJ
www.2qt.co.uk

Cover design
Dale Rennard

Cover Photograph Copyright Dominic and Robyn Quantrill

Thanks to Dominic and Robyn Quantrill for the cover photograph and
to 2QT Publishing for all their help in the production of the book.

Autumn Leaves is a work of fiction and any resemblance to any person
living or dead is purely coincidental

Printed in Great Britain by
Lightning Source UK

A CIP catalogue record for this book is available
from the British Library
ISBN 978-1-908098-44-3

Chapter One

Autumn Leaves

Autumn leaves me all alone
Robbed of my love, my heart is torn...

Wilf sat against the weathered rotting gateway, watching the farmers collecting the last of the straw bales with the huge mechanical aids. How times had changed since he was first a part of this very same field's workforce.

He gazed across the expanse of stubble. The field had been enlarged five years ago when young Jim took over the farm from Mr Potter. Wilf, like most of the villagers, had always called him 'Mr Potter', even though he had known and worked for him for many years. Even his wife Rose had referred to him as 'Mr Potter' in his absence.

Mr Potter had died leaving his son Jim, who was full of new ideas, to take over the farm. His short-lived enthusiasm for making the farm more profitable had proved to be quite a challenge. Hedges had been ripped out here and there and ditches filled in. The fields still seemed to be cowering from the vegetation's mechanical rape and permanent disfigurement, left exposed now to the bite of the cold north winds. Their character had been irreversibly erased apart from this old gate, half forgotten and partially hidden by the long grass, ox-eye daisies and random poppies which entwined the rotting wood.

This was the very gateway where Wilf had first dared to stop and gently, though rather clumsily, kiss Elizabeth on the way back from the village dance. The evening had been perfect. They had danced and danced until Elizabeth finally asked to be walked home, her feet rather sore, having borrowed her younger sister's shoes for the evening. She had felt so excited that evening, wearing the poppy-print dress her aunt had so cleverly made for her from one of her own dresses. Aunt May was rather a large lady, so there had been plenty of fabric to create the flowing, full-skirted frock. She had borrowed some beads from Aunt May and wore some clip-on earrings which had been her mother's.

Elizabeth looked rather shy as she sat in the corner of the village hall with her cousins, fingering the red beads around her neck. The group of girls giggled nervously when the farm workers approached to request a partner for the next dance.

The village held dances, usually every month, and they were well attended. People came from all the neighbouring villages to let their hair down and enjoy the live bands. Some from further afield shared transport to the dance. A local farmer's cattle truck was sometimes used to collect ten or more dancers! The farmer allowed his truck to be used in this way as he knew that his men would clean it thoroughly before they would use this means of transport, so the vehicle was well maintained!

Elizabeth had the bluest eyes Wilf had ever seen. He could see them now, as he stared dreamily towards the infinite horizon of the East Anglian landscape beneath the clear blue sky. The air was warm and the familiar scent of straw greeted his senses like an old friend. Wilf was sitting on rough stubble in the gateway and yet he could have been in a comfortable armchair, for he gained great comfort from this place where he felt at home and where he could relive happy memories. This gateway had become theirs to sit and talk for hours sometimes. It was so peaceful in the long summer evenings and rarely did they see anyone else passing on the quiet country road; such a contrast to today, with the tractors coming and going and the intrusive sound of a radio, when the tractor cab opened momentarily. This gateway was also where Wilf had asked Elizabeth to marry him and she had said 'yes' without a moment's hesitation. Elizabeth had often joked that they should have a little plaque mounted on the gate commemorating the place of marriage proposal. They had only known each other for four months but they knew they had to be together.

Wilf glanced at the gateway and wondered how much longer it might remain here. No doubt a metal gate would be substituted for it soon and the old gate cast aside and more of his precious memories would be further diluted. He might be thought sentimental if he asked for the gate, but he could find space for it at the bottom of his garden next to the bench where he could then sit and relive his memories whenever he wished.

Wilf was stirred from his dreaming as one of the tractors approached, now that 'all had been safely gathered in'. He was thinking of the popular harvest hymn sung at church last Sunday and found himself humming the tune. The trailer had been loaded once more with straw bales. It took great skill to stack it properly to prevent bales being lost on the journey back to the farmyard. Wilf remembered well the hard work involved, tossing straw bales with pitchforks up to the person stacking them back at the farmyard. More machinery, such as elevators, was being used now, but in his day it was tiring work, which 'med yer sweat like a pig' according to Bill, who also worked on the Potter's farm.

Wilf waved to Jim who was driving the tractor; Jim, who was unaware of the significance of his gateway's history as he steered the tractor and trailer cautiously through it.

Wilf had become a little stiff now from sitting too long and cursed his right hip, which was painful at times. He might take an aspirin later if it didn't settle down.

He stood up slowly, straightening his cap which covered the little hair he still had on his almost bald head, and collected his old black bicycle from the hedge. He then set off for his daily visit to the churchyard, his trouser legs neatly tucked into cycle clips, a bunch of yellow chrysanthemums tucked into the old pannier bag attached to his bicycle. He made the daily visit to the churchyard to tend the grave of his love. He felt unable to break this daily ritual, which had started nearly five years ago when Elizabeth had been cruelly snatched from his life. She had been a wonderful wife and they had been so happy together. They had never imagined life without one another.

There had been little warning that Elizabeth had been ill. Wilf had come home from the farm as usual, setting down the enamel churn containing fresh creamy milk on the kitchen sink drainer. He always held the handle of the small churn carefully on the handlebars of his bicycle as he cycled home, eagerly awaiting his well-earned breakfast. It was usually eight o'clock when he arrived back from milking the cows. That morning he found the wooden kitchen table bare. The red gingham tablecloth that normally covered it at meal times was still neatly folded in the drawer and the usual posy of fresh flowers from the garden had not been picked. Wilf's heart started to pound madly, the rest of his body unable to accompany this unknown rhythm gathering pace and strength inside him.

He hurried up the steep narrow stairs and found his sweetheart, *his* Elizabeth, still in bed in their little farm cottage. The bedroom window had been pushed open wide and the net curtains were gently caressing the window frame. Wilf stood over Elizabeth. He felt as though he had been paralysed and could not move for a minute or two. He sensed the gravity of what his eyes were seeing. Elizabeth was dead. Her piercing blue eyes were now distant, staring at the ceiling, her face now pale and clammy.

Wilf knew it was too late, but desperately felt for a pulse at Elizabeth's neck, not wanting to believe the cruel evidence he saw before him. Her skin felt cool and moist. He could feel nothing but wasn't sure if he was missing her pulse because his own was throbbing deafeningly through his body. He had once seen a film at the cinema in which the doctor, the hero in the film, felt for a pulse in a woman's neck and subsequently gave her life-saving resuscitation.

Wilf sank helplessly to his knees, sobbing and crying out loud that God could not do this to him. Then he glanced at his watch, wondering if the doctor would still be at home, and hurried out of the cottage. He jumped on to his bicycle and peddled as fast as he could to the doctor's house hoping that he would become a hero shortly.

Dr Stimpson was about to set off for his morning surgery at Coddleton, three miles further down the road. Wilf had not thought of using the public telephone, which was only about a hundred yards from the cottage, to call an ambulance. He still did not like using the 'modern paraphernalia' as he referred to all such bits of equipment which most villagers now took for granted. He had once tried to telephone the surgery from the telephone box and had got an answerphone. It had made him very uneasy, talking to a machine and waiting for a reply which never came.

Dr Stimpson, smartly dressed in his checked jacket, brown trousers, white shirt and striped woollen tie, was just locking his front door when he saw Wilf come into his driveway, his bicycle skidding on the gravel as he stopped in front of him. He saw Wilf's grief-stricken face and guessed it must be Elizabeth who had taken ill.

Wilf, still breathless, got into the doctor's sports car and started to blurt out how he had found his wife, as they hurriedly drove the short distance back to the cottage. He managed to get his breath back as they pulled up outside their cottage. Wilf struggled to get out of the low car seat, wriggling and kicking his legs like an upturned insect until he was upright again, and hurried inside the cottage. Dr Stimpson grabbed his doctor's bag from his car boot and followed Wilf inside.

The cottage door was wide open as Wilf had left it in his hasty departure. The mail had just been delivered and was strewn over the doormat. More chances to win a fortune, no doubt! The postman's whistling and cheery shout of 'Morning 'lizabeth,' had not been heard this morning. Tiger, Elizabeth's ginger cat, was waiting expectantly in the doorway wondering why she hadn't been fed. Her purrs were ignored as Wilf brushed her aside as he raced upstairs, leading the way for the doctor.

Dr Stimpson confirmed gently that Elizabeth was dead and there was no hope of trying to revive her. Wilf had been about to ask if there was anything the doctor could do but the doctor had anticipated his thoughts. Dr Stimpson thought she had probably had a heart attack in the early hours of the morning.

Wilf began sobbing again and started to blame himself for her death. Elizabeth had only visited the surgery the week before with complaints of chest pain which had just begun to trouble her. She had been given some little tablets to put under her tongue if the angina reoccurred, and was due to attend the local hospital the following week for some more tests. She had played down her symptoms and had told Wilf that it was nothing serious, probably just indigestion. 'That there young doctor needs to study his books a bit more!' she had joked. There was nothing wrong with her, she had tried to reassure Wilf.

He should have known Elizabeth would cover up her

problems. She never complained of any ailments and very rarely gave in to a heavy cold or even flu. She didn't believe in taking to her bed, saying the fresh air in the garden was the best treatment for getting over a little bit of a cold. Wilf looked down at his wife and wished that a miracle would happen. 'Are yew *sure* doctor that... yew know?'

'I'm sure Wilf... and I'm very sorry,' replied Dr Stimpson quietly but firmly, wishing that the truth could be less painful. He put his stethoscope back in his black leather doctor's bag, having confirmed there was no heartbeat present. He noticed Elizabeth's fingers were mottled and her skin cool and moist when he had examined her.

'Is there anyone you want to be informed to come here, Wilf, to be with you?' he enquired, after thinking what he should do next and conscious that he would be late for his surgery.

'Oh... Kathleen, Doctor... yes, Elizabeth's sister.'

'You don't have a telephone, do you, Wilf?'

'No, that I don't, Doctor.'

'Would you like me to call her, Wilf?'

'If yew would, Doctor, that would be helpful, thank yer kindly. Dew yew know her number? I can't think what it is.'

'We will have it at the surgery.'

'Right yew are.'

'Sorry, Wilf, I will have to get off to surgery now, but I will try to sort the death certificate out once I have spoken to the coroner. However, I think the coroner will probably request that a post-mortem is done in view of Elizabeth's sudden death.'

'Oh I see. Oh dear... poor Elizabeth!'

'Here Wilf, there's a sleeping tablet I've put in this envelope, just in case you need something to help you sleep tonight.'

'Right oh. Yew'll ring Kathleen then won't yew, doctor?'

'Yes of course... Goodbye, Wilf, and I'm very sorry this

has happened.'

'Good-bye, Doctor.'

Wilf had not been able to say goodbye to Elizabeth. He had made a cup of tea and left that morning at six thirty a.m., creeping out of the house so as not to wake her. It had been a nice, bright, early autumn morning and Wilf had donned his checked wool cap and set off on his bicycle for the short distance to the farm to greet the cows awaiting his arrival as usual. The creatures were well-used to the routine in the milking-parlour and the usual beasts were at the head of the queue, waiting to offload their milk.

Dr Stimpson left Wilf's cottage. He hurried back to the surgery, which would now be full of his patients waiting for his advice and prescriptions. He would have to greet them all with his warm smile and yet his day had just started with a death, probably another victim of coronary heart disease, another statistic.

His staff greeted him with concern as he was unusually late. He explained the reason for his tardiness and Sally, one of the reception staff, went to the small kitchen to get him a strong coffee. Dr Stimpson asked for Kathleen Berry's medical notes and was relieved to find her telephone number written on the front of them. He then telephoned Kathleen, Elizabeth's sister, and broke the sad news as gently as he could. He would have liked to call at her house on his way to the surgery but he was already late and the waiting room was full as he had expected.

His first customer would have to be old Bill Dobson, who asked the doctor if he had slept in that morning! Dr Stimpson smiled weakly and changed the subject to Bill's symptoms. Bill tugged at his old grey sweater with patched elbows, darned with different coloured wool, which was half tucked into an old pair of black trousers, secured with red baling twine. He said he wanted, 'something doin' about 'this her' swellin' nare me privates... tha's giving me a bit a jip at times.' Dr Stimpson, still a little distracted from the sad start to his day, was roused from his thoughts and examined Bill's large inguinal hernia, which was beginning to trouble him.

Dr Stimpson had to smile to himself, remembering how he had struggled to understand Bill's Norfolk accent when he had first consulted him. On that occasion, he had unravelled an old bit of crêpe bandage securing a piece of lint on his right leg to reveal a large, infected leg ulcer. For a moment, Simon Stimpson thought he could smell the nauseating ulcer now, as he recalled the past memorable consultation, but Bill seemed to be host to an array of different odours and he couldn't quite place the one which was prominent now as he examined him further, although there was an onion-like smell to his clothing. The district nurse had attended to the leg ulcer and finally, after two years and an ongoing battle to get Bill to comply with his advised treatment, it was almost healed.

Dr Stimpson agreed to refer Bill to Mr Bolton, a general surgeon at the local hospital. Bill said, 'He'd better git sharpenin' his knife then, doctor, haden't 'e!'

'You will need two or three months off work, Bill, after the operation to allow the wound to heal properly. You do a lot of heavy work on the farm, don't you?'

'Yis I dew, doctor, and my gardening at home an' all that I dew.'

'Well, it is important to avoid heavy work after the operation or else you could get more problems, Bill.'

'I'll hev to be wholly careful then, won't I doctor, that I will. Pr'aps yew could find me a good woman to look after me an' all!'

'Do you have any help at home, Bill? Any relatives or friends who could help you?'

'Wull, Mrs Coleman next door might be able to help, I s'pose.'

'Why don't you have a chat with her? If not, I'm sure we can arrange for a home help to come in when you come out of hospital. I'm not sure what Mr Bolton's waiting list is like now but it may be six months or so before he can operate, so if you get any severe pain from your hernia or it seems to be getting worse whilst you're waiting to be seen at the hospital, let me know right away.'

'Right yew are, doctor.'

'Your last swab that the nurse took from your leg ulcer was good … looks like that infection has cleared up now. I don't need to give you any more penicillin.'

'Yis, your nurse was right pleased with me last time she saw me, doctor. She says she's soon givin' me the sack an' all she is!'

'Well, it's taken a long time, Bill.'

'Yis, that it has, but I won't miss her nagging at me when it's finally gawn, that I won't!'

'Well you'd better be careful not to get another ulcer when it's healed. It's best to listen to nurse's advice, Bill. If you get any sores, however small, don't leave it so long before you come down and see me or the nurse. Just keep the area clean and cover it with a clean dressing. Nurse has given you some spare dressings, I believe.'

'If my mother had still bin alive, she would ha' cured it long afore with one of her poultices.'

'I never had the opportunity to meet your mother, Bill. You must miss her.'

'That I dew, doctor.'

'Don't forget to make an appointment soon to see the nurse for your tetanus booster. It's best to keep that up to date with your work at the farm and your gardening.'

'Right yew are, doctor. The nurse will look forward to sticking her needle in to my backside again no doubt! Thank yer. Cheerio.'

'Goodbye.'

* * *

Dr Stimpson finished his surgery just after eleven thirty a.m., which hadn't been as late as he had feared. Most of the symptoms brought to him that morning had been only minor problems, which were easily remedied. He often wondered how important what he wrote on the prescription actually was. Most of his patients were happy enough to leave his room with a prescription in their hands, whatever was written on it, and a diagnosis stored in their memory, ready to tell their friends or fellow passengers on the bus journey home. They would later swap stories of their various ailments with a great deal of exaggerating too, no doubt.

Sally came in to the consulting room and told Dr Stimpson that one of his patients, a Mrs Fowler, had just delivered a healthy baby boy in the maternity hospital … but only just! This was her third baby and she had gone into labour whilst out collecting apples from her orchard. Her husband was summoned and he had hurriedly taken her to hospital in one of the farm trucks with his two children in the back enjoying the thrill of their dad's crazy driving! The bumpy ride had not been an experience June Fowler would want to repeat. In fact she didn't plan on having any more children and asked if she could be sterilised in the near future.

Sally commented, 'So one goes and dies and another's born; the circle o' life carries on at Coddleton practice, eh, Doctor Stimpson?'

'Yes, you're right, Sally… nice to get some good news at the end of surgery after a bad start. Mr Fowler will be pleased he's finally got a son, no doubt. Would you get Elizabeth Ford's records out for me please?'

'I hev already, doctor. I put them in your tray there.'

'So you have, thanks, Sally. Efficient is obviously your middle name! Could you put this note regarding Sam Livingstone in the district nurse's message book, please?'

'Yes, o' cors I can, doctor.'

'There's also a referral to type to Mr Bolton here.'

'Right, doctor.'

'Oh … and would you mind getting me a ham roll from the bakery please? I think I left my sandwiches at home this morning.'

'O' cors I will, doctor. Is there anything else yew need from up the street?'

'No, I don't think so, thanks, Sally. Are there just three house calls today?'

'Yis, that's right,' replied Sally, peering at a sheet of paper from beneath a rather long fringe with the rest of her black hair pulled back in a ponytail secured with a red ribbon. 'Brenda Marshall at Freckingham has got a bad chest, her husband says. James Black just down the street is in bed. He apparently has gorn off his legs, old Mrs Black told me. She was in a terrible state when she came rushing down here this mornin' just as yew were finishing your surgery. Poor old dear! I had to git her to sit down for her to git her breath back. She says she hed a right struggle to git Mr Black back on his bed and he seems to be talking strange too, this mornin'. Then there's Barbara Newton at the far end of town, your poorly lady with cancer. Her daughter rang to say she can't get her to swallow her pills this mornin' and she seems to hev taken a turn for the worse. Here's all their notes, doctor.'

'Thanks, Sally. I'll get on with the visits after I've had a quick bite to eat. I'll have a chat with the coroner though first.'

'Right yew are, doctor. I'll hurry on then and git that there ham roll, that I will,' continued Sally. She was married to one of the farm workers on the Potter's farm. She caught the bus every day to Coddleton and enjoyed the work in the surgery. Sally had done a typing course at college when she had left school. Initially, she had found the medical jargon and terminology very difficult when typing up letters for the doctors, but after two years in the job she felt her spelling and her ability to decipher the GP's handwriting had finally been mastered.

* * *

Bill got off the bus, a little disappointed that there had been no one he could tell about his planned surgery, and walked the remaining half-mile to his home, a council bungalow in the village. He used to live in a farm worker's cottage but took the opportunity of a bungalow when one became available in the village as he had wondered how long he could manage the steep stairs in the cottage which also needed some renovation. He soon filled his new home with clutter, but claimed he had no time for housework when he had a garden to tend to. The back garden was a reasonable size but he filled it completely with a vegetable garden, digging up the neat lawn the previous bungalow occupant had maintained.

Bill put his kettle on the stove and took out a penknife from his back pocket. He opened out the blade and started to peel an apple whilst he waited for the kettle to boil. He carefully peeled the apple round from the top until he had the spiralled peel in one piece which he discarded in his compost bucket. He then cut the apple in two, leaving one half on his lap, and sliced the apple into small pieces before eating it. Once eaten, he discarded the core pieces in the compost bowl, wiped the knife on his trousers and put it back in his pocket, wondering if the surgeon, Mr Bolton, might carry his knives in his pockets too.

The kettle's whistle announced that he could make his tea and he poured the steaming water over the tea leaves in his small teapot and reached across to the sink's draining board for his stained enamel mug. His clothes airer, which was suspended from the ceiling and could be lowered down by means of a pulley and its fine rope, had his home grown strings of onions attached to it, as well as two pairs of greying underpants! Bill liked to pickle some of his onions. There were six or seven jars of his pickles in the larder. His bungalow always smelt of onions and his underwear may have too!

He poured a mug of tea, not bothering with the strainer, and was soon slurping his brew. After emitting a loud belch, he filled his pipe with tobacco and lit it, then he picked up the paper and read some of the headlines. He struggled with reading, having missed as much school as his mother would let him get away with, but he could usually make sense of most of the newspaper he bought and would never admit his difficulties to anyone. The paper had the added attraction of pictures of some scantily-clad women, which was as close as he would ever get to the opposite sex. Bill had lived with his mother until she died and had never bothered with actively looking for someone he could marry, although at times he regretted this.

After Bill had finished his tea, having refilled the mug once, he thought he would just have five minutes lie down on the threadbare settee, which had belonged to his mother. He set his pipe aside in a large ash tray, the residue of tobacco smoke now mingling with the aroma of onions in the bungalow. He loosened the baling twine securing his trousers, which felt a bit tight especially with the hernia problem, but left his boots on. He plumped up a cushion and soon fell asleep on the settee and was snoring loudly. His mother used to say that she was sure Bill could fall asleep standing up, given the chance. He had been found dozing on straw bales on a few occasions when waiting for the next tractor load of bales to arrive back at the farm. Bill was always up early though, due to his work on the farm, and latterly a nap was becoming more necessary with his advancing years.

Bill had recently grown a beard, not deliberately, but he had kept forgetting to buy some new razor blades until one day, realising he would save time doing his ablutions by not needing to shave every day, he decided to leave the grey stubble intact. The beard had been a talking point for weeks in the village, but most had now got used to his new hirsute image.

Chapter Two

Goodbyes And Regrets

The courier van delivered a parcel to Cynthia, ordered from the catalogue she used. It helped to spread the cost of bigger items she needed for the family, as she could pay off a sum each month from her bill. As well as ordering some grey school trousers for Michael, she had treated herself to some rather sexy black lacy nylon lingerie. She would wear it for her next meeting with Charles.

She cringed when she remembered the greying old white underwear she had been wearing when her unexpected romantic encounter had occurred in the guestroom at the pub. She was feeling excited about seeing him again, but nervous and guilty of course. What *was* she doing? She was married, but Robert was Robert, and their marriage had lost its spark... if it had ever had it. She felt young again with Charles and... needed... special and feminine. Charles was so gentle and considerate... yet so passionate in his lovemaking. Cynthia recalled Charles' warm muscular body against hers and his fingers caressing and exploring her body, arousing and releasing new feelings which made her heart race again, recalling them now as she sat opening the parcel in her bedroom and wondering what Charles would think of her in this underwear.

She had met Robert when she was still at school and

they had married young because it seemed the thing to do. Michael came along exactly nine months after their wedding and she was happy for a while. She had thought of leaving Robert, but Michael was still young and who else would want her? Now she had found someone without even having to look for him, someone who made her heart pound, and she realised now that she had probably never loved Robert. She had just married him because it was expected of her, perhaps. She hid the lingerie in the bottom of her drawer amongst the untidy array of ageing underwear.

The following day she met Charles, as arranged, and she hoped her headscarf disguise would be enough for her not to be noticed by anyone she might know in Coddleton. She had packed her cap and spermicide cream in the bottom of her handbag. She had been foolish to pretend she had been on the pill during her first passionate encounter with Charles, but surely not using contraception just once would be alright. How would she explain disappearing to the bathroom to fit the cap if their passion resumed today? As it happened, Charles came prepared and suggested he take the precaution of using a contraceptive, just in case… perhaps he knew she had lied about her contraception method.

They spent two or three hours together in Charles's room in the Traveller's Rest inn before Cynthia insisted she must leave to catch the bus home as Michael would be out of school soon. She used the washbasin in the room to freshen up and reapplied her lipstick. Charles gazed at her slender body, her long legs and black lingerie, and complimented her again. He tried to pull her back in to bed, but she managed to resist his advances as the sensible part of her was telling her that she must leave. She kissed him again, leaving her lipstick around his mouth, and then hurriedly finished dressing.

She left the inn, with her headscarf back in place, as discreetly as she could via a fire-escape staircase, the door to which had been left open by cleaners who were still busy on the first floor of the inn preparing the rooms for new occupants later in the day. Vacuum cleaners could be heard further down the long corridor.

Cynthia was soon out in the car park and hurried along the street. She removed her scarf and looked at her watch. She just had time to return her books to the library before going to the bus stop nearby. She handed in her books and decided to grab two more off the shelf near the librarian's desk to justify her trip to Coddleton. She had no idea what the books were or whether she had already read them, but at least they were from the 'romance' section. Cynthia suddenly felt very self-conscious, standing at the desk whilst the librarian took out the tickets from the front of the books. She thanked the librarian once they had been stamped and scuttled out of the library, wondering if her flushed looks might give away her recent passionate meeting.

The bus arrived five minutes later. Once on it, she felt on safer ground and took out her books to try and act normally, discovering that she had already read one of the titles; the other was about a politician who had an affair with his secretary.

* * *

Charles had a meeting to attend that afternoon, but would have happily postponed it if he could have done. He had no ties other than his job. He walked over to the mirror above the washbasin and smiled at the smear of lipstick on his mouth, then washed and dressed for his meeting. How long might it be before he could see Cynthia again, he wondered. He lit a cigarette and sat for a few minutes wishing Cynthia could be a permanent part of his life. What a wonderful tonic she was.

* * *

Later that evening, Cynthia was getting undressed and couldn't hide her new underwear, which she had forgotten she was still wearing. She had intended to change later in the afternoon, but had been in a hurry to catch up on chores at home and her underwear had made her feel more confident and good about herself. She had savoured her romantic encounter for as long as she could. She hardly remembered what jobs she had done as her mind had still been elsewhere.

Robert, who was already in bed reading a car magazine, glanced up having caught sight of her sexy figure in the mirror. Now she was undressed it was as if he were seeing her for the first time. Had he forgotten how attractive she was?

She decided to give him an unexpected treat and, having removed her stockings, slipped in to bed beside him, asking if he liked her new attire she had got from the catalogue. Robert was taken aback by Cynthia's first moves to initiate their lovemaking and they both quite forgot to break off for Cynthia to fit her contraceptive cap.

Robert awoke the next day feeling like a new man and loving his wife, who had been so wonderful last night, even more. He had felt their passion had been more real than their honeymoon attempts when they were very nervous and, of course, inexperienced. He must stop taking her for granted. Perhaps he could work some overtime to help with the household bills. But someone needed to look after Michael when Cynthia worked at the pub.

Cynthia felt confused the next morning. Robert had been different the night before. He actually said how much he loved her and she couldn't remember the last time he had told her that he did. She realised, too, that they had made love without any contraception.

She missed her next period and, a few weeks later, she was feeling sickly, the unmistakable morning sickness. Now what should she do? The pregnancy was ultimately confirmed and Robert was delighted. He was so attentive to her now and their lovemaking became more frequent than it had ever been.

Cynthia browsed through the lingerie section of her catalogue and ordered some more underwear to help fuel the renewed passion, whilst she could still fit in to the lacy attire. Already her breasts were enlarging and her skirts were feeling tight around the waist. She would soon be wearing her flowery smocks once more, which would announce to everyone that she was expecting her second baby. She found her maternity dresses folded up in her chest of drawers and decided to wash them to freshen them up.

Once the morning sickness had passed, Cynthia quite enjoyed being pregnant. Something... some*one* very special was developing inside her. Cynthia gazed at herself in the mirror, rubbing her hands over her expanding abdomen ... wondering. She took all Michael's baby clothes out of the drawers; she would wash them too, once people knew about her pregnancy. She was sure her neighbour, Nancy, would spot the baby clothes on the washing line if she hung them out now and her news would be promptly broadcast. Old Nancy Barker claimed she had very poor eyesight but always seemed to notice things Cynthia would have preferred to keep to herself.

She handled the baby clothes carefully, amazed at just how small they were and feeling that it seemed so long since Michael was able to fit in to them. She wondered if she would have another boy or a girl this time. She really didn't mind, but realised she would need to buy some new clothes as some of Michael's were quite stained. If she had a girl, she would have a good excuse for introducing differently coloured clothes to the mainly blue and white outfits she held before her eyes.

Cynthia decided to make herself a cup of tea and rest for a while, as she felt tired today. She put her feet up on a stool which had belonged to her late mother and said quietly to herself, 'Oh Mother, how I wish you were here to see this new grandchild of yours when he or she is born.' Her mother had died almost eight years earlier and Cynthia had no relatives close to her who would be able to support her when the baby arrived. Still, she would cope somehow. She picked up her magazine and became engrossed in the articles. Having read the problem page, her life seemed quite ordinary really.

Charles rang her at arranged times, so she could be at the phone box just outside their council-house home, but she found herself making excuses now when he tried to arrange to meet her again. She was pregnant but did not know if Charles or Robert was the father. She could not tell Charles and decided that she should speak to him less and perhaps let their fling fizzle out. Yet, she was a little scared at the prospect of spending the rest of her life with Robert. Their refuelled passion might be short lived or their arguing could start again.

* * *

Cynthia was delighted when she gave birth to a baby daughter, a little earlier than her expected delivery date, but she was a healthy baby weighing six pounds, two ounces. They named her Rebecca. She had auburn hair, which Cynthia guessed meant that Charles was more likely to be her father. She had to put this possibility to the back of her mind, however, and get on with life, which was rather hectic with a young son and now a new baby to fill her day.

Time slipped by and Cynthia hadn't contacted Charles for a couple of years now. Often she had hesitated at the phone box, as she passed it frequently, almost drawn to it and wanting to make a call to him. However, the longer she had left it, the more inappropriate it seemed. She had written a few letters to him, but hadn't mentioned that she had a daughter now. He had probably found someone else and perhaps didn't even read her letters. He might even have moved house, as his job may have relocated him to a new base.

Cynthia eventually got a job as a cleaner at the primary school in the next village of Freckingham, which Michael had attended and where Rebecca would later go. Her hours were quite flexible, but she usually did the work as school finished. Rebecca was happy to draw pictures or play in one of the classrooms, whilst Cynthia completed the cleaning in the small school. Cynthia enjoyed having adult company again at work, having become rather bored and a little low at times when she was always at home with the children.

Michael had gone to the secondary school at Coddleton. Cynthia was able to earn a little extra money now, doing the cleaning at the school and continuing to help out at the local pub when she could. The landlord was a family friend who had let Cynthia work there since she was twenty-one. They even managed a few holidays at the local beaches on the Norfolk coast.

Her relationship with Robert had its ups and downs, but they were a family and she didn't want to lose what she had, even though at times she regretted not pursuing her relationship with Charles. Occasionally she tried to imagine what her life would have been like if she had left Robert and she had gone to live with Charles in Appleby. She often wondered what he was doing and half dreaded, half hoped, that he would turn up in the pub once more when he had meetings nearby.

Rebecca was her permanent reminder of the few happy occasions she had spent in Charles's company. He had kept his word, thankfully, and had never written to her, much as he had wanted to reignite the flame of passion he had kept steadily burning for Cynthia over the years.

* * *

Wilf kissed Elizabeth, her cheeks now cold and her skin mottled. He told her rather awkwardly that he would always love her and how he would miss her so terribly. He sobbed, clutching her lifeless hand, his head resting on the bed as he knelt at her side. He could not begin to imagine the emptiness which he would feel without her. Elizabeth had married at nineteen years old; Wilf was six years her senior. They had found such happiness together.

Wilf heard the sound of a moped stopping outside the cottage. It was Kathleen, who lived at the other side of the village. She stood in the bedroom doorway, still wearing her helmet, with tears running down her face. Her usual immaculate make-up was now smudged and her eyes appeared dark and sad.

Wilf was sitting on the bed, still clutching Elizabeth's hand, not wanting to let her go. Kathleen sobbed over her older sister's body, her tears dropping on the crisp white cotton sheets.

'The doctor phoned yew then?'

'Yes, Wilf, what a shock it was,' replied Kathleen, removing her helmet and placing it on the bedroom floor.

'I know… I can't believe this has happened, I can't.'

'When does he think she passed away?'

'Wull, it must have been early… not long after I had gone off to milk, I s'pose. She was a bit restless in the night… I don't think she slept too well, so I didn't mek her a cup o' tea this morning as she was still asleep when I got up.'

'Dear Elizabeth.' Kathleen kissed her sister's forehead, and wiped her tears on a cotton handkerchief that was already in her hand. She studied her face as if seeing her for the first time. She had never seen such a distant expression on Elizabeth's face before, yet this was definitely her dear sister whom she never imagined would be parted from her without any warning.

She placed her hand on Wilf's shoulder. 'I'll make us a cup of tea, Wilf, shall I?' she suggested gently.

'Thank yer, Kathleen. I'll stay with Elizabeth,' Wilf replied, feeling he needed to guard his wife's body… to watch her in case… well, in case she… No, she wouldn't come back to him, but he couldn't leave her.

'I had better feed Tiger too by the looks she's giving us.'

'Blast! I'd forgotten about that cat!'

'Come on, Tiger, come with me,' said Kathleen. She gave her nose a good blow and tried to take in the sad news as she made her way down to the kitchen.

Once fed, Tiger was satisfied and went out in to the garden. Kathleen looked around the tidy kitchen and felt she was intruding in her sister's domain. She made the tea in the brown pottery teapot and called Wilf down when it was ready. He reluctantly left Elizabeth and went down the stairs much slower than when he had last climbed them, and sat in his armchair.

Kathleen passed him his cup of tea and the saucer began to shake as Wilf took it from her. She suggested he put it down on the kitchen table for a moment and took the cup back with its saucer now holding some spilt tea.

'I don't suppose yew've had any breakfast, Wilf, hev yew?'

'No, I'm not hungry.'

'Wull, I'll leave your biscuit barrel next to your tea here, in case you want a biscuit. Or I could make yew some breakfast, of course.'

'No thanks, Kathleen, but may be I'll have a biscuit with my tea. Yis, a shortcake'll dew me.'

Wilf and Kathleen didn't want to move Elizabeth's body from its peaceful resting place, perhaps desperately hoping that she would suddenly stir and that the events today had been a terrible mistake. However, reality had been cruel today and they had to face the harsh situation.

Eventually Kathleen straightened her sister's body, just as Aunt May had apparently done for her mother some years ago. Kathleen washed her sister carefully. She combed Elizabeth's long hair, which was now so grey but had once been a beautiful golden colour, like the fields of barley which had swathed her upbringing. Elizabeth did not dye her hair, she preferred nature to age her gently, and it had. She normally wore her hair up in a bun. Her skin was relatively wrinkle-free, apart from a few fine lines around her eyes due no doubt to her constant smiling, rather than the effects of ageing.

Later, when she got home, Kathleen rang the funeral director at Coddleton and made the necessary arrangements. Wilf sat in the bedroom again, keeping a vigil over his wife. He didn't want the funeral director to take his precious Elizabeth from him. She was only fifty-six years old. How often they had planned their retirement, which had always felt so far distant in their future life together. They had so many different plans, some more serious than others; to travel abroad perhaps, as neither of them had been abroad. Spain sounded nice, from Mrs Potter's accounts of her holidays there. Or maybe a holiday on a canal boat, or a cruiser on the Norfolk Broads. Wilf reckoned that if he could negotiate a tractor and trailer laden with straw down the village lanes, then a boat would be easy to manoeuvre.

They laughed about their wilder ideas, as neither of them had been particularly interested in travel and didn't really understand why people would want to leave the sanctuary of a garden at home. They had often sat on the wooden bench near the honeysuckle at the bottom of the garden during the summer evenings, enjoying the flowers' unique fragrance and drinking homemade lemonade or occasionally a glass of cider or shandy, and considered what they might do in the future. Lack of time and money had prevented them travelling very far but one day they would be able to realise their dreams, or so they had thought. Neither had even considered that one of them might die before they had even collected their pension.

They both worked hard. Wilf had continued work on the farm when young Mr Potter had taken over from his father. Wilf usually milked the cows, which was his main duty. The farm had a dairy herd of fifty Friesian cows. He loved the black and white beasts. As a child he used to visit the farm with his father, who had also worked on the estate. Elizabeth's mother had helped on the Potter's farm during the war. She had died young, too. It was thought she had heart problems.

Elizabeth had started work at the neighbouring village school, a couple of years after she was married. She was the school cook. All the pupils at Freckingham School had loved Elizabeth … and her delicious food that she faithfully and lovingly prepared for them. Among the favourite dishes were her meat and potato pies, stew and dumplings, roast dinners, fish pie, and syrup sponge puddings, bakewell tarts, creamy rice pudding, jam roly-poly and custard. Second helpings of her puddings were always requested by the hungry, sweet-toothed children and school staff!

Wilf and Elizabeth had not been blessed with children, but Elizabeth gained a lot of pleasure from her work at the school. She had a wall in her cottage kitchen devoted to the works of art which the schoolchildren had drawn and given to her. She had received every picture presented to her with great delight. Many depicted her wearing her white apron, serving food to a line of hungry children.

Some of the children would call at her cottage at weekends, if they were playing on the farm estate. They would arrive at her door and proudly present a bunch of primroses or cowslips to her, gathered from the ditches nearby. Sometimes she would be presented with a large daisy chain, which she would wear dutifully around her neck. The children would then sit in Elizabeth's kitchen, drinking her home-made lemonade and munching freshly-baked oat biscuits or shortbread. They would sit and look at their pictures, which were proudly displayed on the wall.

Elizabeth always had time for the children and was pleased to have their company. The children sometimes felt that their parents were glad to send them off to play, not wanting their 'constant noise' at home. Elizabeth never told them off and didn't even remark when they brought mud into her kitchen. She said Wilf made the floor more 'datty' from the muck on his size ten boots than three or four pairs of their little rubber boots put together!

The children would also make a fuss of Tiger, who enjoyed their attention. Wilf had brought her home from the farm. Mrs Potter had pleaded with him to give a home to one of the kittens her farm cat had produced otherwise, she had threatened, they would have to be destroyed. She thought Elizabeth would take good care of a kitten and knew she would accept it, if there was any chance that it would have to be destroyed. Wilf was not fond of cats, but Elizabeth was delighted to have the kitten and decided to call her Tiger as she was a ginger cat with attractive stripy markings.

Chapter Three

Farewell, Elizabeth

What an unbearable pain! Elizabeth pushed open the bedroom window to help get her breath. She took her antacid quickly, probably more than she needed, and thought she would get back in to bed. Lie still for a while. Whatever had she eaten last night? Nothing should have upset her like this.

Once back in bed, she remembered the new tablets the doctor had given her. Oh blast, they were downstairs in the kitchen. Never mind. Give the antacid time. Oh Lord! What a pain! She closed her eyes, the pain crushing now and seeming to radiate down her left arm. The pain was overwhelming, almost suffocating. She found herself praying quietly, asking the Lord to help her.

The morning sunlight was just beginning to filter through in to her bedroom. Elizabeth thought she could hear her mother calling her now. She was drifting, floating somehow, the pain powering her as she drifted into a semi-conscious state. Again she heard her mother; her eyes squinted at the sunlit window and that was unmistakably her mother reaching out to her now, her arms outstretched, ready with their comfort. The pain was being left behind her and she was reaching out to her mother, a young woman again… so beautiful… Mother…

Wilf woke with a start. He was in his armchair next to the open fireplace. The fire he had made earlier in the evening, for company more than its heat, had burnt out. The clock on the mantelpiece gently chimed two o'clock. Wilf sat upright, listening. He thought he heard Elizabeth's voice. Reality reminded him that she was gone forever.

He stood up awkwardly, as his body felt stiff from sleeping in his chair. He slowly straightened up and stretched, knocking over an empty glass. He had drunk a large whisky late in the evening, hoping it would help him sleep. He wasn't very keen on whisky really. He had received the bottle of whisky at the summer fête in the village when he had won the bowling competition. Wilf had opened the bottle last night, discarding the sleeping pill Dr Stimpson had left him. He was not a believer in pills, rarely taking anything apart from an odd aspirin.

Wilf turned off the wireless and lights downstairs and went up to bed, taking the wireless with him. Kathleen had offered to stay in the house with him or suggested he might like to join her and her husband Tom and stay in the spare room at their house, but Wilf insisted he was fine on his own.

'Fine on my own,' he repeated the words now to himself. He knew he would never be fine on his own. How could he be? An inseparable part of his being had been torn away and he would be left to nurse the wound which would never heal.

He got onto the bed, still dressed, and pulled the eiderdown over him. He pulled Elizabeth's pillow to his chest and sobbed again until he felt he could sob no more. He could smell her perfume on her pillow, a delicate scent of roses. Kathleen had wanted to change the sheets but Wilf insisted she leave them. He was glad now that the sheets had been left, as her lingering perfume was all he had left of her.

He wasn't sure if he managed to doze off again, but soon it was getting light and the birds were tuning up for the dawn chorus. He could hear a song thrush near to his bedroom window. He lay in a daze, waiting for his alarm clock to officially tell him that it was time to get up. Yet there was no point in getting up today … would there ever be again, he wondered.

The alarm rang faithfully at six o'clock. He turned it off and continued to lie on the bed. Bill would be doing the milking this morning and would continue to do so until Wilf wanted to resume the job. Jim had assured him that he could be off work as long as he wanted, remembering how distraught he had felt when his own father had died and wondering what it felt like to lose a wife who was far too young to die. He hoped he could help Wilf get through the difficult time ahead. Wilf was such a reliable worker, he never missed a day's work and had needed frequent reminders that he must take time off for holidays. Jim would miss his help on the farm.

Wilf lay wondering if Bill might like some help but he decided he didn't want to hear Bill's account of his latest health problem. Whatever problem anyone had, Bill would always have a problem which he perceived as being greater. He would manage the cows and would get the job done quicker if he didn't have anyone to gossip to. The cows could listen to his swearing and the periodic sounds he produced, belching and others, which could have originated from a tuba, though they were less tuneful, of course.

Wilf turned on the wireless to listen to the news and the weather. Life continued it seemed; political debates and opinions of the famous were still being aired. Miners were threatening strike action, complaining about their poor working conditions and pay. Wilf thought he felt a little like a miner now, blackened with his grief, stuck underground with little light and with little incentive to find a way out back to the surface and to rejoin the unsympathetic crowds who had no understanding of life in the darkness. All those people who had lesser burdens on their shoulders, who were not trapped and weighted down by bereavement. He stared at the empty space beside him, the wireless droned on. He no longer listened to the details of the broadcast. One of the broadcasters was laughing now at something being discussed.

Wilf reached up and abruptly switched off the wireless, feeling that someone was laughing at his misfortune. It hurt to hear someone laughing in a room shrouded with sadness, the happy person apparently mocking his loss. He felt awkward still being on his bed, restless; he didn't know what he should do. His usual morning routine had been interrupted indefinitely and somehow he felt as though he was waiting for instructions. He felt lost and insecure without any structure to his day. Simple tasks now required great effort and he questioned their purpose.

He gazed at the ceiling and watched a spider busily making an intricate web at the end of a beam. He became almost mesmerised by the spider's work and noted several cobwebs in the other corners of the bedroom, which Elizabeth's feather duster had obviously not found.

Eventually he got up and had a wash and changed his clothes. He couldn't believe he had gone to bed fully dressed. Elizabeth wouldn't have approved of that… 'Sheer laziness,' she would have said!

At eight thirty a.m., Kathleen arrived at the cottage. She had walked from her house. Her eyes were red and puffy and she hadn't bothered with any make-up. She hadn't slept well either. She greeted Wilf in the kitchen and they had a cup of tea together.

News of Elizabeth's death had spread round the village. Everyone was shocked. She had been involved with so many activities in the village and she had always attended church on Sundays. Elizabeth and Kathleen took it in turns to arrange fresh flowers on the altar. They both had lovely gardens and took great pride in ensuring the church had a colourful display of blooms. Elizabeth also went to the village Women's Institute. She enjoyed producing home-made jams, marmalades, chutneys and pickles and her produce usually scooped several of the prizes at the village fête. Elizabeth was also a dressmaker. She had picked up this ability from Aunt May, who had been like a mother to her and Kathleen when their own mother had died. She still used her aunt's Singer sewing machine. Since Aunt May's arthritic fingers could no longer tackle needlework, she had passed her handsome black sewing machine on to Elizabeth. Some of the villagers would drop off garments to be altered, at Elizabeth's cottage. She liked to be kept busy with these sewing jobs.

Peter Croft, the vicar, arrived at eleven o'clock to discuss the funeral service. Much to Wilf's amazement, Kathleen told him the hymns Elizabeth wanted for her funeral.

'Well, we've spent many an hour in the church together arranging flowers for weddings and funerals and we used to talk about all sorts, yew know, Wilf.'

Peter was a tall, thin man who was now not enjoying the best of health. He was planning to retire soon, though at seventy-eight years of age, he wondered what he would do once he retired. He had no children and only an elderly brother living nearby. The church was his life. He and his wife Esther had moved to the village when he was a young priest full of enthusiasm for maintaining a large congregation, but it was now rather an effort to take the services in Watton and Freckingham and occasionally help out at the church at Coddleton. Congregation numbers were generally dwindling and he lacked the energy to think of new ideas to boost church attendance. Peter's memory was beginning to fail and sometimes he lost his train of thought during his sermons, or he repeated sections of them. He was becoming increasingly deaf, but refused to consider a hearing aid. He decided he should retire since he was now marrying children whom he had held in his arms to baptise and recently married a young girl whose grandparents he had married!

Wilf had never been a regular church attender but did usually make an appearance at what he classed as the 'main' church services at Easter, harvest time and Christmas. Elizabeth had given up trying to change his ways. She attended church regularly and found Wilf an embarrassment when he did go, as he had been known to fall asleep in the service and once emitted a loud snore! Peter was known for his rather long sermons and Wilf found himself drifting off on more than one occasion before being prodded in the ribs by Elizabeth.

'Poor Peter,' Elizabeth would often say when she came home from church. She told Wilf how, at a recent baptism, Peter had said the wrong name for the baby he held in his arms. The godparents corrected him three times before he could get it right, by which time the young mother began to giggle uncontrollably until she was sternly brought back to her senses by her grandmother, Mrs Coleman, who reminded her of the seriousness of the ceremony. Mrs Coleman, who was also the church organist, had remarked afterwards to Elizabeth that she had felt sorry for Peter having to pronounce the Christian name her granddaughter had chosen: Aureola, after an American pop singer. She despaired of her granddaughter Carol, who had become pregnant before she was married and then showed no respect in the 'holy place'. Mrs Coleman had tutted and shaken her head, repeating, 'These young gals, I don't know, that I don't.'

Peter sat in Wilf's kitchen thinking about the three recent deaths there had been in the village. First there had been Amy, who was ninety-nine years old and only three weeks away from her hundredth birthday. She had never married. She lived next door to the vicarage in a little old cottage, which was rather damp. She had six cats at the last count! If anyone called to see Amy it was hard to know where to sit without disturbing a snoozing moggy! Her cottage was full of clutter. Piles and piles of newspapers lined the hallway. The walls of her small living area were lined with shelves of old books. The yellowing wallpaper could be glimpsed between the dusty shelves.

Amy had been remarkably independent and everyone was amazed she had lived so long. She had often told her visitors how she had been a sick child, having had rheumatic fever. She was one of eight children, the weakest child of the family, and yet she had outlived all her siblings. She had five sisters and two brothers. She used to share the cottage with her brother George, who unfortunately had been killed during the First World War. She would proudly show to visitors his medals, which were on the wall in a wooden case. George had been a good brother to her. She often fondly remembered their school days, although some days had been difficult for her and she had missed a lot of her schooling due to illness.

George would always stick up for his younger sister as she seemed to get picked on in the playground. He would get so angry when the children teased and tormented his sister who was such a small frail child, unable to retaliate. He once ended up in a fight with Tom Benson who had teased Amy one day when she had wet herself. George punched Tom, who ended up with two black eyes. The headmistress was appalled at their behaviour and both boys were severely reprimanded.

The school had been closed many years ago and had since been converted into a house by a couple who had moved into the village from London. Mr Marsden was an architect and had set up his own business locally. Some people on the village parish council were concerned that the local architecture would soon be dominated by modern designs more in keeping with the London skyline. Finally, however, Mr and Mrs Marsden were beginning to feel accepted by the villagers who had initially been rather suspicious of them and other outsiders. Some were worried that the village would be 'taken over' by newcomers to the village.

There had been several new developments in the village. Jim Potter had not been popular when he sold four acres of land to a property developer. He felt he needed to raise funds to update the old machinery he had inherited. Also, there were several properties needing modernisation and renovation, which he rented to the farm workers. The workers now expected modern bathrooms and inside toilets. Jim had despaired of his father when he had been alive, knowing there was a lot of money that needed to be spent on the farm properties. He also had to raise the farm workers' rents to help fund the work, which hadn't gone down well, but they had all eventually realised that they had enjoyed low rent for many years and looked forward to the new 'comforts' that had been promised.

Amy's cottage was now being sorted out by her great nephews and great nieces who were considering renovating the old cottage, and someone had heard they were possibly planning to use it as a holiday home. They all lived on the outskirts of London. Several valuable books had been found in Amy's 'library'. Amy's cats had taken up residence in an old outbuilding in her garden and went over to the vicarage for a good feed once a day.

The second death had been Geoffrey Tunstall, a local joiner and funeral director. He had a very solemn face. Some villagers had remarked that he had been born to be a funeral director! He had never married and never got round to retiring either. At seventy-two, he had still felt able to contribute something to his business, which he had built up over the years following his apprenticeship with the aptly-named Sidney Graves. Recently he had been helped by his nephews, Jonathan and Mark, who would take over the business. At Geoffrey's funeral, everyone had felt uneasy, since Geoffrey had been such a familiar sight at all of the local funerals and some expected him to appear at the head of his own funeral cortège.

Geoffrey was buried in a coffin he had made himself, ready for the day 'whenever it might happen', as he had said to his nephews. He had carved out some joiner's tools in the lid to decorate it. It must have taken much time and skill to achieve. The coffin was rather dusty when it was uncovered in the back of the workshop to take Geoffrey to his final resting place. Jonathan and Mark felt it was a shame to cover Geoffrey's handsomely carved coffin with earth. They had been unaware that the coffin was so ornate. Geoffrey had obviously spent many hours working on it when his nephews were not in the workshop.

The third death was Elizabeth's; how she would be missed by all in the village. She was a very important cog in the machinery of village life. Peter didn't need to get much information from Wilf and Kathleen as he knew Elizabeth so well. The funeral service was discussed and Peter eventually said that he'd better be going home to the vicarage where Esther would be waiting for him.

Esther was a very short stout lady, which made the couple appear rather odd when seen together as Peter towered above her. She had very long hair, which she always wore in braids wrapped round and round her head, secured with numerous hair pins. Esther often wore a green felt hat. She tootled slowly around the village in her black Morris Minor, apparently peering over the steering wheel. Villagers often joked that they didn't think she had found fourth gear yet! She always wore her black leather driving gloves and appeared to be gripping the steering wheel very tightly, her face close to the windscreen since the driving seat was pushed forward as far as it would go and a cushion supported her forward posture. She had had two miscarriages early in her married life and one stillborn baby, after which she and Peter had decided having children was not God's will. Esther had been depressed for over a year following the stillbirth. She had come to terms with her loss eventually, but had been left troubled with anxiety.

Wilf turned down Kathleen's offer of dinner. He didn't feel hungry. The emptiness he was feeling could not be filled with food. Later he set off for a walk across the fields in the village. The air felt fresh and birds were singing. He heard crows making their presence known in the heights of the treetops nearby.

He gazed momentarily at their nests far above him. It reminded him that as a young boy he had been dared to climb to the top of a very tall tree and had almost reached the top before deciding to give in. However, his descent had been very difficult and, once he had finally reached the safety of the firm ground again, he had trembled so much that the boy daring him to dice with death had to give him a piggy back home. Harry Coates also had the task of explaining why Wilf was white as a sheet when he reached Wilf's rather strict mother, who happened to be at the door scrubbing the steps when they got home.

Wilf strode out now across the damp meadows, thankful that he wouldn't have to face any of the village folk. He absorbed the calm from the peaceful surroundings. Rabbits scurried away out of sight when they were disturbed by the solemn lonely figure out walking, trying to make sense of what was happening in his life. He had to clamber over a barbed wire fence and caught his trousers on it. A small tear in the fabric was now apparent, but he didn't really care about such a trivial event. There was an electrified fence around the next meadow where cows were grazing, but he was able to step over the fence quite easily, aware of its venomous sting if he misjudged it. The cows looked up dreamily in his direction but carried on munching the lush grass around them.

He also walked through the small wood at the far edge of the village, which he hadn't done for a long time; he wondered why, as it seemed to instill in him an air of peace and calm. He rested momentarily against a bent tree trunk and felt the roughness of the bark through his trousers. He gave his nose a good blow, which interrupted the peace, and when he put his handkerchief back in his pocket, he found some peppermints deep in his trouser pocket. He put one in his mouth, enjoying the refreshing taste, before setting off again.

Eventually, after walking for five or six miles, Wilf headed back towards the village, joining the road back to his cottage. The road was being resurfaced and the tar had just been spread ready for the loose chippings to be sandwiched on top. The smell of tar was strong and intrusive. One of the workmen, leaning on a shovel, slowly straightened up his posture as if he had a bad back and said to Wilf, 'Grand day, isn't it?'

'Uh, yis, I s'pose t'is. Yew're mekin' a good job of the rood, that yer are. Won't need to skirt the potholes on my old bike now!' Wilf commented, as he concentrated on keeping to the grass bank at the side of the road to avoid the tar. 'That yew won't, sir! That yew won't.'

Wilf got back in to the cottage. He had not locked the door when he had gone out for his walk. It seemed wrong to do so; he had hesitated with the key in his hand as though he might be locking Elizabeth out if she returned. He sighed deeply as he filled the kettle and then made a cup of tea and ate a few biscuits. He read the local paper; although he wondered as he put it down what he had actually read.

At teatime he made some cheese on toast. The toast had burnt a little but he ate it anyway. He made a pot of tea, realising afterwards that he had made a full pot, enough for two. Preparing his meal he felt mechanical, driven by a non-human force which told him it was time to eat even though it seemed pointless and was just part of a routine which no longer seemed valid. He did not enjoy the food and although he ate it with the wireless on, he was not really listening to it. A discussion was taking place about corporal punishment. His heart certainly felt like it had taken a beating. He had switched the wireless on for some noise in his desperately quiet cottage.

He put his used plate and cup in his kitchen sink with cups from earlier in the day. No point in washing up a few things. There was no sign of Tiger this evening; perhaps she was missing the attention from Elizabeth. No doubt she would turn up when she wanted food, if she hadn't feasted on a mouse or two.

Later that evening, Wilf made himself a large cup of Horlicks and went up to bed. He got in to bed and turned towards where Elizabeth would have slept. He stared at the empty space. Minutes passed, and Wilf felt uneasy. Elizabeth would normally be finishing her wash in the bathroom and then joining him. Not tonight. He continued to lie, facing Elizabeth's side of the bed, hardly moving. He tried to recall all the details of her bedtime routine, but couldn't remember them now, and concluded that often he had probably already fallen asleep before she had got in beside him. Eventually he said quietly, 'Goodnight, Elizabeth.' He turned and switched off his bedside light and then lay still, unable to get to sleep.

It was very quiet, apart from the ticking of his alarm clock, which he hadn't bothered to set tonight. He never had problems sleeping normally. The night seemed long and the darkness isolated him. He could have been lying anywhere; his own bed no longer felt familiar or comfortable. After a couple of hours he got up and went to the toilet and then got back to bed, plumping up his feather pillows and trying to find a comfortable position in a bed which now felt alien to him. Again he checked Elizabeth's side of the bed before turning out the light once more.

He must have eventually got some sleep but when he woke he felt exhausted. He looked at Elizabeth's side of the bed ... still empty.

Wilf washed and dressed and made a cup of tea. He made some toast under the grill, having decided he couldn't be bothered with a messy porridge saucepan to clean. The butter was still hard, but he managed to spread it on the warm toast, though rather thickly. He found the marmalade in the pantry and sat down at the table without the tablecloth, not wanting any fuss. He had no one to share the first meal of the day. Normally he was eager to have breakfast after work at the farm.

In the afternoon, Wilf and Kathleen drove in Elizabeth's car to Coddleton to discuss the funeral arrangements and so that Wilf could say goodbye to Elizabeth. He was glad Kathleen had come with him to make final decisions about the funeral. He felt awkward and uneasy in the funeral parlour and, when he had been left alone finally with Elizabeth, he didn't know what to say to her. He sat next to her on a firm chair, carefully positioned by the funeral director. The chapel of rest was small; one high window allowed the bright sunshine to cheer the otherwise solemn room. A bunch of yellow chrysanthemums on a table also helped to lighten the dark surroundings of the heavy mahogany furniture.

'Oh, Elizabeth ... why hev yew left me ... how can I manage without yew?' Wilf kept his voice quiet in case someone in the next room was able to hear him talking. He felt rather self-conscious. He wondered if other people talked to their dead spouses. Elizabeth looked so pale ... distant ... serious ... not the smiling Elizabeth he had married and wanted to remember.

'Elizabeth, I did love yew so ... so very much, my dear... I hope yew know that ... and I always will... I...'

Tears now stopped Wilf's words but he sat gazing at Elizabeth, wishing he could be sure she understood his feelings and that she would be able to embrace him … one more time. He reached in to his trousers' pocket, pulled out a handkerchief to wipe away his tears and blew his nose. He tried to think what else he needed to say.

Wilf sat for another ten minutes just gazing at Elizabeth, still not really believing that she had died. Eventually he stood up and said, 'Goodbye Elizabeth … till we meet again, my dear.' He carefully kissed her forehead and then hurriedly left the building, putting on his cap and trying to disguise his recent expressions of grief.

He went out to the car, where Kathleen was waiting for him. 'Sorry, Kathleen … have I bin tew long?'

'No, not at all, Wilf.'

'Are yew sure yew don't want to see her?'

'No, Wilf… I mean … I think I want to remember her as she was … yew know.'

'Right yew are, Kathleen… Yes, she did look a bit different in there.'

Kathleen still had the image of her late sister in her mind the day she had seen her in her bed and had helped prepare her body before the undertaker took over her care. She had tried to distance herself from the practicalities at the time; she would have been overwhelmed with grief if she had really thought that it was her dead sister she was dealing with. She had been down to the church later and spent some quiet time there reflecting on her loss and praying for strength to get through the next few days.

'Are yew alright, Wilf? Yew dew look tired. Should we go and get a cup o' tea in the café down the road?'

'No, I'd rather get hom', if yew don't mind, Kathleen. I couldn't sleep ag'in last night, that I couldn't.'

'Of course, Wilf. I'm not surprised yew can't sleep, it's hard, isn't it?'

'Yis. I even tried to recall one of Peter's sermons last night and even that didn't work!'

'Poor Peter!'

'That's what Elizabeth says ... *used* to say to me.'

'Let's get home then.'

'Funerals are wholly expensive, aren't they?'

'They certainly are! Can yew manage it, Wilf?'

'I think I can. I hope Elizabeth won't mind not having the best coffin... Cor, blast, what a price that was!'

* * *

Finally the day of Elizabeth's funeral came. Wilf had thought the day would never come and when it did, he found himself wishing it could be postponed for a few more days. Soon the earth would be scattered over her coffin and their separation would be finalised. He would no longer be able to visit the chapel of rest for one last goodbye to the lady he had loved so dearly.

Wilf had visited Elizabeth a second time alone and hadn't told Kathleen. He had caught the bus to Coddleton rather than use Elizabeth's car. The car felt odd as he had not driven it very often, and it didn't seem right to use it. He had been to the butcher's shop to buy a pork chop for his dinner. Then he had stood opposite the funeral director's for several minutes, feeling uneasy but somehow drawn to the place. It was as though Elizabeth was quietly calling his name. He could not ignore her calling him and eventually plucked up the courage to enter the funeral director's and awkwardly asked if he could see Elizabeth again. He was asked to wait a few moments in the reception area and sat clutching his cap and the string bag with the meat he had just bought.

After about fifteen minutes, Mark appeared and told him he could enter the chapel of rest. Wilf stood up and left his shopping on the chair with his cap. He pushed his hand over his head, checking his hair was lying flat, and went in to the room to sit near Elizabeth once more. Her expression was unchanged. Of course she hadn't been calling him, but he felt reassured that he had come. Wilf just sat and gazed at his wife. So many happy memories, but the hope of many more years together, which now would never be. He wondered how he could function without her.

Mrs Manby, the secretary who had been typing efficiently on her sturdy black typewriter in the reception area, had told Wilf there was no rush, he could stay as long as he wanted. So he sat for nearly an hour, drawing comfort from being with Elizabeth before saying his final farewell to her and giving her his last kiss on her cool forehead.

On the way back to the bus stop, he realised he had just missed the bus and the next one was not for another hour and a half. Wilf decided to walk home, it wouldn't take long. He was nearly half way home when Mrs Potter spotted him as she was driving home and offered Wilf a lift, which he accepted. She asked him how he was and they chatted for the remainder of the short journey home. She offered advice on how Wilf could cook his chop, knowing that he probably didn't know what to do with it.

Wilf ate the chop, having cooked it as advised by Mrs Potter, but he didn't enjoy it. The potatoes he had mashed quite well, though he did find a couple of lumps. The carrots and cabbage were alright, but something was missing from his meal. He guessed it must be Elizabeth's company he was missing most. Meals just didn't taste the same any more and were lonely events. No pudding today, either. He had so enjoyed Elizabeth's puddings. Treacle sponge and custard was probably his favourite, although it was no doubt responsible for his expanded waistline.

He sighed as he washed up the saucepans and grill pan. What a lot of mess he had made in the kitchen and all this just cooking for one. What would Elizabeth say if she could see her kitchen now, he wondered. She always kept things clean and tidy. He had rarely helped her tidy up, as she described washing up and putting things away. She often insisted on doing that herself, telling Wilf to sit down and rest after a long day. Elizabeth had always appeared to have endless energy and was content even doing the mundane chores.

* * *

Wilf dressed in his dark suit, which he kept for the rare occasions he needed to look smart. The trousers were a little on the tight side, he thought, as he was only just able to fasten the buttons. He hardly recognised himself as he caught sight of his reflection in Elizabeth's dressing table mirror. He was not used to wearing smart clothes, feeling more at home in comfortable clothing suitable for farm work.

Wilf stood looking at himself; he was pale and he felt he had physically aged, though he rarely examined his face apart from when he was shaving and that was to check that he hadn't missed any stubble rather than wondering how old he might appear.

He pictured Elizabeth's face in the coffin at the chapel of rest a few days ago. Although it was undoubtedly her, she had looked so much younger again. Wilf wondered whether she was now free to run in the golden heavenly fields of corn, with her mother watching over her again. Elizabeth had strongly believed that she would be reunited with her mother again when she died, although she had never contemplated that their reunion might happen so soon.

Wilf finished buttoning up his crisp white shirt with the starched collar, which had been laundered carefully by Kathleen, and went downstairs using the oak banister for support.

Tom, Kathleen and her elderly father, Leonard, arrived. Soon afterwards, Mark and Jonathan Hayton came to take them to church in the large black funeral cars, which shone in the hazy autumn sunshine.

Kathleen went to help her father out of the car, as he was crippled with arthritis and gout. Today, however, he seemed to have summoned a new strength and strode ahead with the aid of his sturdy walking stick, which he had made himself. They all followed the coffin into the little Norman church and were amazed to see it was full. Peter was lucky if he got a third of the number in the congregation today for his weekly services.

Kathleen gazed at the altar and the flowers she had arranged for her sister. A few white lilies with dark green foliage, which she had bought, looked stunning with the sunlight just beginning to filter through the stained glass windows above them; she hoped Elizabeth would have approved. She started to remember the happy times she and Elizabeth had spent here together arranging flowers, and the not so happy memories of their somewhat lonely teenage years. Kathleen had visited her mother's grave one day and suddenly Sam Livingstone appeared from behind a grave stone. Sam had Down's Syndrome. He had exposed himself to Kathleen in the churchyard, as she was about to get on her bicycle to go home. She had been rather shocked and upset by the experience and didn't know who she should turn to.

Sam's mother had thought she was going through the change of life, having given up hope of ever having a child. She had become very tired and had put on rather a lot of weight but thought nothing of it. Then one day she sent for the doctor as she had severe stomach cramps. She had the shock of her life when old Doctor Bates told her she was in labour! She was transferred to the small cottage hospital at Needham and finally gave birth to Sam, weighing a good

8lbs 8oz. Her husband was amazed that he finally had a son, and went around in a stunned daze for many days! Later it was announced that their son had Down's Syndrome, but it didn't matter to Millie; she had a beautiful baby son at the age of forty-three and she was the happiest she had ever been.

Sam grew up to be a loving son, but he was beginning to be additional strain on Millie now that her husband Jack suffered from dementia, and it was becoming a full time job to care for him. Recently Jack had started attending a day-care centre at Coddleton three days a week which, together with Sam's days spent at the adult training centre at Needham, meant Millie finally got a bit of a break. However her days seemed to be spent washing and ironing. Jack had become incontinent but worse than that, he would urinate in inappropriate places. Millie had once opened the teapot and the unmistakable smell of urine met her. She had also found urine in her flower vases and in a bucket under the kitchen sink. She had to follow Jack now wherever he went, but at least she usually managed to catch his urine in the daytime by offering him the bucket now devoted to the purpose.

Millie had saved up to buy a twin-tub washing machine which was now her pride and joy, so she felt life was getting a little easier. However one day, thirty years or more ago, Harry Smith had called on her. He looked awkward as he twisted his cap in his hands. He finally explained how Kathleen had told of her experience with Sam in the churchyard. Millie broke down in tears and said she didn't know how she should handle the matter. Harry asked if she would like him to talk to Sam, as Sam helped on his farm at weekends and during the busier times of the farming calendar. Millie gladly accepted his help. A red-faced Sam had later apologised to Kathleen for his behaviour, with Harry present for support.

Kathleen and Elizabeth had gone to live with their Uncle Harry and Aunt May when their mother had died. Their father, Leonard, had not coped at all well when he lost his wife. He had taken to the whisky bottle and started to neglect himself. Aunt May already had three girls and two boys, but thought two more mouths to feed wouldn't make much difference; it was the least she could do for her late sister, Mabel.

May and Harry lived in a large draughty farmhouse on their farm where they reared pigs. They also had lots of chickens and some geese who wandered around the farmyard. They fattened a few turkeys to be sold at Christmas locally. They sold eggs at the farm gate, together with surplus vegetables and sometimes flowers. Kathleen had loved the bright yellow yolks of the eggs the hens produced. She and her sister usually had a boiled egg for their breakfast with some freshly-baked bread made by their aunt. They had often giggled and joked that they ought to be clucking after all the eggs they had consumed over the years!

Wilf, Kathleen, Tom and Leonard sat down in the front pews of the church. Elizabeth's coffin was in front of Wilf's misted eyes, adorned with simple wreaths of white and pale pink flowers. Wilf couldn't really absorb what was going on around him. Peter's voice appeared distant and then he thought he heard Elizabeth singing, but he realised that it was Kathleen standing next to him. Wilf tried to sing and his lips were moving, but he could not muster any sound.

Peter said some wonderful things about Elizabeth in his eulogy. Wilf knew all of it to be true and he could tell plenty more stories of how she had touched the hearts of so many. As Wilf sat there, he wondered if he had told Elizabeth how much he had loved her. He had taken her love and presence for granted, and now she was gone. He felt jealous that she was now with the Lord she had worshipped so faithfully all her life. He had nothing and nobody.

Peter was coming to the end of his eulogy. Finally he drew attention to the bunch of forget-me-nots he had noticed in the church porch. The flowers were tied together with a blue ribbon and had a note attached. They were from Rebecca Mason, an eleven-year-old former pupil at the school where Elizabeth had worked. Rebecca had been very fond of Elizabeth and had been a frequent visitor to her cottage even when she had left the primary school.

Rebecca had passed her eleven-plus examination and moved to the girls' grammar school at Foulsham. She was sitting in an English lesson gazing out of the window and thinking about the funeral happening about the same time. Rebecca had wanted to attend Mrs Ford's funeral but her parents had said that funerals weren't for children and that was that. However, Rebecca had slipped away from home early that morning, having hurriedly picked a bunch of forget-me-nots from their rather basic garden and tied them with her blue ribbon, which she normally used to tie up her long auburn hair. She had written a little verse using her fountain pen, which she had attached to the flowers. Peter now read it to the congregation:

> Mrs Ford has gone away.
> In the graveyard she will lay.
> The village is now very sad.
> She was the best lady it ever had.
> I will miss her friendly smile
> And her pleasant chat,
> The visits to her home
> And playing with her cat.
> I will bring flowers
> Whose names she used to test
> To this peaceful spot
> Where she will be laid to rest.
> She will be loved in Heaven

But how she will be missed
By her little friend of eleven.

Love from Rebecca xx

Mr and Mrs Mason sat stunned in the congregation, realising now why Rebecca had left earlier than usual that morning for the school bus. They felt very proud of the touching gesture from their daughter. Even Peter seemed moved by the child's words and the significant flowers chosen by Rebecca. As he now concluded, all would forget-her-*not*; they would all remember Elizabeth.

The congregation filed out solemnly from the church and most stopped to look for themselves at the now rather withered forget-me-nots in the porch. Rebecca had no idea that her bunch of hastily gathered flowers and the simple verse would have made such an impact. She was sitting in an English literature lesson. Miss Pearson was droning on about the wonders of Shakespeare's works. From what Rebecca had heard so far, she was wondering what all the fuss was about and wondering if she would ever make sense of his plays. Her thoughts kept drifting elsewhere … to the village church where she wanted to be paying her last respects to the lady who had meant so much to her. She recalled her parents' parting words as she was leaving the house: 'funerals weren't for young 'uns.'

Elizabeth had been so pleased for Rebecca when she had passed her eleven-plus. She had given her a five-pound book token and a little congratulations card she had made with pressed flowers. Rebecca had been the only pupil at her school to have passed the exam and was very apprehensive at the thought of starting a new school without any friends alongside her. Rebecca felt that Elizabeth was really proud of her, more so than her own parents, whose first reaction to her examination success was how were they going to afford the school uniform?

The Masons had christened Rebecca as a baby, but Rebecca didn't know who her godparents were. She had once asked Elizabeth if she would act as her godmother. Rebecca probably felt Elizabeth to be more like the fairy godmother figures she read about in fairy tales.

Rebecca's mum was a cleaner at the village school and worked in the village pub; her dad was a lorry driver, delivering farm feedstuffs for Hastings Ltd. around the county. He was a tall thin man with thinning dark hair. He always wore Brylcreem to keep his fine hair in place, brushing it across his growing bald patch.

Rebecca had an older brother, Michael, who was often in trouble with the police. He had recently left the secondary modern school at Coddleton. He had said school was a waste of time and had often been absent. His dad kept reminding him that he was unlikely to get a job unless he 'bucked his ideas up' and started to take some responsibility for his life. However, Michael did have one interest: he was a very good artist. His ability to draw people had initially got him into trouble when his maths teacher had realised Michael was paying no attention at all to his lesson, but was obviously busy drawing something. When he confiscated Michael's exercise book, he discovered a rather good sketch of himself. He had been very cross about it at the time, but later commented to the art teacher in the staff room that, having seen his maths book portfolio, Michael Mason could be a potential portrait painter! Michael left school with grade I CSEs in art and technical drawing, and one grade A O-level in art. Unfortunately he had got in with the wrong crowd at school who had introduced him to petty thieving.

Mrs Mason despaired of her son and couldn't believe how different her two children were, though secretly she assumed that Rebecca was conceived during her brief affair with a travelling salesman who had been staying at the local inn where she sometimes worked behind the bar to earn extra cash. Robert Mason had never suspected anything and luckily her few passionate encounters had not been discovered by anyone else, which was extraordinary in such a small village. The salesman was unaware he had fathered a child, having believed Cynthia Mason when she said she was on the pill. Her usual means of contraception was, in fact, still in the bathroom cupboard. Cynthia now religiously dyed her greying hair auburn to look like her daughter's to reduce suspicion. Her natural colour had been a light mousey brown.

'…ashes to ashes…dust to dust…' Peter was saying. How often Wilf had heard these words, but never had they felt so blunt or affected him so personally. It was as though reality was now slapping him in the face.

He dropped one of the roses picked from their garden onto Elizabeth's coffin, which was now in the depths of the double grave. Wilf had asked for the double grave to be dug so that one day he could join Elizabeth… How he wished it could be now. He felt a little dizzy and then he felt a steadying arm; it was Kathleen's. Will stared at the deep grave, wanting the funeral service to stop, to ask that Elizabeth be brought out of the damp ground. He felt as if there was a knife in the back of his throat… Panic flashed through his body and he tried hard not to cry, it wasn't a male emotion to display in public… Then he lost control and heard himself sobbing. He could see a black blur of people as he was helped to the funeral car. One of the concerned faces he glimpsed was his brother, Stanley, with his sister-in-law, Alice.

Wilf sat in the car, feeling as though everything around him was spinning and he felt a little nauseous. He closed his eyes and rested his head against the back of the car seat and soon felt cool air as the car set off; someone had opened one of the car windows. Wilf took a few deep reviving breaths and tried to calm himself during the short journey.

All of the mourners had been invited back to Kathleen's cottage for the funeral tea. There was not a lot of space but luckily the weather was fine and some people drifted outside to the little garden. Kathleen had been overwhelmed with the thoughtfulness of her friends in the village who kept arriving the day before the funeral with pork pies, sausage rolls, tea-breads, ginger cake and scones. As she looked around her cottage, now crammed with people, she was thankful the gifts of food had been so plentiful. She had made some ham sandwiches, two fruit cakes and two Swiss rolls. She had smiled to herself when the Swiss rolls had rolled up beautifully and had said to herself, '*Nearly* as good as your baking, Elizabeth!'

Mary, Kathleen's only daughter, appeared with a tray of cups of tea, which she handed out, then she disappeared into the kitchen to refill the tray. Kathleen had borrowed some extra cups just in case more people came back after the service than she had estimated, but she hadn't dreamed so many would.

Peter was knocking back his third sherry (at least!). He was sitting next to the stove in the armchair where Tom normally resided and, as Mary remarked, he looked like he might be there for the night! Eventually, Esther pulled on her driving gloves and declared it was time to go. Luckily she was teetotal apart from a sip of Communion wine every Sunday. The next intrusive noise which disturbed the mourning party's subdued conversations was the revving of Esther's Morris Minor and much gravel being thrown up as she eventually lurched forward and out of the driveway, driving over the edge of the flower bed as she did so.

Wilf was sitting in the garden, a cold cup of tea in Kathleen's best china by his feet. His brother Stanley had been sitting with him, catching up on the past few years since they had last met. He lived on a small farm in Lincolnshire and grew vegetables, supplying many local shops. He was always busy and rarely had time to visit family. The brothers regretted this now as they talked about the old days. Stanley's Norfolk accent was now much less pronounced than Wilf's.

They talked about their younger brother, Ernest, who was disabled, having had polio as a child. He lived alone in sheltered housing in north Norfolk and was unable to get out of his bungalow without a great deal of help. He had written a letter to Wilf, when he heard of his bereavement, which Wilf let Stanley read. Luckily Wilf had put the letter in his pocket in case Stanley was able to get to the funeral.

Stanley had tears in his eyes as he passed the letter back to Wilf. 'That's a lovely letter our Ernest has written to you, Wilf.'

'That it is. I must try and visit him.'

'I haven't seen him either for about nine months. Time flies and work doesn't get any easier. It's hard keeping up with all the shop orders. Anyway, Wilf, I must find Alice in the kitchen and get going now. I think she was doing some washing up last time I saw her.'

'Right yew are, Stanley, and thanks ever so for cummin.'

'Well of course I would come. We must try to keep in touch. The last time I saw you was at Ben Foster's funeral.'

'So it was. Oh dear! Right, yis please, come and see me again when yew get sum time.'

'I will, Wilf, goodbye.' Stanley patted Wilf's shoulder, wondering how he would cope if Alice were taken from him. He hoped he and Alice would have many more years together and decided to ensure they spent more time together when work would allow.

The bench had not long been vacated when Leonard's stooped figure approached Wilf, aided by his walking stick. He sat down next to him on the wooden garden bench. Leonard felt uneasy, but managed to say, 'It should ha' bin me, shouldn't it, Wilf?'

Wilf looked a little vague but roused himself from his thoughts of his brothers and realised what Leonard was saying and replied, 'No, no… I don't think that at all, Leonard. Cors' I don't.'

They both sat silently together for a while. Wilf eventually broke the silence and remarked how they had both lost their wives at a young age.

Leonard said, 'Wull… don't yew a' going following my example will yer, Wilf… Yew must look arfta yerself… Look what I've done to m'self… what a fool I've bin! But Mabel was everything ta me and I was too blind ta see it. I don't believe I ever thanked 'er for all she did. But how was I ta know she would be taken from me so young, an' all… Life's a sod at times… but this isn't what I should be saying to yew… Yew know how it feels… I just want to say… sorry, I s'pose… wull… to Elizabeth for abandoning her rear-lly… but it's too late a cors'. I dew feel bad… but also… thank yew for finding her and loving her as yew did… She was a great gal… like her mother, yew know in many ways… I just didn't know what t' do with two gals to raise who needed a mother, not a fewl like me, to put them on the right path.'

Wilf broke his gaze from the neatly-trimmed hawthorn hedge; Tom had obviously been busy in the garden. 'Wull, Leonard, yew should be prowd that both Elizabeth and Kathleen turned out fine, didn't they?' Wilf was amazed at Leonard's conversation, he was normally a man of few words and he realised that he must have been blaming himself for his daughter's death. He was touched by his frankness and wondered whether he had rehearsed expressing his feelings.

'Yis, they did an' all, but no thanks to me, although I loved 'em so… I just couldn't show it I s'pose. I just hope it wasn't my fault that Elizabeth never had children… Yew know how she was always fretting over me and gitting me straight at hom' when she should hev been with yew.'

'Leonard, yew know that Elizabeth loved to mother yew

and she could never keep still… liked to be kept busy she always said. I don't know why we never had children… she would have been a perfect mother, that she would. I'm not sure whether I would have been a good father or not… it frightened me a little at the thought of it… But any way, it was not meant t' be. Elizabeth used to say it was God's will. She got talking to Esther once in the church and apparently she had problems having a family too. Having children must be wonderful if yew're able, but then raising them can be difficult too. Family life used to be much simpler in my day. We didn't have a lot when I was a child, but we didn't go without anything important. What yew don't hev, yew don't miss, I s'pose.'

'It was the same with rationing during the war; mealtimes were special and what we did hev we made the most of. Mother was so good at making meals out of very little and mekkin do with what little we had.'

John, Mary's husband, appeared, which interrupted the conversation. He was carrying two fresh cups of tea and said that Mary and Kathleen kept thrusting cups of tea at him to deliver to anyone who needed one. Wilf commented that he was awash with tea, having drunk more over the last few days than he would normally consume in a month. John told Leonard that a lady called Ann Catchpole had wished to be remembered to him. He didn't know who she was, but she had been at the funeral. She had to catch a train back to London, so hadn't been able to call at the cottage.

'Ann Catchpole! Wull I never did, that's a rummin!'

'Who is she?' enquired John.

'Ann was an evacuee who stayed with her mother with me an' Mabel during the war. Fancy her a'cuming all that way to our Elizabeth's funeral. Ann was only a baby when she was staying with us. Mabel an' I often said we saved a fortune on dolls cos 'lizabeth and Kathleen used to push Ann around in the pram all day. Kathleen could hardly see over the top of that old pram! Ann's mother, Lillian, died about three years ago, I think. She used to help on the Potter's farm. She had a hard life an' all. I wish I'd sin Ann, though I doubt I would ha' recognised her. Kathleen must ha' wrote an' told her 'bout our 'lizabeth.'

Leonard had cheered up a little, remembering the happy times they had, despite world events during the war. 'The war brought a lot of people tergether as well as separatin' a lot of others. Mabel used to write often to Lillian, they got very close. As for Ann, she was like a baby sister to Kathleen and 'lizabeth. I wonder if Kathleen saw her to speak to.'

'I don't know, Leonard, but Ann said she would contact you soon and that she would try and visit when she could get some time off work. She has found some old photographs which she would like to show you too,' John said.

'Wull, I'd best be goin'... Dew yew keepa troshin, Wilf.'

Friends from the village Women's Institute had helped Kathleen and Mary to wash up and clear away the tea cups and residue of the funeral tea. Most of the food had been eaten. They finally sat down and breathed a sigh of relief that all the guests had gone home and they could enjoy the quiet time together.

'So, Mary, when am I to become a grandmother?' Kathleen suddenly asked.

'Mother! Are you serious? You know that I'm not ready to have my body stretched and disfigured for nine long months and to go grey overnight. Isn't that what yew claimed happened to yew because of having me?' replied Mary.

'I wouldn't have said that, Mary!'

'Wull yew did, and many more of your aches and pains and worries have been attributed to me over the years!'

'Yew know I didn't mean it, Mary! Don't leave it too long though...'

'Yes, I know ... in case we're not blessed with children ... like Aunt Elizabeth. Yew've told me many times.'

'Alright, enough said… And here's my *favourite* son-in-law!'

'Ha, ha, Mother-in-law, I am your *only* son-in-law!' added John, having now come in from the garden. 'I'm surely off duty now from tea delivery, aren't I?'

'Yes, of course, we've just shut up shop, John! Thank yew. Tell me how work is going.'

'It's alright, though at times I wonder how I'm going to keep control of some of the classes. They have no respect for us teachers. I wouldn't have dared act like some of the fewls in my classes at present.'

'Yew will have to make it clear who's boss!' laughed Kathleen.

'Easier said than done, but still I'm glad to have a job. It's strange working in the school where you used to be yourself … and your mother-in-law, come to that. The graffiti you scrawled on the desks still exists, you know!' teased John.

'I don't think so, John… my feather quill could never make any mark on the desks!' retorted Kathleen.

'Very quick-witted aren't you!' laughed John. 'Talking of ancient times… seriously now… Ann Catchpole was at the funeral and she said she was going to get in touch soon. I have just been hearing how she was like a baby sister to yew and Aunt Elizabeth.'

'Gosh, that's who it was! I saw her and knew she looked familiar but just couldn't place her. And then I was helping Wilf and Dad into the cars to come back here and I missed seeing her to talk to. I wish I had spoken to her; we have a lot of catching up to do. I haven't seen her for years. I'd forgotten I'd informed her about our Elizabeth. I wrote so many notes to the people we normally send Christmas cards to, but haven't seen for ages. I wonder who else I missed seeing. The church was so full wasn't it? I was rather overwhelmed by all the people that made the effort to come. Don't suppose there'll be so many at my funeral!'

'Mum! For goodness' sake, be quiet. Can yew change the

subject?'

'Actually, Mary, I had to smile to myself earlier. I was remembering the time that I helped Esther with the special tea she was preparing after the Synod meeting, at the vicarage some years ago now, shortly after I started helping her in the vicarage. She left me making a trifle, whilst she went to get some shopping she had forgotten. Her last words were, "Just help yourself, Kathleen, to what you need … most things should be in the pantry." So I started making the trifle and well… you know me… a trifle isn't really a trifle without sherry, now is it? So I started looking for some sherry and eventually found what I thought was Esther's cooking sherry and let's say I was fairly generous with it, which flavoured the trifle. I thought no more about it. On the Sunday after church, Esther was full of praise for my trifle, which had gone down very well with the Synod members. However, she commented how Peter seemed a bit frantic at the altar since his Communion wine stock seemed rather depleted. He was sure he had plenty when he had last checked the pantry shelf at the vicarage!'

'Oh, Mother! I hope you confessed!'

'What do yew think?'

* * *

Rebecca got off the school bus and walked home. The door was locked so she went to the back of the house and lifted a large pot holding a withered plant, which was now hard to identify. A spare house key was revealed and she let herself in, dropping her school bag at the door.

She poured a glass of orange squash and drank it rather too quickly, then opened the biscuit tin. She took out three custard creams, shut and locked the door, returning the key to its hiding place and walked down the road, munching her biscuits. She wished she had taken more as she was always hungry at this time of day, especially when she was on first sitting for school dinner. It was the First Years' turn for early lunch this week.

She wandered down the road to the churchyard and paused at the gateway leading to the graveyard. There was no one around. She walked to the mound of earth covered with flowers, which she guessed must be Mrs Ford's grave. She stood staring at the flowers that not only covered the grave but were laid alongside it, as there were so many. Then she noticed her withered forget-me-nots. Someone had moved them here to be with the rest of the flowers. Oh dear, she wished she had picked flowers which would have stayed fresh. They looked overwhelmed by the beautiful sprays and wreaths of flowers around them.

Rebecca whispered, 'Mrs Ford, I'm sorry I couldn't come to the funeral. I will miss you… I…'

Rebecca heard someone walking down the gravel pathway to the churchyard, so decided to cut short her visit and leave, feeling rather uncomfortable being here on her own. She didn't recognise the person who was approaching her holding a bunch of flowers, but said 'hello' as they passed each other on the path. She decided she could return here soon to visit Mrs Ford's grave again.

* * *

Rebecca decided to walk back through the wood, which was ablaze with autumn colours. She feasted her eyes on their extensive palette of golds, reds and browns. She was glad she had kept her school blazer on, as the sun was fading now and it struggled to penetrate the dwindling foliage, precariously holding on to the branches. As a slight breeze rustled the trees, a few more leaves were released and fell gracefully to the ground. One leaf tickled Rebecca's face on its journey to join the growing carpet of leaves. She held her blazer tightly around her, rather than fasten the buttons. It was rather too big for her still, but Mum said she would grow in to it and, as the uniforms were so expensive, it would have to last her several years. She pulled up her long beige socks for added warmth and continued through the wood. She had often walked here, perhaps more reluctantly in the past, with Mum and Michael.

Rebecca thought she had better hurry back now and get on with her homework. She had a history test tomorrow on the ancient pyramids. History was not one of her favourite subjects, but she knew Miss Parker would give her a hard time if she didn't get at least fifty per cent in the test. Who would want to be a teacher, she wondered.

She didn't know what she wanted to be when she left school; it seemed to be such a long way off that it didn't matter right now. She couldn't imagine being an adult and having to work. Her dad had told her recently that 'school days are the best days of your life', which seemed a frightening prospect. At least when she left school she wouldn't have to study subjects like history which seemed so useless to her and no help with her future adult life. Elizabeth used to encourage her with her homework and lend her books. She had a set of very useful encyclopaedias, which were a great reference source and easier to use at Elizabeth's than carry home to use. She would really miss Elizabeth.

As she walked towards the row of council houses where she lived, her parents were just returning home from being at the funeral tea. It was strange to see Dad dressed smartly in a dark suit, as he usually wore the Hastings brown overalls and brown cap.

Chapter Four

Lessons

'How rich art is; if one can only remember what one has seen, one is never without food for thought or truly lonely, never alone…'

'These are the words of Vincent van Gogh… a letter to his brother Theo, written in 1878,' said Miss Price. Rebecca was enjoying a history of art lesson. These words were more meaningful than Shakespeare's!

She thought for a moment of her brother Michael and reflected upon his change in character when he was painting or drawing. He definitely displayed the better side of his nature when he was involved with his artwork. Perhaps she should encourage him to paint more, but he never listened to his little sister. The people Michael hung around with didn't have time for creativity, unless it involved scrawling graffiti on a wall somewhere, and Michael didn't tell his mates about his hobby. He was rather modest when it came to his art and preferred to be alone when out sketching. If anyone came along the country lanes or fields where he was working, he would hastily cover up his work or pretend he was involved in some other activity.

Rebecca wondered if she should call and see Wilf tonight on the way home from school, but she didn't know what to say. She imagined he must be feeling lost without Elizabeth. Rebecca wondered what the cottage would be like without Elizabeth's radiant presence. She was sure that Tiger would be missing her already.

Rebecca realised her thoughts had been wandering from the lesson... now back to Van Gogh... He had shot himself. How crazy! She tried to visualise the scene... maybe wheat fields... a black sky... crows noisily circling overhead... She could hear the gunshot, a common sound in the country when rabbits were being shot ... and Van Gogh dragging himself to his home, bleeding and distraught ... and eventually dying. Why would anyone want to kill themselves, she wondered? Rebecca had a vivid imagination, or so many people kept telling her, including her mother. What a waste of life and talent. She wished she was able to draw or paint. Van Gogh must have been brave, she thought to herself, to have pulled the trigger. Why would he do it, though?

'Rebecca Mason, why haven't you tied your hair back?' asked Miss Price, now looking at Rebecca.

'Well, Miss... I, er... couldn't find my ribbon this morning and I... er... sorry Miss.'

'Use this elastic band for now and make sure you're better presented tomorrow, will you?'

'Yes, Miss Price,' replied Rebecca and realising now where the ribbon had gone.

She couldn't help smiling to herself. She had looked all over the house that morning for her ribbon and eventually gave up, fearing she would miss the school bus. Now she remembered she had used it for Mrs Ford's posy of forget-me-nots. Her parents had told her that her flowers and little rhyme had been the highlight of the funeral service. Rebecca couldn't quite believe that, nor could she believe her parents telling her about it. They had *actually* appeared proud of her.

She liked making up rhymes. Sometimes, when she had visited Mrs Ford, she would tell her a rhyme or limerick she was composing and ask her to suggest a final line or verse. Sometimes they would laugh hysterically when one of them suggested a rather silly line. Rebecca loved that about Mrs Ford; she was almost like an older sister to Rebecca in the way she had such fun with her.

Rebecca's mum always seemed serious and stressed and, when Rebecca thought about it, she very rarely laughed. It was as though she was carrying a heavy burden on her shoulders.

Rebecca had preferred the company of Elizabeth to friends of her own age. She was a bit of a loner really. There was Clare Franks in the village who she used to spend time with, but she didn't see much of her now that she attended the secondary modern school, along with Rebecca's three other friends who had been in her class at primary school. Elizabeth had tried to reassure Rebecca many times that she would make new friends once she started at the grammar school. She did have some good friends but they lived seven miles away so she didn't see them very often since her mum couldn't drive and the local bus service wasn't very frequent. Occasionally her dad would collect her from one of her friend's houses on his route home in the works' lorry. How embarrassing that had been, clambering in to the lorry with 'Hastings Farm Feeds' emblazoned on the truck.

Her friends from the grammar school seemed to live in a different world to the one in which she had grown up. Their mothers didn't seem to be working all the time and her friends' parents drove smart cars, unlike her dad's rather rusty mini that he said would last forever! Fortunately her friends rarely asked to go to Rebecca's house. She wasn't ashamed of living in a council house, she had known nothing else, but she had been amazed at her friends' smart houses. They all had televisions. Dad said they might be able to afford one soon, but there always seemed to be some unexpected expense which came along preventing the purchase.

Perhaps she would try and visit Clare again when she

wasn't entering a gymkhana. They used to spend a lot of time together and Clare let Rebecca ride her pony. Rebecca used to dream about having her own pony but realised that dreaming was the closest she would get to owning one.

Chapter Five

Life Must Go On

Wilf turned the sand egg timer over as he released a large brown egg carefully from a metal spoon in to the boiling water in an old saucepan on the cooker. He sat down and found himself staring at the sand trickling through its narrow route to the glass chamber now standing on its head. The egg-timer had been a present to Elizabeth from Rebecca. She had bought the souvenir from Great Yarmouth, when she had visited the golden sandy beach one summer on a school trip. Elizabeth had gone to help the class teacher, together with a few willing mothers, to cope with all the excited pupils.

Wilf was mesmerised by the sand, never having watched it before, although the timer must have been in the kitchen for nearly four years. He was watching time pass. He roused himself from his stupor as the last grains joined the top of the miniature conical sandcastle. He rescued the egg from the boiling water and tipped it in to an eggcup on a plate, already half covered by two thick slices of bread and butter. He cut off the top of the egg and shook a little salt and pepper on to the golden yellow yolk. Wilf had successfully boiled one of Kathleen's hens' eggs for his breakfast. Not bad for a first attempt! Who said he couldn't cook!

He listened to the wireless while he ate his breakfast

and looked across at the empty space at the table where Elizabeth should be sitting. She had never gone away during their married years and it seemed so lonely sitting at the table with no one to talk to. He wondered what they had talked about at every mealtime; they had always plenty to talk about… the vegetables which were nearly ready to gather from the garden, the particularly pleasant colouring in the flower beds… or snippets of conversation Elizabeth had reported from school.

She came home with some wonderful stories. One day she had told Wilf about the school's visit to an open farm park, which was about twenty miles away. The class had watched some lambs being born. One little boy looked astounded as a lamb emerged from its mother and had remarked, 'How did it git in *there*?' How Wilf and Elizabeth had laughed at the story and often recalled the tale.

Wilf looked at the children's drawings on the wall and thought he was unlikely to receive any more artwork. He had often thought Elizabeth would have been a good teacher as she had such patience with the children and enjoyed teaching them about wild flowers, trees and nature. She was often the supplier of exhibits for the school's nature table. She would sometimes help the teachers in class too, when her kitchen duties had been complete. She was happy to give her own time to help at school, gaining much pleasure from the children's company.

Wilf finished his breakfast. It wasn't the usual hearty breakfast he used to enjoy which Elizabeth had cooked for him, but it satisfied his small appetite that morning. He felt restless and decided he would go back to work tomorrow. He just didn't know what to do on his own in the cottage and felt he would rather be kept busy.

He got on his bicycle, which had been returned to him. He wasn't sure who had dropped it off, unless it was Bob Mason who often delivered feedstuff to the farm next door to the doctor's house.

Wilf cycled the short distance to the farm and found Mrs Potter in the kitchen. He told her he would return to his duties the following morning. Life must go on. Rose tried to dissuade him, saying it was too early after losing Elizabeth and he needed time to himself. Wilf hesitated at the thought that all his remaining years would be 'time to himself' and what a lonely feeling it was. Time to himself was already making him feel insane and he thought that he would cope better if he had a routine to follow, so that he wasn't left thinking too long on his own, wondering what might have been…

Rose, of course, could sympathise with Wilf, having lost her husband. She had never really been on her own though, since her bereavement. Her son, Jim, stepped into her husband's shoes to run the farm and farm life was always so busy. At times, Rose still expected Mr Potter to appear at the kitchen doorway asking what was for dinner. She had often laid an extra place at the table, forgetting that her husband could no longer sit at his usual place.

'Oh, I've been meaning to ask you, Wilf, if that was your brother I saw at the funeral?'

'Yis, Stanley was there.'

'I thought he had to be your brother. You are very much alike.'

'He is five years older than me. We have a younger brother, Ernest, but he couldn't manage to come.'

'I didn't know you even had brothers, Wilf. I suppose we don't often have time to chat about such things, do we?'

'No, we don't. The funeral has made me realise, though, how important our family is and I am going to try to keep in touch with them from now on.'

After the inevitable cup of tea with Rose, Wilf cycled down to the churchyard. It was so peaceful there and it was as though time stood still as he reached what would become an arena for regular reflection. It was nine thirty and there was heavy dew on the grass and Elizabeth's flowers still looked quite fresh on her grave.

Wilf read the cards attached to the wreaths once more. He had done this on the evening after the funeral but he felt more composed now and wanted to read all the nice things that had been written about his wife. He felt very proud that she had been a part of his life, but could not accept that she had been cruelly snatched away from him. It took about twenty minutes to read all the cards, some of which were difficult to decipher now that the dampness had partially obliterated the kind words, probably so carefully thought out before being written by their sender. However, Wilf could remember the odd word which was now just an ink splodge and he would reflect upon the kind sentiments over the many visits he would make to Elizabeth's grave in the weeks and months to come, long after the flowers had died and been reluctantly discarded in the bin in the churchyard.

He found himself making the graveyard visit every day and felt oddly close to Elizabeth here. He talked to her too, once he was sure no one was in the churchyard, hoping that she might be able to hear him. If only he could get a reply… to hear her voice once more… to have answers to all his questions… for her to acknowledge that she was missing him too.

* * *

Charles was in his car at a road junction just outside Freckingham, having been at a meeting in Coddleton. Which direction would he go? He longed to turn left towards the village of Watton, where Cynthia might just be working in the pub… He hesitated. A car tooted its horn impatiently behind him and he found himself driving away from where his heart wanted to take him. He continued his journey home.

Chapter Six

Cookery Lessons

'Thanks, Elizabeth, for having Rebecca. We will be as quick as we can. You be good now, Rebecca.'

'Yes, Mummy. Bye bye.'

'Bye bye, Becca.'

'Bye, Cynthia, now don't yew worry… we'll be fine, just fine. Won't we, Rebecca?' asked Elizabeth.

'Of course we will, Mrs Ford,' replied Rebecca without hesitation. She loved spending time with Mrs Ford, who had endless patience and never got cross with her.

Cynthia and Robert Mason were in fact going shopping to buy Rebecca a new bike for her eighth birthday, which was fast approaching. Cynthia had done quite a lot of extra hours of work at the pub to help fund the bicycle.

'I think your mum might be a while shopping with your dad, Rebecca. Would you like to bake some bread with me?'

'I'd love to do that!'

'Come on, my dear, then. Let's find you a pinny. Here, if we pull the ties at the back and attach it to the neck tape, it won't be tew long will't… How's that? Oh dear! Well at least it will keep you clean!' laughed Elizabeth, looking at Rebecca in the oversized apron, which was still covering her ankles despite the adjustments.

'Let's wash our hands first shall we, my dear? I hope you

haven't been in those ditches collecting flowers on the way!'

'No, not today.'

'Good. It won't take long then, to get your hands spick and span. Here's the towel.'

'Thank you.'

'Can you help me measure the ingredients now?'

'Yes, Mrs Ford.'

'Climb up on this chair, my dear. Yew go carefully now… Here are the scales … now then … we need a pound and a half of this here strong bread flour. If you start tipping the bag over the bowl on the scales, I'll tell you when to stop, OK, my dear?'

'Yes.'

'That's it … keep you a' goin' … slow down … yes that's it, well done. Right, a couple o' teaspoons of salt … yes that's it. Right … I put the yeast and sugar and warm water to mix a little while ago and it's ready to use now. Look at the froth on the top. We just need to tip it in and mix it all together. Not forgetting a bit of elbow grease!'

'Urrh, what's that?'

'I mean a bit of effort, that's all! I tell you what, I'll mix it up a bit more first and then we'll divide it up so you can manage kneading the dough. There's too much dough for your little hands to cope with.'

'Alright, Mrs Ford. What's that funny smell?'

'It's the yeast, no doubt. It helps the bread rise. Right, here yew are… a piece of your own. Watch me a minute… see… keep pushing your knuckles in to the dough and then push the dough away from you… and keep on doing it… and turning it… like this… to make it quite elastic… A little more flour if it gets tew sticky… Yew can get rid of all your frustration with this, yew know!'

'What do you mean, Mrs Ford?'

'Wull, yew know how yew are always telling me that your brother Michael gits orn your wick… Wull, yew can beat this dough and get rid of your angry feelings if yew like!'

'That's a good idea… like this?'

'Oh steady, my gal… poor Michael, I think he felt that! Look at the flour cloud!'

'Sorry, Mrs Ford, I didn't mean to mek a mess,' giggled Rebecca.

'That don't matter my booty, we're having fun aren't we?'

'Yes, I am.'

'Yew've got the hang of it… that yew hev.'

'It's hard work, isn't it?'

'Yes it is, 'specially for yew, my dear. I think that's nearly enough kneading now. We will leave our dough here by the stove to prove.'

'To prove what, Mrs Ford?'

'Sorry… to rise I mean. That's lovely, Rebecca. Put the dough in this bowl, that's it. We just need to cover our bowls now with these her' cloths. Shall we wash our hands again and get a well earned drink?'

'Yes, please.'

'What would yew like, my dear?'

'Some of your lovely lemonade if you have any, please.'

'That's fine. There's plenty here in the larder. An oat biscuit or two an' all?'

'Oh yes, please, Mrs Ford. Can I blow some of my bubbles now I brought?'

'Of course yew can, my dear. I'll git on with my washing up.'

'Can I sit on your kitchen doorstep?'

'Yes of course, my dear. Here hev this cushion to sit on.'

'Thank you. Ooooh, look at this one… it's ginormous!' exclaimed Rebecca later, as she gently blew a bubble from the plastic loop which formed it, having been dipped in the soapy solution.

'It certainly is, Rebecca!'

Rebecca and Elizabeth held their breath as they watched

the large delicate bubble drift out of the doorway into the garden, almost bouncing in the air, until it finally burst.

'Oh, that's a shame, it was heading to see Wilf at the farm!' giggled Elizabeth.

'It would never have got that far!' said Rebecca laughing.

'Yew never know!'

Rebecca sat contentedly making bubbles. Every time she blew another one she watched mesmerised as it floated away. She noticed purple and pink colours as the sun highlighted the film of soap bubble.

'Oh, my bubbles have run out now!'

'Never mind, let's top them up with some washing up liquid, it will make bubbles... possibly even bigger!'

'Thank you, Mrs Ford.'

Elizabeth finished clearing the kitchen.

'Right, my booty, what would yew like to do now?'

'Um ...what about hopscotch?'

'Hopscotch? Goodness! It's bin a while since I played hopscotch... but I dare say I can give it a go! I'll have to find some chalk. I'll have a look in the outhouse, I think we might have some there,' said Elizabeth as she disappeared out of the door.

'Any luck, Mrs Ford?'

'Yes, I've found a little bit. This is probably what Wilf used for the fête signs on the blackboards for the stalls; I think it'll dew. Right we'll have to use this little bit of concrete path. Let's see now... how do I do this?'

'Start with one square, then join on two, I think.'

'What, like this?'

'Yes, Mrs Ford. Now one square... yes, keep going up to ten.'

'Dew yew want to write the numbers in?'

'Yes, I will do it!'

'Oh dear the chalk is getting small now, isn't it?'

'Well it's almost done, we can pretend there's a number

ten in the last square.'

'Cors we can! Right yew start and remind me what to do.'

'First I need to find a stone and you do too, Mrs Ford.'

'Right… is this one alright?'

'Yes, I think so.'

'Right, we have to roll the stone on to the first square and if it lands in the square… I'll try… ooops, too far!'

'Have another go… yew are just explaining to me what to do.'

'Alright… yes! That's it, now I have to hop like this… to the end… and then back and then I roll again to the two and so on till we reach number ten… or the blank square!'

'Oh, I see.'

'The first to get to the end wins.'

'Do yew play this with your mum?'

'No, I have never asked her. But we play it at school a lot.'

'Oh, I'll have to look out of the kitchen window at school and pick up some tips then!'

'There! I missed the three, so now it's your turn.'

'I hope Wilf doesn't come home now, he'll think I'm wholly daft!'

Elizabeth carefully rolled the stone and it landed perfectly on the one.'

'Well done, Mrs Ford!'

'Thank yew… beginner's luck!'

'Now the hopping!'

'That's the difficult bit… Oh! Oh, my goodness me, oh, Rebecca, I feel a bit silly… is that right?'

'Yes, you did it. Now try number two.'

'Oh dear, I've missed two. At least I can catch my breath whilst yew hav' your turn again!'

Rebecca and Elizabeth continued playing hopscotch amidst much giggling and eventually Rebecca won, although Elizabeth probably purposefully rolled her stone too far on the final blank number ten square, which ensured Rebecca caught up again and won the game.'

'Oh well, I hope it doesn't rain tonight, so I can get some practice later before yew challenge me again! Mind yew, if Ivan the postman sees this in the morning, he will think I'm daft, won't he? Perhaps the rain had better wash it away!'

'He might be a hopscotch champion! I'll have to remember to bring my chalks round another time.'

'Right, we had better check on the progress in the kitchen. Let's wash our hands and have another cold drink though first. Phew I'm fair whacked!'

'I feel a bit thirsty after that… It was fun.'

'Oh dear me, let me just sit down a minute!'

'Your cheeks are very red!'

'I'm not surprised after that! Phew, I'll get that drink I promised yew in a minute.'

'Thank you. That lemonade was lovely,' declared Rebecca as she gulped down the cold drink.

'Right, I must pull myself tergether! Now then, we need to knead this again.'

'Goodness. I never knew bread took so long to make!'

'It will be worth all your hard work, when you have some later with some strawberry jam.'

'I can't wait.'

'Here's your dough again. Look how well it's risen.'

'Oh yes, almost to the top of the bowl. It's magic! It feels different, doesn't it? Quite spongy.'

'That's right. It won't take too long now. Hev yew got any energy left? I'm tired out!'

'I've got a little left! Oh, it's getting smaller again… the dough is disappearing!'

'It's just the air being knocked out of it, but it will come back! That's it… you are quite an expert baker, my dear! Perhaps teacher will let yew help me in the school kitchen when I need some extra help or when Mrs Smith is poorly.'

'It's fun. I think I want to be a school cook like you when

I grow up.'

'That would be good. Right shall we put the dough in the tins now?'

'Yes.'

'Here's a small tin for your loaf.'

'Thanks.'

'We have to leave the loaves again now to rise again.'

'That sounds like Mr Croft speaking about Jesus at Sunday school!'

'Oh Rebecca, yew silly billy! Hev yew got any of your rhymes for me to finish whilst the bread rises?'

'No, but I'll think of one in a minute! What about… There was a young girl from Diss…'

'…who dreaded her very first kiss…'

'…she wore… a mask… to cover her face…'

'…and hoped her boyfriend would miss! Oh dear, perhaps that's not the best ending!' laughed Elizabeth.

'It'll do, Mrs Ford!' laughed Rebecca.

'Shall we play "I spy"?'

'Yes, yew start.'

'I spy with my little eye something beginning with… oh dear… C…'

'Um… ceiling? Or does that begin with S?'

'Not ceiling, but yew were right, ceiling does begin with C. Well done.'

'Uuuumm… let me think… that can… of peaches?'

'No.'

'Cat? Though I can't see her!'

'No.'

'Cabbage?'

'No.'

Rebecca scanned the kitchen looking for potential words. 'Carrot?'

'No.'

'Uuurrrr… cutlery?'

'No... should I give yew a clue?'

'Yes please.'

'Yew were close when yew said ceiling...'

Rebecca looked up and said, 'Oh, is it cobweb?'

'Yes, I'm afraid it is! The spiders in this house have been busy, haven't they? I'll have to get that cobweb down when we've finished baking. Right, your turn.'

'I spy with my little eye something beginning with H!'

'Hopscotch?'

'No!'

'Hoover?'

'Yes! Your turn again.'

'I spy with my little eye... something beginning with B.'

'Bread?'

'Yes, first guess! Yew are too good!'

'I spy with my little eye something beginning with... T.'

'...tired old woman!'

'No silly!'

'Tin?'

'Yes! Your turn again.'

'I spy with my little eye something beginning with... oh yes, B...'

'Bowl?'

'No.'

'Bin?'

'No.'

'Oh, I can see what yew are looking at! It's a bishi barni bee!'

'Yes it is, where did she fly in from I wonder?'

* * *

Rebecca called the following day to see Wilf after school. She hesitated at the door waiting to be asked in. It was not the same without Elizabeth being there. Rebecca used to knock at the door with the brass doorknocker, which was always well polished, and just walk in, calling to Elizabeth as she did so. She felt a little awkward now standing on the doorstep.

Wilf looked surprised to see her and nearly said, 'Elizabeth's not here,' but realised that she must have called to see him. Rebecca explained that she had made some rock buns in the cookery lesson at school and wondered if he would like to have a few cakes.

Wilf was touched by her thoughtfulness and invited her in. They sat down together sampling the spicy buns. Wilf later asked for the recipe, saying he would have to try some baking! Rebecca found herself laughing at Wilf, knowing that he had often said it was a woman's domain in the kitchen. But he was determined to give it a try, feeling he had something to prove perhaps. Rebecca knew that normally Elizabeth had done all the cooking, which wasn't surprising since she was so good at it.

'Perhaps you've been a frustrated cook for many years, Mr Ford,' she suggested.

He laughed and said, 'No, o' cors not.' However he was already planning his first baking session. Rebecca told him how she'd heard that all the boys at Coddleton School had to do cookery lessons, which surprised Wilf. There had been no cookery lessons in his day, that was for sure; but then he hadn't attended school for any longer than he had to, preferring to help at the farm whenever possible. It had just been assumed that he would work on the farm as soon as he was old enough. He had two brothers and they had always expected their mother to make all the meals, because … well, wasn't that what mothers did? Apparently not any more, according to Rebecca.

Wilf was amazed to hear that Rebecca would be having some basic woodwork lessons next year at her girls' grammar school. 'What was happenin' to tha world?' he wondered.

A few days later he cycled down to the village shop where his niece Mary worked, with his list in his hand with all the ingredients he would need for his rock buns!

Mary was amazed at her uncle's need for mixed spice and self-raising flour. She asked if her mum had called to do some baking for him, to which he replied, 'No ... I er ... wull, I thought I might try my hand at bakin' myself. I don't know what yew women make all the fuss about, I'm sure it's not that tricky.'

'We'll see, won't we, Uncle!'

The shop sold most things the villagers needed, from tins of baked beans to elastic! Mary quite enjoyed serving in the shop and knew most of the customers by name. They very rarely had passing trade. Old Miss Millicent Brown, the owner, served on the post office counter. She looked so frail and was past retirement age, but wanted to keep working for a 'year or two yet', as she kept saying. Mary smiled to herself whenever she heard Millicent stamping letters or pension books as her frailty seemed to disappear when in charge of a rubber stamp!

Mary had tried to influence Millicent's stock in the shop by suggesting she introduce some more modern lines, but she was reluctant to risk stocking items which might not sell. Mary felt like reminding her of the old stock she had recently dusted down and tidied from the little storeroom still price-marked with old currency, but thought better of it.

Mary had to write down the prices of the goods people bought on a notepad and add them all up in her head. She found this easy now, but when she started work she had felt the eyes of her customers who were trying to tot up the figures to check she got her sums right! Maths hadn't been her best subject at school.

The till was a wooden drawer which needed a sharp pull to open it and it gave a satisfying ring each time this was done. Mary longed for a modern till, which would save her having to do her mental arithmetic. However, the shop had character and it was the only one for three miles, which meant Millicent had a good business and would ensure she had a comfortable retirement. She lived alone with her poodle, Sooty.

The doorbell jingled noisily to announce the arrival of the next customer, Esther Croft. She had her wicker basket on her arm and peered at the counter displaying half-price cakes.

'The sell-by dates expire today, Mrs Croft,' explained Mary, 'which is why they are reduced.'

'Oh I see. Well, I'll take this jam sponge cake then. That will be nice for a change. I also need a quarter of red cheese please and a quarter of ham.'

'Of course, Mrs Croft, I'll just go and weigh those for yew.' Mary tore a small piece of greaseproof paper from the roll and cut the large cheddar cheese with the metal wire cutter. 'The cheese is just over, Mrs Croft,' called Mary from the back of the shop. 'That's five an' a half ounces … is that alright?'

'Yes, I expect we'll eat it… Thank yew, my dear… How is your mother, Mary?'

'Not too bad, thank yew,' replied Mary concentrating on slicing the ham now. 'We really miss Aunt Elizabeth though. Uncle Wilf was just in the shop before you came.'

'Yes, I saw him cycling up the hill with his shopping, he gave me a wave. He looked a bit weary… but then we probably all do! Now then… right… ham and cheese, I've got… a packet of custard creams, please… a tin of peas… oh, and a tin of Spam too. Now what have I forgotten?'

'Do yew need any fruit today, Mrs Croft?'

'Of course! Thank yew, my dear, yes… A tin of peaches and a pound of those Golden Delicious, please.'

'That's one pound and four ounces or I can take an apple off, if you want just under the pound, Mrs Croft,' said Mary, concentrating on the big metal weights which balanced the silver coloured weighing pan holding the apples.

'Oh I don't know… just under the pound I think, please… All these decisions! Oh… and perhaps I'll take a packet of those trifle sponges… they are half price too, I see. Oh yes, and I had better take two more cans of cat food. Those cats of poor old Amy's keep coming back to be fed. At least they seem to be keeping the mice numbers down, so I can store my cooking apples in the outbuilding. Now that really is all. How much do I owe yew?'

'That's four pounds, ten pence please, Mrs Croft.'

'There we are… four crisp pound notes straight off the washing line! I told yew how I washed Peter's trousers the other day with his money in his pocket, did I?'

'Yes, yew did!'

'Oh dear me! Peter's face when he found me in the garden drying the notes. He thought I'd lost my marbles, as yew young 'uns seem t' say!'

'Easily done though. My mum always checks my dad's pockets before she washes his trousers and she says she can keep anything he's been daft enough to leave in his clothes. It's her laundry allowance, she says! Knowing Dad, I bet he doesn't leave much change in his pockets for her!'

'Now then what did yew say…. ten *pence*, oh fiddlesticks, I'll never get the hang of this new money! Two shillings, isn't it?'

'Wull yes, yew're right, that's what it's worth! Thank yew, Mrs Croft, that's great… Four pounds, ten pence exactly, that'll save the change which is running short in the till.'

'Thanks, my dear. Goodness, my basket is heavy, I'm glad I brought the car. Bye, Mary.'

'Good-bye, Mrs Croft.'

Mary smiled to herself. She had heard that tale of the washed pound notes several times this week. Mary liked Esther. She often said she would have things 'for a change' yet seemed to buy the same things most weeks. As it was Thursday today, it would be ham salad at the vicarage. Perhaps peaches and tinned cream for pudding! Tomorrow she would be back to buy a parsley sauce mix for her plaice, which she would buy from the mobile fish shop. Saturday would be shepherd's pie and a nice apple crumble, no doubt!

Mary hoped she wouldn't be quite so predictable in her later years. She didn't particularly like cooking and quite often bought something ready-made from the shop freezer. Aunt Elizabeth had always teased her about it… but not any more. John had dinner at school but could always eat whatever was put in front of him when he got home. He had a good appetite.

The shop bell rang again and it was Rose Potter who came through the door. She went to the post office counter to buy some stamps and to get a parcel weighed. She had just knitted a little cardigan for her new baby great-niece and was sending it through the post. Her great-niece had been called Fiona Rose, so she was really touched that the new baby had a middle name in common with her first name. The baby lived in Lincoln so she hadn't seen her yet, but hoped that she might be brought over soon to meet her great-aunt. Or she might take the train when the farm work settled down a bit if she got impatient waiting to be introduced to Fiona. She needed to be around to make the workers their tea and see to the vet if he called. There was never a dull moment in her kitchen, which was as busy as the farm itself.

'Hello, Mary, how are yew?' she enquired, as she came back to the shop counter.

'Alright thank you, Mrs Potter. How are yew?'

'Oh just fine, thanks. Hev yew heard about my great-niece?'

'Yes, Mum told me your good news. Lovely names too, Fiona Rose.'

'Wull yes, but then I would be biased in favour of them, wouldn't I? Oh, here comes the post van. That was good timing, I've just caught the post, good. I've just seen your mother, Mary, heading towards Coddleton on her moped.'

'Speeding along at exactly thirty miles per hour, no doubt! She's probably gone to collect a prescription for Grandad.'

'Always busy, that mother of yours.'

'Yes, she is. She never sits still, or so Father says anyway.'

'I can quite believe it. Well, I think I will gather some blackberries on the way home. I spotted a lot on the hedge just down the road. I just fancy a blackberry and apple pie.'

'Oh that sounds good, you're not like me who normally buys a pie. They're never the same as home-made are they?'

'I suppose not, but then I never buy them to know the difference, dear. Oh, I mustn't forget … I need a tin of custard powder please, Mary.'

'Large or small tin?'

'I had better have the large tin … it won't last long in my household! How much do I owe yew?'

'That's fifty-nine pence please.'

'There you are, dear.'

'Thank you … and your penny change!'

'Thank you. Well, bye bye, Mary, I'd best get along now.'

'Bye, Mrs Potter.'

'"…And there is a season… turn, turn, turn…" Morning ladies! How are we this fair morning?' enquired Ivan the postman, breaking off his version of the Mary Hopkins' song.

'We're fine, thanks. Hey, Miss Brown, the singing postman's here!'

'Now listen, "Molly Windley", give me twenty No. 6 so I can "smook loike a chimley"… there's a good girl!' retorted Ivan.

'You're quick this morning!'

'Well yew might hear one of my songs on your wireless

yet, my dear!'

'There yew go.'

'Thank yer, my dear. There's the right money unless you've put up yer prices overnight!'

'No that's *just* enough today, thank yer,' smiled Mary as she put the money in the till.

'Morning all,' said Bill Dobson after the doorbell rang loudly and he burst through the shop door.

'Morning, Mr Dobson. What can I get for yer today?'

'An ounce o' bacca... Old Holbourn, if yew please, my dear. Oh and some cuckoo... I'm right owt. Can't git to sleep at night without a nice cup o'cuckoo, an' hav' yer got somethin' for this her' corf, Mary?'

'Owbridges cough expectorant?'

'If it'll git rid of this barkin' that'll do fine, ta.'

'Two pounds, twenty-five pence then please, Mr Dobson.'

'Cor blast, that fiver won't last long then, will it? P'raps yer grandad'll buy me a pint tonight! Her' yer are. Thank yer kindly. I can't stand mardlin' so fare y' well tergether!'

'Thank you. Bye, Mr Dobson.'

'Oh hello, Mr Marsden, how are yew?' asked Mary, as another customer came in.

'Very well, thank you, and how are you?'

'Not bad, thanks. Not a bad day out there, is it?'

'No, it's keeping fine.'

'What can I get for yew today?'

'I would like a half pound of your roast ham, please.'

'Right yew are, sir, won't be a minute... there yew are. Anything else?'

'Just a packet of cornflakes, please.'

'There yew are... that's one pound and twenty-six pence, please.'

'Thanks... oh, put the odd coppers in the charity tin, I can't be doing with too much change rattling around in my pockets. Thanks, bye.'

'Thank yew, cheerio,' replied Mary as she pushed the small coins into the charity tin in aid of guide dogs for the blind.

Mary used the break in customers to catch up on some restocking of the shelves. After about thirty minutes, however, Sam came in, straight from pigsty duties by the smell of him!

'Hullo, Sam, how are yew?'

'Fine, thank yer! Can I hev' a quarter of pear drops please, Mary?'

'Course yew can. I'll just weigh them for yew.' Mary reached for the large jar from a shelf of assorted boiled sweets. She carefully shook the pink sugary contents on to the scales until they balanced at a quarter of a pound and then tipped the metal dish from the weighing scales into a paper bag and twisted the top, to secure the contents. 'There yew are.'

'I'll hev a quarter of barley sugars an' all, Mary.'

'Right, Sam... there yew are ... looks like I need to order more of those... just enough for yew today though. That'll be thirty-six pence, please.'

'Can yew take it from this, Mary?' Sam held out a handful of change amongst sweet wrappers and an assortment of pocket debris.

'That's it, thank you, Sam... the rest is yours!'

'Thank yer, I'll git gorn. Cheerio.'

'Bye, Sam.' Mary reached for the air freshener spray, which was kept beneath the counter for the unwanted aromas which accompanied some of their customers!

The bell jangled again and Mrs Coleman entered. 'Hello, Mary.'

'Hullo, Mrs Coleman, how are yew today?'

'Fair ter middlin' I s'pose, my dear. How are yew teday?'

'Fine thanks.'

'Good. Now then, I told Carol I was coming to the shop,

so here's her list first, if yew don't mind.'

'Right yew are, Mrs Coleman.'

'Whilst you're getting those things tergether, I'll git my pension.'

'I'll just call Miss Brown then. She's just letting Sooty out for a run in the garden I think… Ah, here she is. Alright… which sort of apples does Carol want? Golden Delicious or Granny Smith's?'

'Oh Golden Delicious, I should think. Those Grannys are probably a bit bitter… like some of us other grannies!' mumbled Mrs Coleman under her breath as she approached the post office counter.

* * *

'Look at these, Rebecca!' called Elizabeth as she carefully placed the loaves on top of the stove with her oven gloves.

'The bread smells wonderful.'

'It does. We'll just let it cool down a little even though it's tempting to eat it now. Wilf would eat it right away given the chance. Then he'd be complaining that he'd got indigestion later! Have yew finished reading your *Twinkle* comic yet?'

'Nearly, Mrs Ford. What do yew think of the bracelet I got with it?'

'Oh, very glam, my dear!'

'Pardon, what did you say, Mrs Ford.'

'Glam… yew look glamorous!'

'I'm a little princess! Next week I'll get a little crown thing.'

'Dew yew mean a tiara? Princess Rebecca?'

'Tee-arrara… is that what it's called?'

'Yes, this Princess Elizabeth…. or I could be Queen Elizabeth, of course! I keep my tiaras locked away in the towers of the attic!'

'With real diamonds?'

'Diamonds, sapphires and rubies!'

'Oh, we will have to try them on.'

'Goodness, is that the time?' asked Elizabeth, more to herself rather than expecting a reply from her young assistant, as the sitting room clock chimes reminded her that it was half past four. 'I should think your mum and dad will be back soon. Come, Princess Rebecca! Let's have some bread and jam. I'm sure even princesses like bread and jam for tea! Yew can take that little loaf home with yew that you've made to share with your family when they have tea later.

'Mmmmm, this bread and jam is *really* good, Mrs Ford,' said Rebecca, licking a stray dribble of the sweet preserve from around her lips.

'Well, it must be all your expert kneading which has made the bread so good. Yew hev done well.'

Rebecca beamed back at Elizabeth as she was complimented on her achievement.

* * *

Rebecca had continued to call on Wilf on her way home from school. Usually it was on Wednesdays, after her cookery lessons, but sometimes she called whenever she felt like a chat or thought that Wilf might like a chat. She was very perceptive for an eleven-year-old and, although she hadn't talked at length to Wilf before Elizabeth's death, she now felt she had known him well for years and she could tell when he was a bit low.

It was now five months since Elizabeth's death, but Wilf was still feeling traumatised. He could not get the image out of his head of Elizabeth lying in their bed, so pale … and yet so peaceful. He had confided in Rebecca that he had been lying in bed one night unable to sleep and had felt Elizabeth gently touch his shoulder as she used to do, to

90

reassure him when he was worried about something.

After he had told Rebecca this, he wondered whether he should have, but she replied, 'That must have been comforting, Mr Ford.' To which he replied, 'Wull, yis it was really, but I thought yew might think I was mad or somethin'.'

'I would never think that. I would only think yew mad if you didn't miss your wife… like we all do.'

'I appreciate yew keeping me company, Rebecca, but don't yew go feeling sorry for me. Yew should be enjoying yourself with all your friends.'

'*Yew* are my friend, Mr Ford. Anyway, I need to know how yew got on with last week's recipe!'

'Shepherd's pie, wasn't it?'

'Yes, that's right.'

'Wull, let's just say it was more successful than my first attempt at those rock buns! Do yew remember those?'

'Was that the time I needed urgent dental treatment?'

'Very funny! Any way, Mrs Fanny Craddock, what have yew prepared earlier to tell me about today?'

'Lemon meringue pie.'

'Forget that, my dear, tha's far tew fancy!'

'Well, you can sample the one I've made, but it's probably not the sort of thing you would want hanging around in your pantry for a week.'

'Does your mother not mind yew giving away your culin'ry delights?'

'No, not at all. She is still amazed that yew've been trying to cook.'

'Yew cheeky madam, what do you mean *trying* to cook?'

'I didn't mean to say that… it's just that your Elizabeth used to tell Mum at work that yew always said it was women's work, cooking an' all that.'

'I did an' all, but if I didn't cook now I'd starve. Wull, maybe not starve, but ploughman's lunches dew get a bit monotonous arfter a few days, they dew. Mind yew, our village pub does dew a nice ploughman's lunch and wholly good homemade soup too when I'm feeling really lazy!'

'Mum said she'd seen yew with Leonard Chatham the other day having a meal.'

'Yes, we had a lovely hotpot, and the cook must have felt sorry for us two wifeless men cos she sent second helpings out for us! Must say, I have lorst a bit o' weight since Elizabeth passed away though. Of course I needed to lose a few pounds, I s'pose.'

'Well try this her' pie and you might replace a quarter of an inch to your waistline!'

'Yew are getting cheekier, young lady. You used to hardly say a word when I got hom' from work and you were sat her' in the kitchen.'

'Maybe that was because I always had my mouth full of your wife's wonderful baking. I wish I could cook like she did.'

'Wull, I have to say this her' lemon pie is rather nice.'

'Yew sound so surprised… and it's a lemon *meringue* pie, if yew don't mind!'

Wilf and Rebecca's unlikely friendship continued. She still sometimes called in to use the books Elizabeth had on the shelves, which she had probably bought for Rebecca's benefit. Rebecca liked the way Wilf treated her like an adult and always had time for her, unlike her own parents. Whenever she got home from school, her Mum would shout, 'Get on with your homework, Becca. I'll make your tea in a minute or two but I'm really shattered today, so I'll just have a lie down in my room for a few minutes to recharge my batteries.' The minutes turned into an hour or more. Her Mum would often fall asleep or else shout down the stairs to Rebecca later, could she start peeling some potatoes for her. At other times, her mum would have a bad migraine and would lie on her bed with the curtains drawn and Rebecca and Michael had to remember to keep quiet and Michael could not play his records.

Rebecca's brother eventually got a job in an advertising company. He settled into his work and lost interest in his old wayward friends. Rebecca found the amount of homework she was given hard going, but managed to keep up with her studies. Her marks in the end of year exams were never the highest in her class, but she usually managed to get grade Cs. She was pleased to get an A in cookery and a B in English literature. Wilf had said he would award her an A in cookery in any case. Rebecca had replied in her serious tone and imitating one of her teachers, Miss Finch, that she would award Wilf a B in his cookery, but with continued application he might get an A in the final exam!

Chapter Seven

Bad News

One day Rebecca arrived home from school to see a police car outside her house. Her heart sank. Oh Michael, why couldn't he stick at anything, she thought. But when she went inside, a female police officer approached her. 'You must be Rebecca?' she asked.

'Yes, that's right. What's up, Michael?' she hurriedly asked her pale-looking brother.

'It's, it's…' he attempted to explain, but couldn't continue.

'I'm afraid that your father has been… killed in a car accident… and your mother… is very seriously injured.'

Rebecca dropped into a chair, her legs feeling like jelly. 'She'll be alright though, won't she?' Rebecca asked the police officer who had now come to sit near her.

'We don't know yet, Rebecca. We will take your brother to see her in hospital. Who can you stay with for a while? Do you have a relative nearby?'

'No, no! I want to come to see her. I have to see her, she's my mum too!' Rebecca blurted out, rather louder than she intended, but desperate to be included in her unfolding family crisis.

'Are you sure you want to come? She was transferred to the specialist head-injury unit at Appleby. It's quite a journey. Is there someone you can take with you?'

'Yes, Uncle Wilf,' suggested Rebecca, surprised at how natural it had been to suggest Wilf Ford.

'*Uncle* Wilf?' Michael enquired. Then he quickly realised how close Rebecca had become to Wilf Ford and so continued, 'Oh yes, Uncle Wilf, I'm sure he will come with us.'

The police car took them to Wilf's house. It was just starting to rain. Rebecca ran up the path to explain quickly to Wilf what had happened and could he pretend he was her uncle, '*Please,* Mr Ford,' Rebecca had pleaded, her expression desperate.

Wilf was so taken aback by the urgency of the situation that it wasn't until they were on the journey to the hospital that he realised what Rebecca had asked of him. Could he pose as her uncle? He felt touched that she felt able to come to him when she needed support. The Masons didn't have any relatives nearby. Wilf thought that Mrs Mason's sister lived in Glasgow, but wasn't sure what other relatives they had.

The journey took about an hour and a half. It rained heavily for most of the journey. Rebecca was mesmerised by the windscreen washers and stared ahead from the middle of the cramped back seat of the car, with Wilf and her brother next to her. She wondered if the rain would ever stop and was feeling a little travel sick, but did not want to make a fuss.

Wilf had never been to Appleby and tried to absorb the gloomy countryside set against the grey skies. The last time he had travelled in the back of a car had been for Elizabeth's funeral. Once again he felt he could not control their destiny; he was a powerless passenger being taken to face reality once more. As the gravity of the situation began to sink in, he sensed that this journey would not have a happy outcome. Mr Mason had been killed and Mrs Mason was seriously injured. He had to be strong for Rebecca. What if

Cynthia didn't pull through?

Questions flashed through his head. He wasn't keen on hospitals and had always tried to avoid having to visit anyone from the village who had been in the local hospital. Elizabeth had willingly done her share of taking flowers or fruit to their hospitalised friends. Now he had to be strong and supportive whether he liked it or not.

They got out of the car. The rain had eased to a light drizzle. The female police officer accompanied them in to the hospital and they walked along long corridors with well-polished floors. Signs indicated they had passed several wards, which were named after the Norfolk Broads.

They were led into Hickling Ward, the neurosurgery ward, where a clinical smell of disinfectant was apparent. They were taken into the ward sister's office and asked to sit down. The police officer said she would join her colleague downstairs in the canteen near the main entrance and they could take as long as they wanted. Wilf thanked her for her kindness, which seemed inappropriate to Rebecca, as bringing them bad news had hardly seemed a kind act.

Rebecca swallowed hard and focused her attention on the ward sister who explained, particularly for Rebecca's benefit, that her mum would look very different and that she shouldn't be worried by all the tubes and drains she might see. She could not breathe unaided so had a ventilator to do that for her. Her head was bandaged and she had various monitors and drips attached. Was she sure she wanted to see her mum so poorly? Of course she did. Why were these people trying to stop her seeing her mum? She had no father now and, apart from her brother, Mum was all she had left.

* * *

Rebecca felt almost as if she were underwater, hearing distorted voices and questions being directed at her but

96

unable to reply. She had sometimes submerged herself in the bath, seeing how long she could hold her breath, and had been interrupted a few times by her mum calling her and getting cross when she didn't reply. She found the ward sister looking at her now, waiting for a reply. Everything was quiet. Michael nudged Rebecca and whispered, 'Well, do you want to see Mum?'

Rebecca nodded.

'Well if you're sure, dear,' the sister went on, 'but there is a day room at the end of the ward near the door if you need to have a little break. There's a TV in there, too.'

Shortly afterwards, Rebecca saw for herself why the ward sister had tried to discourage her from visiting her mum and had tried to prepare her. She was stunned. Was that her mum? There must have been a mistake. They were led into a single room. A nurse got up from a chair and smiled weakly in Rebecca's direction. Rebecca didn't remember taking hold of Wilf's hand, but she felt his strong grip now. A chair was placed by the bedside and Rebecca sat down. Two more chairs materialised and Michael sat down too. Wilf hesitated but Michael asked him to stay, so he sat next to Rebecca.

The nurse said, 'You must be Rebecca.' How did everyone seem to know her name, she wondered. She mouthed 'yes', but only a whisper came from her lips.

'My name's Sandra… you can talk to your mum, Rebecca,' the nurse suggested.

Rebecca was wondering how on earth Mum could talk to her, when the nurse added, 'She might be able to hear you… but she can't talk to you.'

Rebecca felt very self conscious and cleared her throat a few times, doubting whether she could even speak herself, but after a few minutes she eventually started. 'Hello, Mum… hope… you're not… hurting in there.'

Michael added after another awkward silence, 'Mum, it's

Michael and Rebecca here. We… want you to come home soon… pl-please… get well,' he stammered and broke down in tears.

Wilf gave him a gentle pat on the shoulder as Elizabeth used to do to him, and passed him his handkerchief, which luckily was clean. Rebecca was shocked to see Michael in tears and found that she too was crying. She reached into her pocket and brought out one of her own handkerchiefs with 'R' embroidered on the corner and dabbed at her eyes. She had another spare handkerchief in her other pocket and was glad she was prepared. Whenever she left for school, her Mum would shout had she got a clean hankie and had she picked up her PE kit, etc. etc. Rebecca often took a hankie without checking her pocket stock and would sometimes find she had three or four hankies stuffed in to her blazer pocket.

She felt a bit out of place now, still wearing her school uniform, but she hadn't even thought of changing and anyway there hadn't been any time to do so. The nurse looked sympathetically in their direction and asked Wilf if they wanted to go out for a moment, but Michael spoke first and said between tears, 'No, no please, we want to stay, don't we, Rebecca?'

Rebecca was looking at the nurse, and nodded in agreement with her brother. She sniffed, trying to stop crying, and gave her nose a blow, with her further armoury of hankies ready to be drawn very soon, she anticipated. She looked at the nurse's uniform to distract herself from her mother's pitiful, motionless profile. She wondered if the nurses ever put coloured clothes in with their brilliant white aprons and caps when they were washed, or perhaps the hospital washed them for the nurses. The uniform certainly wouldn't remain white for long if it was laundered in the Mason household. Goodness… uniform when you worked! Rebecca vowed to herself that she wouldn't become a nurse.

Fancy having to wear a uniform once you'd left school. How awful.

Rebecca remembered then that she had had a nurse's uniform when she was younger for dressing up, complete with plastic fob watch. She used to pretend to give Michael injections and he got mad with her irritating play. She wondered if he was remembering this childhood memory too. She had to administer the jabs to her teddy and golly who never complained like her reluctant patient called Michael.

Rebecca tentatively took hold of one of her mother's hands, something she hadn't done for probably six years, and felt its limpness. Her mum had painted her nails with bright pink varnish, which was now chipped and unsightly. How Rebecca longed for Mum to grip her hand tightly, to reassure her that it was really her beneath the bandaging and clutter of equipment.

The rhythmic sighing of the ventilator interrupted the awkward silence. Rebecca looked at the cardiac monitor and tried to make sense of the wiggly lines being sketched over the screen. A bag of fluid was dripping slowly into a chamber connected to clear tubing, which disappeared under the crisp white cotton sheet covering her mum and which had the hospital name stamped on it in red lettering. The tubing in her mother's mouth looked cumbersome and too big for Mum's delicate lips to enclose. A few strands of auburn hair had escaped from the head bandage. Rebecca could hear her mum's voice in her head, 'I'm just going to have a lie down.' This time it didn't look like she would ever get up again.

The nurse, who wore a tall veil-like starched white hat, returned. She kept coming back into the room, checking the ventilator equipment and writing down some figures on a chart. She took blood pressure and pulse measurements and recorded them on the charts too. She shook a thermometer sharply before placing it under her mum's armpit, then shone a small torch in Mum's eyes. After the nurse had left again, Rebecca stared at the charts, trying to decipher the graph-like records.

Wilf asked the nurse, 'How is she doing?' He handled his cap nervously.

'Mrs Mason's observations are stable at the moment,' the nurse replied. 'I will continue checking them half hourly now. Would you like me to get you a cup of tea?'

'Yes, please, nurse, that would be nice… two sugars please.'

'Anything for you two? Squash or tea?'

'Tea please, two sugars for me too. Rebecca?'

'Squash please.'

'Right, Carol the auxillary will bring those for you shortly, she is just finishing the hot drinks round in the ward. I'll have a word with her now.'

'Thank yer kindly, nurse.'

Wilf was glad of the drink, having just brewed a pot of tea which he had to abandon when Rebecca had called on him earlier. Rebecca munched two rich tea biscuits, remembering she hadn't had her usual drink and biscuit-tin raid when she arrived home after school that day. She felt a bit light headed; a mixture of being hungry and the shock of trying to absorb what was happening in her previously ordinary life. She drank the rather weak orange squash quickly in two or three gulps. Michael drank his tea, having chosen it as a more grown-up choice rather than actually preferring it to squash.

They all sat quietly together, the clinical stillness continually interrupted by the reassuringly rhythmic sounds of the ventilator. The nurse's reappearance every half hour helped the time pass and reassured them that Cynthia's readings were still satisfactory, as the pulse and blood pressure recordings were linked in a fairly even line now.

Wilf thought the nurse's regular visits reminded him of the Potters' Swiss clock in their hallway. On the half-hour, two wooden figures would suddenly spring in to action. He tried, but failed, to remember what activity they did so regularly, possibly a dance.

On the main ward, the visitors to those who were making a good recovery were now leaving after the ward sister had authoritatively rung the bell to announce that visiting time was at an end. Someone was heard being sick in the main ward and curtains were briskly pulled around the patient's bed. Michael recalled the last time he had been very sick, after drinking rather a lot of cider with the crowd he used to hang around with. His mother was annoyed at the mess he had made in his bedroom and his father had banned him from going out with his friends for a whole week.

'We'll get you an injection for sickness, Mrs Baldwin; we'll be right back and then we'll clean you up, alright? Here's another bowl. Oh, you poor thing! Won't be long.'

Michael heard the sympathetic voices of the nurses and wished he had received more sympathy when sick, even though it had usually been self-inflicted. He had gone off cider for a long time, but too much lager had the same effect on other occasions. Though an injection would not be welcome at any time, he thought!

Patients' buzzers sounded, summoning help from nurses on the ward and Michael looked at his mother wondering how she would summon help if she needed it.

Daylight was fading. Wilf asked if Michael and Rebecca were ready to go home and they reluctantly agreed, realising that their Mum was not going to suddenly open her eyes. They felt helpless being here and also a little guilty with all the activity nearby on the ward as patients were being settled for the night. Commodes and bedpans were being distributed behind curtains, the crude form of privacy here, attempting to shield an activity which normally would be behind closed doors. Rebecca wondered how her mum would use the toilet.

Sandra Binks, the nurse looking after Mum assured them as they stood to leave that she or a colleague would telephone them if there was any change overnight. Kathleen's telephone number was given to her, since the Masons and Wilf didn't have a telephone. The ward's contact details were given to Wilf, who the ward staff assumed was looking after Michael and Rebecca.

Sandra watched Rebecca leave with her family and felt very sorry for her. She hoped that her mother would recover. Sandra sighed and started her observations again. She bathed Mrs Mason's eyes with saline-moistened cotton wool balls, then freshened her mouth with swabs, moistened with a pink mouthwash solution and applied yellow soft paraffin to her dry lips. Sandra chatted, as always, as she did these things, warning her patient what she was doing and telling Mrs Mason that she should be very proud of her children who had just visited and that they had gone home with their uncle.

Outside the ward, Wilf telephoned Kathleen from the public phone using the little change he had in his pocket, thankful he could recall her number. He quickly explained the Masons' situation and Kathleen suggested she make a bed up for Rebecca at her home. Wilf thanked her but then was cut off as the pips went and his money was used up.

A patient from the ward was now waiting to use the phone. She wore a thick, dark blue dressing gown. Rebecca noticed part of her head was shaved and she was very pale. The lady smiled at Rebecca and seemed to be looking at her blazer badge, probably not recognizing the uniform as her school was not a local one.

As they approached the canteen, the police officers stood up, having seen them heading in their direction. They smiled weakly, not knowing how the visit had gone, but looking at

Michael and Rebecca's pale faces and Rebecca's red eyes, guessed that they had been shocked by seeing their mum.

Wilf thanked the police officers again for their trouble and they walked outside to the police car, which was parked in a no parking area. The air felt quite fresh after the rainfall and refreshing after the stagnant clinical air of the hospital with its unpleasant smells.

Eventually they were on their way home and the homeward journey didn't seem to take as long as the one to the hospital. Nobody spoke, but intermittently the police radio broke the silence and reminded them that other people were experiencing troubles of their own. They all got out at Michael and Rebecca's house and the police officers left them with 'Uncle' Wilf.

Wilf told Rebecca of his sister-in-law Kathleen's offer to provide a bed. She was happy to do something to help. He told Rebecca to pick up some overnight essentials and then he walked her up to Kathleen's house, where there was a hurriedly prepared bed for her.

'Will yer stay for a drink, Wilf?' enquired Kathleen.

'No, thank yer kindly, I'd best get home to bed. I'll see yer tomorrow. Good night, Rebecca, yew must be tired.'

'Good night, Mr Ford... yes I s'pose I am tired... and thanks for coming with me.'

'Glad I could help yew, my dear.'

'Now then, my dear, yew must be hungry. Can I get yew something to eat and drink?' asked Kathleen.

'I don't think I'm hungry really, thank yew, Mrs Berry.'

'Wull how about a bit of fruit cake and a glass of milk may be?'

'Well just a small piece, thanks, and yes, a drink of milk would be nice, thank yew.'

'Right yew are, dear. Then I'll show yew to your room.'

Rebecca ate the cake, anxious not to offend Kathleen. She hadn't been in Kathleen's house before but noticed that the curtains looked familiar and realised they were the same pattern as Mr Ford had in his front room.

Michael wanted to be on his own for a while. He couldn't quite take in the events of the day. As far as he knew, his mum and dad had gone off shopping to the supermarket which had opened recently at Wexham. His dad would have been driving his trustworthy Mini... unless his mum had finally attached the learner plates which he had noticed in the boot and driven under Dad's supervision. Michael had suspected his mum might secretly be having driving lessons with his dad, so she could surprise them all when she had gained confidence and was ready to take her driving test. What could have gone wrong, he wondered? Had his parents been arguing, and his father... or perhaps his mother... been distracted whilst driving? All the police were able to tell them was that a lorry was also involved; the driver had been taken to hospital and was thought to be alright, apart from some minor injuries and severe shock.

Michael lay awake all night wondering how his mother was. He began to wonder if this was how she had felt when he was late home or hadn't returned home on the odd occasion. His parents had been very angry with him and his mum had said she was 'sick with worry'. Now he understood how she must have felt. It was weird being in the worrier's situation and he wished he could say sorry for the anxiety he had caused his parents in the past.

The house felt so empty and quiet. At two a.m. he got out of bed and went to the telephone box, which was right outside the row of council houses where he lived. He telephoned the ward as he had been told to do if he wanted to see how his mother was. Wilf had given him the telephone number. The nurse on night duty said there was no change in her condition. Michael wished he could just see for himself how she was, but Appleby was too far and he couldn't try hitching a lift at this time of night from the village. The nurse said they would ring the contact number given, if there was any change in his mother's condition and then the pips went and Michael had no more change to feed into the telephone. His link to his mum had been abruptly severed.

The night air was chilly. He ran back in to the house and locked the door this time, having forgotten to do so when he first went to bed. He grabbed another blanket from the untidy shelves of the airing cupboard and hurriedly got back to bed, pulling the extra blanket up to his neck. He felt comforted by the weight and warmth the covering provided to his vulnerable being. Perhaps he should leave a light on in case Kathleen called round with a message from the hospital. He decided to leave his bedside light on, as his bedroom was at the front of the house so the light would be noticed; also, the light somehow made him feel less alone.

Meanwhile Rebecca lay awake for hours in Mary's old bedroom at Kathleen's house. It was a very small room with a low ceiling. It felt odd being in a strange house lying in an unfamiliar bed. Rebecca had not slept anywhere other than her own bed apart from two holidays that she could remember, spent in a caravan at the seaside, when she was five and six years old. They had used a static caravan belonging to a friend of their dad's. They were good holidays and she recalled the happy days they had spent on the beach as a family.

She remembered how Dad had got very sunburnt on a particularly hot day and had to spend the next day in the caravan with the curtains pulled and the windows opened wide. She could almost smell the calamine lotion that Mum insisted on applying to Dad's burnt back and which seemed to permeate the whole caravan. To some of her school friends, holiday memories portrayed images of exotic locations, sun, sand and sea. Rebecca always associated holidays with caravans, calamine and Cromer crabs! She could still remember her mum reprimanding her dad for not using the sun cream with which the rest of the family had ritualistically smothered their bodies at regular intervals during the day. Michael had referred to Mum as 'Sergeant Sun Cream'! She remembered how the sand had stuck to her skin where she had been too generous with the sun cream and its abrasive feel against her skin.

Rebecca thought of Michael and could picture the spectacular sandcastles he had made on the beach, with their paper flags flying proudly when the construction was completed. Mum would sit in a deckchair wearing her purple bathing suit, engrossed in a romantic novel, and reluctant to look up to admire her children's sandy creations whilst she hungrily devoured her book. They had a stripy windbreak, which was always erected by Dad when they arrived at the beach whether or not it was windy. This seemed to mark the Mason territory, which sometimes took a great deal of time and argument to locate. When the beach wasn't busy, Rebecca could never understand why a certain patch of sand was any different from its neighbour, but siting the windbreak was obviously an adult thing and she learnt not to pass comment.

She remembered the fun she had when she flew a kite with Michael on the beach. Michael liked to take charge of the flying most of the time, as he felt only boys were able to master the skill. Sometimes he allowed Rebecca to take control, although he constantly told her how to hold the string which cut in to her fingers. She tried not to complain. Her usual job, however, was to run along the beach until Michael gave the command to let go of the kite, which she had gripped carefully in her hand, and it would rise successfully into the air. She would gaze up at the lightweight blue nylon kite dancing in the wonderful expanse of blue sky, enjoying its apparent freedom, until finally the string was reluctantly wound in and the kite packed away for another day. Her neck was often stiff after watching the kite's effortless display. Michael had once made a kite from brown paper, strengthened with dowelling, which had needed a lot of adjustments and experimentation with tying on small pieces of driftwood onto its tail to get its weight just right. Their father had helped with the kite making; he remembered his own father making a kite for him many years earlier.

On the walk back to the caravan they sometimes stopped for fish and chips, which they had to eat outside the shop from newspaper wrappings as they always had too much paraphernalia to carry back to the caravan from the beach. Rebecca had a habit of collecting shells and stones, which she always regretted once the walk back was underway and her hands became cramped from trying to carry her share of the essential beach kit along with her latest collection of shells in a small bucket. Sometimes, they bought a fresh crab and ate it in the cramped caravan. Michael spent ages trying to remove every morsel of white meat from the crab's claws, which he broke open using nutcrackers that he found in the caravan kitchen drawer.

In the evenings they played board games such as Snakes and Ladders or card games such as Happy Families… *Happy families… they* had been happy, hadn't they?

Rebecca roused herself from the memories and wondered why she had thought about holidays. Perhaps it was lying in this small bedroom. However, it was still bigger than the little room she had to share with Michael in the caravan, where the seats where they ate their meals became their beds at night. Perhaps the stripy blanket at the end of the bed had reminded her of the windbreak. Kathleen had hastily made up the spare bed and had been worried that she would be cold.

Rebecca pulled the reserve blanket up over the candlewick bedspread and noticed the extra warmth the stripy layer now gave her.

The blanket's colours also reminded her of the tri-coloured birthday cakes Elizabeth Ford had made for her birthdays. Mum wasn't that good at baking and Elizabeth often offered to make the cakes when Rebecca's birthday approached. Rebecca loved to see the colours of the three-layered sponge cake as it was cut – a chocolate layer, a bright pink layer when Elizabeth had been a bit too liberal with the cochineal and then either a plain golden sponge or sometimes a bright blue sponge! The layers were 'cemented' together with a sweet butter-cream.

She remembered too the stripy ice cream, again similar to the cake, when they had Neapolitan ice cream. Her pronunciation had been 'nealopitan' as a younger child, despite being corrected many times. Sometimes they had raspberry ripple for a change, or if the shop's supplies were limited. The ice cream had to be bought just before they were ready to eat it, as they didn't have a freezer. Michael was often asked to go and get it, which he usually moaned about, but usually gave in if he was allowed to spend the change on candy cigarettes or bubblegum. She remembered her mum's toffee 'Rice Crispies' cakes, which were sometimes rather hard, and the toffee once brought the tooth fairy to one of her party guests sooner than expected!

Rebecca turned over again, trying to find the most comfortable position in the unfamiliar bed. Kathleen had worried that the bed wasn't aired properly, not having expected to accommodate any guests. The hot-water bottle Kathleen had given her was now cold so Rebecca discarded it on the bedside table.

She heard a distant peacock calling from the Hargreaves' estate, which sounded like someone calling out in pain. She wondered if her mum was in pain and what might be happening in the hospital ward… If only she could just take a peep in to the ward, glance at the charts' recordings or hear the ventilator breathing for Mum. Would she ever talk to her again? Had that really been her mum she had visited? If only it was a terrible mistake and she had only woken from a bad dream. But sadly not this time.

Rebecca clasped her hands together and began to pray that God might help Mum… give her another chance… she needed her mum. 'Please God, let Mum live… she doesn't deserve this… and Dad has already left us… Please don't take Mum too, please let her live.'

She began to cry now, silently, her tears dampening the pillow. Surely God wouldn't let her down. She remembered her regular past attendance at Sunday school at the little chapel in the village. Would this be enough for God to help her now? She had tried to be a good Christian, but now realised that her chapel and church attendance had been very poor. Since starting grammar school, she had homework to do and very little spare time. Her parents had not attended church, apart from weddings, christenings and funerals. Perhaps God was now punishing her for their lack of commitment.

Rebecca remembered the lady's smiling face outside the hospital ward and wondered if she had also had a car accident. She may have looked as her mother had done a few weeks earlier. She tried to imagine what might have happened to cause her parents' car accident. Her wild imagination had created several different scenarios. She wondered if anyone would ever know what really happened.

She eventually managed to doze for a few hours and then woke with a start at about five o'clock. She wondered why she had woken up. Maybe Kathleen's cockerel had announced daybreak. Perhaps her dreaming had disturbed her. The various possible causes of her parents' accident may have been re-enacted in her semi-conscious state.

She thought that as she was awake, she might as well go and 'spend a penny', as her mum always described going to the toilet. At least Kathleen's toilet was upstairs, not downstairs like at home in a converted room where the coal used to be stored.

She had just crept back to bed, when Kathleen gently tapped on her door.

'May I come in?'

'Of course … sorry, did I wake yew?'

'No, I haven't slept well either and I have been wondering if yew were awake. Have yew been cold in that bed?'

'No, it's alright, thank yew. I have only just pulled up this blanket and it's really quite cosy.'

'Good. Shall I refill the hot-water bottle?'

'If yew like, I don't mind, I'm warm enough.'

'Do yew fancy a hot drink?'

'That would be nice, thank yew.'

'I'll bring it up to yew.'

'Oh no, I'll come downstairs with yew, Mrs Berry,' Rebecca replied, anxious for some company. She pulled on her cardigan over her pyjamas and picked up the hot-water bottle in case they decided to fill it. She didn't want to be any trouble. She hadn't brought the dressing gown she had outgrown both in its size and its childish print.

'OK. What shall we hev then?'

'Hot chocolate would be nice if yew have any,' suggested Rebecca rather awkwardly.

'Good idea. I fancy some too.' Kathleen measured two mugs of milk into a saucepan and heated it on the electric hot plate on the Baby Belling oven, which she had in addition to her Rayburn. She watched the milk carefully for the first signs of bubbling and steam when it reached boiling point. How often Tom had left saucepans of milk unattended on the stove and they had boiled over causing such a mess.

'There yew are, my dear … careful it'll be very hot.'

'Thank yew.'

They sat in the chilly kitchen sipping the hot chocolate,

warming their hands on the mugs. Kathleen plugged in an electric fire; its two bars of heat smelt as if something was being scorched, probably due to the dust which had settled on it through lack of recent use.

Kathleen remembered the last time she had sat in a similar position with her daughter, Mary, who had not slept one night worrying whether she was doing the right thing marrying John.

'Am I too young? What if he isn't "Mr Right"? What if he falls in love with one of his brainy work colleagues … and what did he see in me, who just works in the local shop?' she had sobbed.

'I'll put the kettle on too to fill that water bottle again later.'

'Alright, thank yew, Mrs Berry.'

Rebecca realised Kathleen looked different because she normally wore quite a lot of make up and it was strange to see her wearing an old nightdress and a pink nylon quilted dressing gown.

She was still sitting with Kathleen in the kitchen, listening to a clock ticking somewhere in the house, probably the sitting room, when the peace was suddenly disturbed by the shrill of the telephone ringing. Kathleen and Rebecca stared at each other for a few seconds, both realising who the early morning phone call would be from.

Kathleen rushed in to the hall and reached for the large black telephone receiver.

'Yes, it *is* Kathleen Berry speaking… Yes, Rebecca Mason is staying with me at present… Yes… yes… oh… I see… has she? Oh dear, I think I understand… Yes, I will go and see Michael… yes… thank you, Doctor Jamieson. Good bye.'

'Is it Mum, Mrs Berry? What's happened? *Please* tell me,' demanded Rebecca anxiously. Kathleen hadn't noticed that Rebecca's eyes were such a beautiful hazel brown before as she now stared in to them, pleading her to explain.

Kathleen led Rebecca back to the now warmer kitchen. 'I'm *so* sorry my dear... Your Mum had a... brain haemorrhage... a bleed... a complication of her head injury, apparently. The doctors did all they could, but she... has just... passed away... peacefully... she never regained consciousness after the accident. I'm *so* sorry, Rebecca.'

Rebecca was crying quietly, silent tears trickling down her pale freckled face. She felt stunned and sick. Yet somehow she had anticipated the news.

Kathleen took hold of her shoulders. Then Rebecca started to sob and she let Kathleen hug her. She felt secure, yet a little uncomfortable in her embrace. Rebecca felt Kathleen's body shuddering a little against hers and sensed she was crying too.

It was now nearly six a.m. and they decided to go and break the news to Michael. They hurriedly pulled on some warm clothes and walked briskly towards Rebecca's home. He was lying awake as they had expected.

He told them how their mum had been OK when he had phoned at two a.m. He felt immediately betrayed by the hospital staff.

'Wull 'pparently the brain haemorrhage had started suddenly, Michael. Her condition hadn't changed till about five a.m., she was taken back to theatre shortly after and they tried to treat the problem... I'm really sorry, Michael...'

'Thanks, Kathleen, I... wish I'd stayed with Mum now; the nurses said her condition was poor... but stable... and there was no point staying... Why *didn't* I stay? If only...'

'Michael, *don't* blame yourself... Yew couldn't have sat there all night... the complication happened, but nobody could have predicted if... or when it might happen. Appleby is a specialist hospital for neurosurgery... she was in the best place to be cared for... they did all they could.'

'I suppose...'

'What will we do, Michael?' asked Rebecca sobbing

again.

Michael gave her a hug, which surprised her.

'I don't know yet, Becca, but we'll be OK. We'll manage.'

'Rebecca, let's take you home... I mean back to my house and let's try to get some rest,' Kathleen said. 'Is that OK with you, Michael?'

'Yes, thanks Kathleen... I'll um... well, I'll have a think about things ... and speak to you later.'

'Will you be alright? You can come back too if you want. I have plenty of blankets... you could have a rest on the sofa or...'

'No, no, Kathleen, thanks... I... well... just take care of Becca please.' Michael was struggling not to cry in front of Kathleen and Rebecca.

'Of course, come on, Rebecca, we had better get home.'

'I want to see Wilf,' said Rebecca.

'Oh...' Kathleen seemed surprised. 'Yes... later, Rebecca ... it's still only about ten to seven I would guess!'

'OK... but he'll be up now, won't he?' persisted Rebecca.

'Yes, I expect he will, but let's go back to mine first and think things over, shall we?'

'OK, yes... sorry, Mrs Berry.'

'Sorry, Kathleen... this can't be... you know... easy for you either,' said Michael.

'That's OK, I just can't believe the news yet... Both your parents passed away... Life *is* going to be hard for you. Rebecca is welcome to stay with me as long as she wants...'

'Thanks. I don't know who else we can... you know... turn to really.'

'I understand, Michael. Come on, Rebecca, we'll see Michael later... and may be Wilf too,' said Kathleen, leading Rebecca away.

* * *

Tom hadn't been able to sleep since the early phone call and was making breakfast when Kathleen and Rebecca got back, so they joined him at the table. He expertly cut slices from a loaf of brown bread with 'Hovis' lettering standing proud on its surface. Rebecca managed to eat a little buttered toast, though she did so more through politeness than being hungry, even though her last proper meal was yesterday's school dinner. Their discarded hot chocolate mugs were in the deep Belfast sink.

Rebecca felt exhausted and wondered what else could go wrong now. Surely, there would be no more bad news... she felt saturated with bad news and was unable to receive any more. Her eyes ached from crying and she wondered if they had produced all the tears that they possibly could. Kathleen passed her a small box of tissues and then silently filled the hot-water bottle for her. Rebecca whispered 'Thank you' and went upstairs to the room she was staying in.

She lay down on the bed, pulling the stripy blanket over her, placing the tissues next to her in case she needed them and, hugging the hot-water bottle with its fluffy cover, stared at the ceiling. She was in a daze; everything around her seemed out of focus. She felt that someone had just snatched her fairly smooth childhood path away from her and a rather rockier adult route was now being laid before her. There were no signposts to guide her in the right direction or show her how to negotiate the hazardous path she envisaged she would have to tackle.

* * *

Wilf had had a restless night, worried at seeing Rebecca so distressed. During the night when he had been awake he had pulled open one of his drawers and lifted out a pillowslip, which still hadn't been washed. It had been on Elizabeth's pillow the morning she had died and he still couldn't bring himself to wash her perfumed memories away. He took out the pillowslip occasionally and held it to his face and inhaled the distant perfume and smell of his late wife. Somehow this was reassuring and it felt then that Elizabeth was not so far away.

Once more he hugged and held the pillowcase. 'Oh, Elizabeth, what shall I dew? That poor little mite,' he said out loud. If only Elizabeth were here with him now she would know what to do for the best.

* * *

Sandra arrived for her early shift on the ward at seven thirty a.m. and was upset to see the bed empty in the high-dependency unit where she had cared for Cynthia Mason just the evening before. At report, she was told how a brain hemorrhage had started and Cynthia had needed emergency surgery to reduce the raised intracranial pressure and attempt to arrest the haemorrhage, but unfortunately she had died in theatre. The post-mortem would explain what led to the complications and maybe explain more of the damage sustained in the car accident.

Sandra felt stunned and recalled Rebecca's sad face the evening before. She wondered what the child would do now both parents had died. This week had been awful on the unit, this would be the third death… all young people. It made Sandra feel that life was for living and perhaps she would go to Jane's party tonight after all. Who knew what life would throw at her tomorrow… life was precious and good health should never be taken for granted.

'Sandra, can you finish preparing the high-dependency room? There will be a lady coming back from theatre today following excision of a brain tumour. She's been prepped and had her pre-med. It's Jennifer Platt, currently in bed three.'

'Yes, of course, Sister Mills,' replied Sandra, having to shelve her sad reflections and take note of report.

* * *

Later, Rebecca went to see Wilf. She knew he would understand just how she felt. She hadn't been able to sleep, but had felt the quiet time thinking on the bed had given her some strength to try and sort out how she would manage the next few days, now she was an orphan. She had thought about the label 'orphan' which made her feel like a subject from a Dickensian novel. She didn't know anyone who had no living parents.

Kathleen had agreed that Rebecca could go and speak to Wilf at about nine o'clock. He was really upset to hear the news and he gave her a hug, not knowing what to say to her and feeling inexperienced with dealing with adolescents... If only Elizabeth were here, he thought again, she'd say the right things.

'I'm so sorry, Rebecca. That's *terrible* news, that it is... Your mum did look wholly ill though didn't she... when we saw her?'

'Yes, I know... but I didn't think that would be the last time I saw her... I hadn't told her that... I... well... yew know... loved her...' sobbed Rebecca, feeling awkward saying the word *loved*.

'Wull... I'm sure she knew yew did and may be... wull p'rhaps she knew yew were there visiting her last night. There were lots of things I hadn't said to Elizabeth yer know... I regret that I didn't say many things... that I do, but... wull, I s'pose we don't get... warning that these things are about to happen. Here hev this her' handkerchief... it's a clean one,' said Wilf, producing a large white handkerchief from his pocket.

'Thanks,' replied Rebecca, giving her nose a blow and

realising she no longer had someone to remind her to keep her pockets filled with clean handkerchiefs.

Wilf thought for a while and then suggested, 'P'rhaps yew could see yer mum in the chapel o' rest. Then again... I don't know if yew'd like that, but... wull... I think it helped me a bit... yer know... to tell Elizabeth things I needed to say.'

'Oh yes. Would I be allowed? I must see Mum again.'

'I'm sure it would be possible. I'll tell yew what, we'll speak t' Michael and see what's to be arranged abowt the funeral and so on... I wonder whether your auntie has been told the bad news yet? Michael says he thinks she was the next close relative to your mum.'

'I don't know. She's my godmother too I think, Auntie Ann... but I can hardly remember what she looks like... apart from having to spend most of her day in a wheelchair. I can't remember much about her as we hardly ever saw her. She lives in Glasgow. Dad has a brother, Uncle Alan, but I don't think they got on... we never saw him.'

They chatted for a while, Rebecca felt at ease with Wilf and somehow secure at last. He really was like an uncle to her and she knew he would help her through the difficult times ahead of her. Wilf went to make some tea. He finally came back, having made a great effort to set out a tray with Elizabeth's nice china. He had found some shortcake and custard cream biscuits, which he had arranged on a plate, remembering Elizabeth's words that presentation was very important, especially to young eyes. However, he found Rebecca had fallen asleep on the settee. She had finally given in to the tiredness which had been dragging her down, enveloping her in its energy-draining grasp.

Rebecca needed someone to give her a lifeline; she had felt drawn to Wilf. Would he be able to rescue her from her deep pit of despair? He was struck now by her pale complexion and the greyness of the skin beneath her reddened, puffy eyes. He felt a strange emotion within him. He felt deeply sad for this young girl and also, strangely, he now felt that she was his responsibility.

He put the tray down and poured himself a cup of tea from the big brown teapot. He dipped a shortcake biscuit in to his tea and just managed to get the softened biscuit to his mouth before it broke away. Wilf gazed at Rebecca for a while, wondering what he should do. He finished his tea and then found an eiderdown from the spare bed and carefully placed it over her. She appeared to be sleeping peacefully. He scribbled a note to her on an old envelope that he would call to see Michael, but he would be back soon, and left it on the tray of tea and biscuits.

Michael was pleased to see Wilf. They sat down together and started talking about the practicalities of arranging the transfer of Cynthia's body to a funeral director's, arranging a funeral and contacting the few relatives they had.

Michael remembered that all the family's important documents were kept in his dad's bureau, an old piece of furniture which had belonged to his dad's grandfather. It was very ornate, with hand-carved birds on the drawers, and smaller drawers revealed when the top pull-down section was opened, housing lots of envelopes of bills. The bureau looked out of place with the rest of the furniture in the room, but his dad had loved the antique piece and often claimed it would be worth a lot of money if he ever sold it. However, he would never have parted with it as it was a reminder of his late grandfather, and where it used to stand in his house, and how he had spent much of his youth with his grandfather whom he had loved dearly. There had been an equally handsome grandfather clock, but Uncle Alan had been given that when things were sorted out after Robert Mason's grandfather had died.

Michael soon found details of a solicitor who should be contacted in the event of anything happening to either parent. He had felt uncomfortable looking through private papers, and in his dad's bureau, which had never been accessible to him or Rebecca. Michael wondered if his parents ever contemplated that they might both be dead within two days of each other. Michael couldn't believe so much had happened in the space of two days and that he and Rebecca were now about to plan a funeral for both their parents.

He felt a deep sense of regret. He knew he had been a difficult son to raise and that he had got involved with the wrong crowd, but just as his life was becoming more orderly and he was beginning to feel he was achieving something … something which his parents might be proud of … it was too late to prove himself to them.

'Thanks, Mr Ford, for helping us, especially Becca… She pretended yew were our uncle when the police came to tell us about the accident. She is very fond of yew… and I know she still really misses your wife.'

'Wull… I was touched that she treats me like an uncle, that I was. I must say that she has been a great help to me, trying to get used to life without Elizabeth. I really looked forward to her visits after school and yew no doubt heard about all the cookery tips she's given me!'

'I think she mentioned something about cooking, but I can't say I was always listening to my little sister. Now… she's all I've got.'

'Wull, she's a lovely girl, that she is… and yew should be prowd she's yer sister. Kathleen and I will do our best t' help yew both as long as yew need us. Your mum was a good friend of Elizabeth's as yew know, and I'll try to help yew all I can, that I will. Should we telephone the solicitor? I've got plenty of change in my pocket.'

'Yes, Wilf, that's a good idea. If only we had a phone.'

'Do yew know, even I'm beginning to think they're not such a bad idea myself now. We could always use Kathleen's phone if we need to… and yew could give Mr Wilkinson her number as a contact if yew like.'

'Right, thanks. Come on then. Will yew come with me?'

'O' course.'

Wilf and Michael squeezed into the phone box together and phoned the solicitor's office.

Chapter Eight

More Grief And New Beginnings

There was quite a delay before the double funeral could take place, due to the need for post-mortems and an inquest. Cynthia was found to have had a brain tumour, an astrocytoma, but whether this had caused the car accident by causing a seizure, was unclear. The post-mortem had not been conclusive, but she had had a brain haemorrhage in Appleby Hospital. Cynthia was in the driving seat, apparently learning to drive with Robert. Neither of them were wearing seat belts, which had resulted in their serious head injuries. Robert's injuries had been so severe that he had died at the scene of the accident. The lorry driver remembered only a car suddenly coming towards his vehicle head-on as he came round the bend in the road just two miles from Wexham.

Michael had been told the outcome of the post-mortems and inquest with words that Kathleen and Wilf hoped would not cause him any further upset. Whatever words they chose or whatever had led to the accident, the outcome was no different: their parents were dead. They felt Rebecca didn't need to know all the details.

Finally Cynthia and Robert Mason were laid to rest in the village churchyard. Their shared grave was directly behind Elizabeth's grave, which somehow comforted Rebecca. She felt Elizabeth was watching over her parents in some way. The funeral was to be the last Peter Croft would officiate at, since he retired at the end of that September.

* * *

Rebecca felt rather uncomfortable in the borrowed black velvet jacket which she wore over her own black needle cord pinafore dress, which was a little tight for her now, and a white blouse with fancy frills down the front. She didn't like the blouse, preferring plainer clothes when she was given the choice.

She sat in church looking at the congregation, mostly wearing black mourning 'uniforms'. A few ladies were wearing navy clothes. She wondered who had decided on the mourning colour and why it seemed most of the people present today had complied with the 'uniform' rules. Did everyone have a mourning uniform in the back of their wardrobe, to bring out whenever they needed to pay their respects to someone who had died, she wondered. Rebecca thought there was a strange smell in the church today and could only guess it was the smell of mothballs from the recently disturbed dark clothes, stored for so many months in their cocoons of tissue paper or hidden in the depths of a large wooden wardrobe, but which now shrouded the sombre people around her.

She couldn't concentrate on what was being said during the funeral service. People around her were sobbing and using handkerchiefs to dab their eyes and blow their noses. She felt sad and empty, but the reality of what was happening around her had not sunk in. She felt detached from the rest of the congregation; it was as if she were watching a play, but just couldn't understand the point of the story or how to interpret it. She remembered how her parents had stopped her attending Elizabeth's funeral and could now understand why. However, she *had* to be at her own parents' funeral, although she didn't know what was expected of her and whether it was alright to cry.

She stared at the coffins in front of her in the church. She hadn't visited her parents in the chapel of rest as Wilf had originally suggested; after chatting with Kathleen, she had advised her that she felt it was best to remember her parents during the happier days of their family life together. Kathleen had feared that Rebecca may have been further traumatised if she had seen both her parents' injured faces after the accident and the scars from her mother's further surgery before she had died.

Rebecca still fixed her gaze on the coffins. Could they really hold her parents' damaged remains, their identities concealed by their wooden caskets, soon to be buried in the cold Norfolk clay-choked soil? Rebecca shuddered at the thought of the earth smothering the coffins and wanted to stop it happening. For a moment she thought that she couldn't breathe and felt a sense of panic shoot through her body. She took hold of Kathleen's hand and gripped it tightly, hoping that the continued nightmare would soon end.

Rebecca was pleased to see Auntie Ann at the funeral, but the journey had not been easy for her, and her husband had to lift her in and out of their car and directly into her wheelchair. She had explained that her multiple sclerosis was advanced now and life was a constant struggle. Her husband, Bruce, had been made redundant from an electrical appliance store and had decided to look after her at home rather than rely on carers coming and going all day. It was obvious that they couldn't look after Rebecca and anyway she felt this village was her home. She hoped she wouldn't be made to sever her childhood roots which now felt so fragile.

Many of the congregation, mostly people from the village,

commented that Rebecca and Michael were very brave at the funeral. Kathleen, Tom and Wilf were close beside them throughout for support. Michael looked very smart in his black suit, which Kathleen had helped him to buy, saying he could pay her back what he owed any time. He was grateful for her help and thought the suit would be a useful addition to his rather empty wardrobe of clothes. He usually wore jeans and was surprised how the suit had given him added confidence; he felt and looked like an adult. Many of the villagers had been struck at how much Michael resembled his father and how Michael had apparently matured in the last few weeks.

After the funeral, the mourners went to the village pub, The Cock and Pheasant, where Cynthia had worked, and where today Kenneth had provided some light refreshments. There were corned beef and tomato sandwiches, cream cheese and cucumber sandwiches, egg and cress sandwiches, all cut into small triangles and arranged neatly on trays. There were also sausage rolls and a large fruit cake bought from Coddleton bakery.

Ann and Bruce were staying at the pub for the night, as there was a ground floor bedroom suitable for disabled people's use. Kathleen had offered to accommodate them, but realised Ann would not manage the stairs in her home, so the pub had proved very convenient for them. Bruce commented that this was the first night that they had stayed away from home in about six years. He regretted that it had taken a sad occasion to get them away from home.

Ann was very tired from the emotional day and a very early start to ensure they made it to the funeral on time. She had enjoyed finally getting to know her niece and god-daughter whom she hardly knew and also Michael, who had been going through his difficult phase the last time Cynthia had written to Ann. Their letters had not been very frequent and Ann now regretted that she had drifted apart from her sister.

Ann decided that she and Bruce should stay an extra three days in the village so she could talk again with Rebecca and Michael and perhaps participate in the discussions about their future care and meet the solicitor who held the wills. It was the least she could do for her sister.

It was at times such as these when she felt particularly frustrated with herself, that her body would not do what she wanted it to do. She felt like a discarded puppet, which had just been discovered in an attic. New faces were peering at her once more with high expectations of what the floppy figure might be able to do, but she knew that her 'strings' had long since been damaged. Her friends in Scotland were often bringing her newspaper cuttings which talked of new treatments and 'miracle' cures for multiple sclerosis, but she knew deep down that life would never get any better for her.

Ann was still stunned to learn that her late sister had had a brain tumour. Cynthia had recently complained of frequent headaches, but never imagined they might have been caused by anything so serious.

Ann wondered what life might be like if they moved to this village. So far everyone she had met seemed very friendly and concerned, but a niece and nephew would be her only connections to the area. Besides, Bruce would never leave his beloved Scotland. He couldn't get over how flat the landscape was around here.

She invited Rebecca and Michael to their home in Glasgow whenever they liked and promised to keep in touch by letter, even if it meant Bruce had to write them for her. They had a spare room, known as the 'box room', which tended to get lots of junk stored in it but it could be cleared in honour of any guest who came to stay.

A few days later, Rebecca became unwell. She was still staying at Kathleen's. She was due to go back to school the next day, having had extended compassionate leave. She woke with a terrible sore throat and high temperature.

'Gosh, Rebecca, yew look dreadful, what ever's the matter?'

'My throat feels very sore and I feel really hot.'

'Goodness, your head does feel wholly hot! I'll find my thermometer, just a minute. Get yourself back to bed, I don't think yew'll be going to school tomorrow, my dear,' said Kathleen, very concerned about her temporary house guest.

She returned with the mercury thermometer. 'Here put this under your tongue, my dear, and be careful not to bite it. Whilst that's there I'll just get yew a drink o' cold water,' said Kathleen before she disappeared again. She returned with the promised drink and set it down next to Rebecca's bed. 'Right let's see … oh dear, yes, your temperature is one hundred and three degrees. Here, have a drink and we'd better pull back some of these blankets to cool yew down.'

'Thanks, Kathleen. Oh, it really hurts to swallow this!'

'Yew poor thing. I think we should call the doctor, yew are wholly flushed, aren't yew?'

'I don't know but I feel awful… Sorry Kathleen, I don't want to be a nuisance. Weren't yew goin' to your father's today?'

'Wull I was, but I can see him later. I need to change his bed and do the laundry. But I will ring the doctor. Do yew see Doctor Stimpson?'

'I don't remember ever seeing a doctor.'

'Wull I'll give the surgery a call. I don't know who'll be on duty today as it's Sunday. Yew try and sip some more of that water if yew can. Dew yew want any breakfast, Rebecca?'

'No thank yew. I feel a little bit sick and I don't think I could swallow it anyway. It feels like there's a knife in my throat!'

'Wull, just rest till we get the doctor then, my dear. I will bring a bucket up just in case, yew know…'

'Thank yew, Kathleen.'

Kathleen went downstairs and consulted her address and phone book next to the telephone. 'Oh hello, it's Kathleen Berry here. I am looking after Rebecca Mason whose parents died recently and she really isn't well today.'

'What seems to be the problem?' asked the receptionist.

'Wull, she has a temperature of a hundred and three and a terrible sore throat.'

'Just hold the line a moment, Mrs Berry, please.'

'Alright I will, thank yew.'

'Hello, Mrs Berry.'

'Hello.'

'Doctor Hardy is on duty today and he will call to see Rebecca later this morning. Would you give me Rebecca's home address and your address too, please?'

'Of course. Rebecca lived at number two, Laurel Bank, Watton and my address where she is staying at present is Orchard Cottage, Freckingham Road, Watton. It's near the post office.'

'Thank you, Mrs Berry. The doctor will be with you as soon as he can, but he has another call to do before he can see Rebecca.'

'That's alright, thank yew, goodbye.'

Kathleen was hanging out some washing on the line when Doctor Hardy arrived in his blue Ford Escort estate car, which looked like it had been recently washed and polished. He was a tall man, nearing retirement. He greeted Kathleen with a welcoming smile. 'Good morning, Mrs … Berry isn't it? How is she?'

'Yes, morning, doctor. She's in bed, I'll show yew her room. She looks wholly ill doctor.'

'Ah Rebecca, I'm Doctor Hardy… How are you feeling now?'

'Oh sorry… I think I must have gone back to sleep! Um… well my throat feels bad and I just don't feel like doing anything.'

'Let's have a look at you then. Oh yes, your glands are rather swollen in your neck. Sorry, that hurt did it?'

'Yes, when you pressed my neck just then.'

'Can you open your mouth wide please? Say "aaah!"'

'Aaaah.'

'Looks like you've got tonsillitis, my dear.'

'What does that mean?'

'Well, your tonsils are inflamed due to an infection and it's making your throat feel sore. I will give you some penicillin. Is she allergic to anything, Mrs Berry?'

'I don't know, doctor. Rebecca, do yew know if yew are allergic to anything?'

'I don't think so, but I don't think I've had medicine before apart from cough medicine and may be an aspirin.'

'Well, take this antibiotic but if you have any problems with it, ring the surgery again, please. Take an aspirin too, which will help bring your temperature down. I'll just check your temperature now. Let's just put this under your tongue whilst I finish writing your prescription. Right, let's see… yes a hundred and four.'

'Oh dear, Rebecca, it's even higher than earlier this morning.'

'Don't worry she'll soon pick up. Here are enough tablets for today and then you can collect the prescription tomorrow for the rest of the course of the antibiotics.'

'Thank yew, doctor.'

'Try and drink plenty, Rebecca, if you can. An aspirin will also help that sore throat. Have you got some in the house, Mrs Berry?'

'Oh yes, I'll go and get her one.'

'You'll need perhaps a week off school, Rebecca, but I don't suppose that will be a problem, will it?'

'Well no, not really, but I have already been off for three weeks.'

'Oh dear, why's that?'

'My mum and dad died and their funeral was just last week,' said Rebecca, her eyes filling up with tears.

'Oh, I *am* sorry Rebecca, I didn't realise… of course… dear me, I'm so sorry. Well you've had a lot to cope with then, haven't you, so you may need a little longer off, but I'm sure Mrs Berry will take good care of you. Try to eat some soup or something light when you feel up to it and remember to drink plenty.'

'Yes, alright. Thank yew, doctor.'

'If you don't start to pick up in two or three days Mrs Berry should ring the surgery. Alright?'

'Yes, thanks. Bye, doctor.'

'Goodbye.'

'Let me see you out, doctor.'

'Goodbye, Mrs Berry. Poor girl, what a lot she's been through.'

'Yes, poor Rebecca, she's such a nice girl and no trouble at all. Thanks again, Doctor, goodbye.'

'Goodbye.'

Kathleen went back to Rebecca. 'Here's that aspirin I promised you, it's dissolved in this water.'

'Thanks, I'll try to drink it.'

'Good girl.'

Rebecca was soon fed up of being ill, lying in Mary's old room where she had already had enough sad experiences to reflect upon. She didn't often sleep well. She felt uneasy, as if something else was going to happen. She worried about Michael sometimes. What if he had a car accident when he was out with his friends? She would have no one.

She sometimes read the local paper which was delivered daily to Kathleen and got really absorbed in the reports, sometimes coming close to tears when she read of other people's misfortunes. A young girl had gone missing in Appleby and this story was in the paper most days. No one had seen her since she had set off to do her paper round early one morning the previous week. The reports seemed to suggest that she was unlikely to be found alive now. Rebecca thought about the girl when she was lying in bed. She prayed silently that she would be found and that she was safe. Wouldn't it be great if she turned up in Watton and Rebecca could help her return to her parents? She thought of the frantic parents desperate to have their child returned to them. She felt a connection with them, even though she didn't know them. She felt their pain and anguish.

* * *

Everyone was talking about the missing girl in the village. Wilf cycled down to the village shop to buy a few things and decided to get something for Rebecca to cheer her up.

'Oh dear, it is a shame about that there missing girl. I see from the paper this morning that she is still missing.'

'Yes, Wilf, it is terrible isn't it,' replied Miss Brown. 'I don't think the police have had any leads, have they? Those poor parents must be beside themselves with worry.'

'Yes, they must be in a terrible state.'

'What can I get for yew this morning, Wilf?'

'What shud I get for Rebecca, do yew think?'

'Oh, is she still not well?'

'Wull, she's a bit better now but still not her usual self.'

'Poor Rebecca, what a lot she's been through.'

'She has, the poor little mite.'

'What about these little novelty boxes of sweets, Wilf? These are new in this week. Liquorice allsorts, dolly mixtures or jelly babies?'

'I'm not sure what she likes.'

'Or I have these boxes of chocolates. These are one pound, twenty pence though. It depends how much yew want to spend.'

'Oh yes, they might be nice for her. She deserves something special. I think she might like this box. Yes, thank yer, that'll do nicely. Can I hev a quarter a' pound o' cheese an' all?'

'Red or white, Wilf?'

'Red please, Miss Brown.'

* * *

Rebecca had cut out the report from the local paper about her parents' accident and kept it in a tin box under her bed. When she couldn't sleep she would turn on the bedside lamp and look at it again, reading the report and still wondering what had really happened. Her dad's precious Mini was barely recognisable as a car in the photograph. She would stare at it, trying to discover a new detail or a clue which would explain how or why the accident had occurred.

Kathleen was so good to her, but she wanted her own mum and dad to be with her; even Michael's company would be welcome now. The poor missing girl's parents needed their child back, Rebecca needed her parents back; flaws and all, they were her parents and she was too young to be without them.

She kept herself occupied reading books off the shelf in Mary's old bedroom. She didn't feel like getting up but after three days of the penicillin and Kathleen's care and attention, she finally made the effort to get dressed and sat in the sitting room reading. She was nearing the end of her second book now, *Anne of Green Gables*.

Kathleen had gone to take her father's clean laundry to him when there was a knock on the door.

'Uncle Wilf, hello!'

'Hullo, my dear, how are yew?'

'Better today, thank yew. I finally got dressed today. I've been so lazy.'

'Wull, yew can't help being ill can yer. Here's a little present for yew.'

'Thanks,' replied Rebecca, excitedly opening the brown paper bag. 'Yum! Thanks, I will enjoy these.'

'I thought yew liked chocolates.'

'Of course I like chocolates, but I don't think I've ever had a box given to me. I'm just starting to eat properly again. I couldn't swallow food at the weekend, my throat was so sore. Even jelly was a little hard to get down.'

'Kathleen told me. She was worried abowt yew, that she was.'

'She is very kind. I feel bad making her more work.'

'She is happy looking after yew. I think she likes to have a young lady at home again.'

'Shall I open these?'

'If yew want to, o'course. Thought I would try to cheer yew up!'

'The box is pretty. Those little kittens are cute. Not as cute as Tiger though, of course! Would yew like one, Wilf?'

'Don't mind if I dew! I'll try this one, thank yer.'

'Oh, I've got a caramel.'

'Mine is a strawberry cream! I haven't eaten a chocolate in a long time. Mmm not bad! Hev yew bin reading the paper?' asked Wilf noticing the local paper on the table next to Rebecca.

'Yes, I am so worried about the missing girl Anna.'

'Oh that is a rum ole dew, that it is. I was speaking to Miss Brown in the shop just now about her. I dew hope she is found safe an' well soon.'

'So do I. She's almost the same age as me. I can't stop thinking about her. Poor girl. Shall I make you a cup of tea, Uncle Wilf?'

'That would be nice thank yew, if yew feel up to it.'

'Of course, it's nice to have a visitor.'

'Where is Kathleen this morning?'

'She's gone to help her father and take his clean sheets and clothes.'

'She's always busy, just like poor Elizabeth was, but she has it all to dew on her own now, o' course.'

Eventually Rebecca recovered fully and went back to school, wondering how her friends and teachers would treat her. No one mentioned her parents and everyone seemed to avoid conversations about home life, which was unusual especially for Alice Walters, who was constantly moaning about her mum with whom she didn't get on well, it seemed. Alice was born at a stage when her mum thought she was starting the menopause and it seemed she had struggled to cope with another child when there was a fifteen-year gap between the birth of her second child and Alice arriving.

After a week at school feeling she didn't really belong there, Rebecca decided that she would talk about her parents. Her friends all looked relieved that she had brought them into the conversation. It still didn't really seem real to her that both parents had died and that she would never see them again. Rebecca had managed not to cry when she told her friends what had happened and felt better for having talked to them. All of them had seen the article about the accident in the local paper and the incident had been much talked about at the tea table.

It was decided that Rebecca should stay with Kathleen, and Michael would continue living in the council house. The house would be rather large for him alone, but it held so many memories for him and Rebecca and it was too soon to expect them to box up their past. They would keep in close contact and Kathleen hoped that Michael would join his sister for Sunday dinner whenever possible at her cottage. She invited Wilf too and, in the months that followed, they had many enjoyable meals together. Kathleen was amazed at Michael's appetite and how he really enjoyed the meals she had prepared. Michael had become used to convenience foods and fish and chips bought at Coddleton, since he started living on his own. He was very appreciative of the 'real food' Kathleen had cooked and recalled awkwardly that his mother had not been a very good cook.

Rebecca still visited Wilf at his home as often as she could, as she felt so happy and relaxed in his company. She knew Kathleen was always busy, especially with caring for her elderly father and besides, she felt at home with Wilf.

Elizabeth's presence was still evident in the cottage and Rebecca felt she would always be there. Sometimes Rebecca imagined that Elizabeth would suddenly appear in the kitchen like she always used to, back from picking flowers from the garden or having brought the washing in from the clothes line. Elizabeth had always seemed to be proud of her washing, pegged out on the line in an orderly fashion; Wilf's socks pegged in pairs and pure white sheets neatly tethered, billowing in the wind like the sails of an old ship. A wooden prop made by Wilf would hoist the 'sails' high into the beautifully fresh air.

Rebecca remembered the washing in their household had been much less orderly. Her Mum would often be heard to curse when she had discovered that she had put something brightly coloured in with the 'whites' wash. Rebecca had rarely kept a white T-shirt for very long. She had felt self-conscious during PE lessons wearing her aertex T-shirt, which was now a rosy pink instead of its original white. Pairs of socks also had a habit of getting separated when they were washed and dried in the Mason home, so that it became a challenge to find a pair of matching beige socks in the morning when getting ready for school.

Wilf had kept many of Elizabeth's treasured things. Even the children's paintings were still displayed on the kitchen walls. The paper was now looking rather tatty and the paint fading. Rebecca would suggest they take them down when the time was appropriate.

Wilf occasionally dabbed a little of Elizabeth's rose perfume on one of her handkerchiefs and put it near his pillow at night, which somehow comforted him. Her jewellery was still in her jewellery case in her dressing table drawer as she had left it. A treasured locket belonging to her mother was among the strings of beads and pearls. Wilf kept meaning to pass on the locket to Kathleen.

Wilf had very few recent photographs of Elizabeth but had framed a very nice photo of her, found by Kathleen, and he placed this near to his bedside. He had been unable to sort out Elizabeth's personal drawer next to her side of the bed together with her handbag, which was still where she had left it under the dressing table. Wilf didn't think he should look in the handbag, even though it only contained Elizabeth's rose-pink lipstick and face-powder compact, which was all the make-up she ever wore, a purse with a five-pound note and some loose change, a handkerchief, a cartridge pen and a diary with dates of her church flower duties and events associated with the Women's Institute.

Wilf and Rebecca often visited the graves of Elizabeth and Rebecca's parents together, having gathered flowers from Wilf's garden. At other times, Wilf would go alone on his bicycle, devoted to what he felt was his duty to visit Elizabeth's grave daily and have a chat to her when he was alone. He told her what had been happening and asked her advice about Rebecca. While he knew he couldn't get a response, he felt he had consulted her and she would guide him somehow to do the right thing.

Wilf and Rebecca had their grief in common. They both had good and bad days, but seemed to manage to keep each other going. They both felt their grief was reduced by supporting each other and keeping one another company when possible.

Rebecca felt rather uneasy at Kathleen's house. She didn't know how long she would have to stay in Mary's old bedroom. What other option was there for her? She wasn't old enough to go home and be with Michael. She had most of her treasured things with her now, but she couldn't relax in someone else's home. Her environment still felt unfamiliar. She would get off the school bus and wonder where she would go. She wanted to be with her family. Everyone who passed her seemed to have parents driving them home, or children would be holding their mother's hand as they walked along the village lanes. She felt lost and lonely.

She slowly wandered back to Kathleen's home, struggling to carry her satchel which was heavy with her school books. She had a lot of homework to do and wondered what was the point of all the school work? Who would be proud of anything she could achieve?

'Hello, Rebecca. Come and hev a drink. I was just putting the kettle on for a nice cup of tea. How was school?' asked Kathleen.

'Alright I suppose,' answered Rebecca, rather wearily.

'Are yew hungry?'

'Yes, starving.'

'Do yew want a piece of this coffee cake then?'

'Oh yes, please, Mrs Berry. It looks lovely,' replied Rebecca. 'School dinner was awful today. It was meat balls and I really don't like them with lumpy mashed potato.'

'Never mind, I hev made a chicken pie for tea with the chicken left over from our Sunday dinner… yew like that don't yew?'

'Yes, thanks…oh this cake *is* delicious.'

'Good. Here's your tea. I think I'll sit down with yew for a few minutes whilst I drink my tea. It's been all go today! I have at least got all the washing dry, there's been a good blow today. My father's ironing is almost done now. Oh, I needed that cuppa!'

'Mmmmm, that's better. Yew should come and cook at school! Not that yew have time for any other work, poor yew! I probably haven't worked as hard as yew today by the sounds of it, but I still feel tired. I had better start my homework now, I suppose. I have got loads today. It's so unfair! I have got to do geography, maths and English all tonight. I think I will start with English.'

'Oh dear, poor yew. I will clear this table for yew then. Do as much as yew can before teatime and I will give yew a shout when we need to lay the table, dear.'

'Alright. Is there a little more tea in the pot?'

'Of course… there yew are.'

'Thanks. Right… to the homework!'

'Mary never got as much homework as yew do.'

'Lucky Mary! Oh well, at least English is OK. I have to write a short poem, that's not hard. Elizabeth used to make up rhymes with me, yew know; she made me laugh. Geography should be OK too, but maths is tough.'

'Don't ask me, Rebecca, I can't help yew with maths, I'm afraid. I don't even hev my sister's ability to make up rhymes.'

'It's OK, I'll just have to do what I can.'

'That's right. Could Michael help yew with the maths?'

'I doubt it. He never paid much attention to any of his subjects apart from art. Perhaps Miles in the year above me will explain it to me tomorrow if I can't figure it out. He is on our school bus and other people ask for his help with maths. He is very intelligent and always gets grade As for maths and sciences. He gets the maths prize most years at school prize giving. He is a bit of a bore really.'

'Wull, he's lucky to be so clever, even if he is a bore! I'll let yew get on, dear. Just do your best, that's all anyone can ask of yew. I know it can't be easy for yew dear, after the difficult time yew've had. Your teachers must understand what yew've been through.'

'I don't know, they don't say much to me.'

'Wull, if yew want me to talk to them, of course I will,

dear.'

'No, it's alright; I am just a bit fed up today.'

'Anything in particular bothering yew my dear?'

'Well, I dunno ... p'rhaps it's because it would have been... Mum's birthday tomorrow. What can I do to show I remembered?'

'Oh Rebecca, my dear girl, what a shame! Wull how about when yew get back from school tomorrow we gather some really nice flowers and yew can take them to her grave?'

'Alright. I was wondering if I should write her a little verse, but I hev so much hom'work.'

'Don't yew worry, Rebecca. Try to get your homework done. I'm sure your mum would understand and she would be so proud of yew; how yew've coped with your sad loss of both parents and made such good progress at the grammar school. Here ... hev a big hug sent from your mum. I'm sure, if she could, she'd send yew one.'

'Thanks, Mrs Berry. Actually she didn't... well... *hug* me that much, yew know.'

'Well, what a shame. There's nothing like a hug for making things feel right, I think.'

'Yew could be right.'

'I was a little bit older than yew when my mother died, but I had Elizabeth then of course and we became very close.'

'Oh, Mrs Berry, I had no idea... I'm sorry.'

'Not at all dear... but I do know how yew feel. My Aunt May did her best, but we both missed our mother so much. Anyway, I mustn't keep talking, I'm keeping yew from your homework. Tom might be able to help you with the maths when he gets hom'. He's certainly got more of a math'matical brain than me... Although, I could write a letter to your teachers if yew like, to excuse yew from your homework perhaps?'

'Oh no, I'll get on with it now. Boring Miles the

mathematician can always be consulted in the morning if needed! Thanks, Mrs Berry, though. Yew are very kind to me.'

'How about yew call me Kathleen?'

'Well... perhaps *Auntie* Kathleen, if that's OK?' suggested Rebecca, anxious not to be disrespectful.

* * *

Months passed and one day Wilf was sitting in his armchair holding the local newspaper, but not really reading it, thinking... wondering. Rebecca was at the table doing her homework.

'Rebecca, I er... I've bin wonderin'... wull, I...' started Wilf.

'What?' asked Rebecca bluntly, still engrossed with her history homework.

'Wull, I don't suppose that yer would want to... wull...'

'Wull... spit it out!' demanded Rebecca.

'Wull... live her' with... me, would yer?' asked Wilf, rather nervous and desperate that he shouldn't get a negative response.

'Live with yew!' Rebecca leapt off her chair, pushing aside her homework. 'I would *love* to live here with yew, Uncle Wilf, more than anything. I can't believe it! Are yew sure yew really mean it?' she asked excitedly.

'O' course, I mean it... I just didn't know what would be best for yer.'

'Oh Uncle Wilf, thank yew so much, yes... please let me stay.'

'We'll need to write to your Auntie Ann, o' course, and I'll have to have a chat with Kathleen, but I know she has been worried that you're not happy at hers.'

'Wull... she is so kind, but I feel I might be in the way sometimes, and what with her father being so frail now and needing lots of help... and... then there's the garden and the chickens and she helps Mrs Livingstone with the cleaning and she does the church flowers... but... oh, I can't believe it!'

'Do yew ever stop to draw breath, gal?' asked Wilf, so relieved that his offer had not been turned down.

'Wull, Auntie Ann said what a nice man yew were and that we seemed to get on so well,' continued Rebecca, further justifying why she should accept the invitation.

'Oh, did she now? Tha's a rummin'... I aren't the cleverest fella... as yew know, so don't expect help with yer homework for a start, but I feel Elizabeth is telling me to look after yew.'

'Wull, I could look after *yew!*'

'I have a few years left in me, before that might be necessary, I think!'

'Thank yew... *seriously*, Uncle.'

'It's nice... yew calling me, Uncle, yer know. Hey, how abowt we tricolate the spare bedrum for yer?'

'What...? Oh... yew mean *decorate*... that would be great! I *love* that bedroom overlooking the fields and it's much bigger than mine at Kathleen's... *and* mine at hom' come to that.'

'Wull, I don't s'pose tha's many of yer fancy friends can say they have a choice of sev'ral bedrums that they could stay in!'

'No, that's true! Come on let's go and speak to Auntie Kathleen. And I must write to Auntie Ann.'

'Not till yew've done yer hom' work young lady!'

'Oh I think I've changed my mind; you're sounding bossy already!'

'Cheeky madam, stop your squit! Go on, git it finished and then we'll go.'

'OK and... well... thanks again,' said Rebecca, giving Wilf a quick hug, rather awkwardly.

Chapter Nine

Hope And Happiness

Ann was agreeable for her niece to live with Wilf and he would ultimately become her legal guardian. Rebecca settled well in her new home with Wilf, who became a happier person again, just when he had thought life had lost all its true happiness. He had felt so lonely and his life seemed so black and white. Rebecca had brought back the colour in to his life and he so enjoyed her company and youthful energy.

They decorated the spare bedroom. Rebecca helped to strip off the old pink flowery wallpaper, which was now rather faded and a little damp in places near the window. Wilf put on the new wallpaper she had chosen, a pale blue. He was relieved that she had chosen a plain paper. He remembered, soon after getting married, when he had put on the pink patterned paper, that he had grumbled at Elizabeth because it had been impossible to match up the pattern when applying it to the corners of the room, since the walls were uneven in the old cottage. They had disguised his less than perfect workmanship by placing the bedroom furniture carefully to hide the distorted roses.

Wilf whitewashed the low ceiling and put a fresh coat of gloss paint on the door and skirting boards. The carpet had covered most of the floor space, but again was highly patterned, so was replaced with a plainer one that Kathleen had rolled up in her spare room. The carpet had belonged to her late Aunt Agnes. Kathleen knew it would find a good home eventually. She had offered it to Mary, when she had set up her home, but she had refused it saying it smelt of Aunt Agnes! Kathleen didn't tell Rebecca this comment. Nor did Kathleen tell Rebecca that Aunt Agnes was probably the last person to stay in the room which was now hers, and that she always left a trail of mothball odour wherever she visited. Not that much other than gloss paint would be smelt for a while in the newly decorated, or 'tricolated' as Wilf kept saying, bedroom.

Old grey linoleum surrounded the carpet, but was barely noticeable. Kathleen made some new curtains for the room and Wilf bought a new candlewick bedspread for the bed, which they had spotted reduced in the sale at Harper's, the small haberdashery shop in Coddleton, when choosing the curtain fabric. Kathleen was amazed at Wilf spending his money quite so liberally, remembering how Elizabeth said moths flew out of Wilf's wallet, when he rarely agreed to part with some of his hard-earned notes! Wilf had actually had a small win on his premium bonds, and this helped finance the room decoration, but he hadn't told anyone apart from Elizabeth, of course. Kathleen would report to Elizabeth, next time she visited her grave, on her brother-in-law's quite out of character spending behaviour.

Rebecca was pleased with her new room and felt it now belonged to her. A large dark wooden ottoman, also belonging to Agnes, stood beneath the window and housed a lot of Rebecca's clutter and keepsakes from her childhood. She couldn't help thinking that it looked a bit like a coffin. She had dreamt on several occasions that her Mum had been buried alive and, as she woke from the nightmares, she would focus on the ottoman, convinced that she heard her Mother banging and shouting to be let out of it. Foolishly, she had found herself lifting the lid on more than one occasion to check. Only the eyes of her old doll and Golly ever met her own scared and still sleepy eyes. Golly's wide grin remained fixed and somehow reassuring.

Sometimes she couldn't get to sleep, lying in bed trying to recall the last few days of her parents' life. On other occasions she thought she could hear their raised voices in the room next to hers.

Sadly Anna, the missing girl who had been in the news, had been found murdered in Thetford forest. Rebecca was devastated when she saw the article in the newspaper confirming everyone's suspicions that the girl would not be found alive.

Rebecca also had nightmares about this event, but didn't feel she could talk about it to anyone. She felt she wanted to write to Anna's parents to try to offer them some support and to tell them how she had felt when she heard about their tragic loss. She still felt she had a connection with the family and that they shared immense grief, which most people could not begin to comprehend. Her friends were upset when their goldfish died or other pets such as a cat or rabbit. These were indeed sad occasions, but people dying, was in a different realm and she wished she had not had to experience the harsh effects of bereavement.

Wilf's own bedroom was in need of redecoration, but he couldn't bear to change the imprint on it, which was still so obviously Elizabeth's. The curtains were quite faded and the lavender print barely apparent now with the damage from the sun and from washing them over the years. He had eventually removed the net curtains, which had become too tatty, deciding not to replace them as he liked to look out of the window without net obscuring his view. He had never been keen on the net curtains, but didn't like to comment when Elizabeth had made them and proudly hung them up, claiming they would help prevent the sun fading the curtains and wallpaper in their bedroom.

Elizabeth's handbag was gathering dust, still in the same place where she had left it. Her clothes remained neatly folded in the large chest of drawers they had shared. The top two drawers were Wilf's and the lower two Elizabeth's. Wilf had opened Elizabeth's drawers on several occasions, intending to sort out the clothes, but he couldn't bring himself to discard them and somehow leaving them there felt like her parting was merely temporary. Kathleen had offered to sort the clothes for him. Part of Wilf knew he should accept her offer but it still seemed too soon to remove more evidence of Elizabeth's fading presence. Wilf's wounds still felt too raw and too fragile to be touched or treated. Rebecca helped him to think less about the pain he was feeling and to focus on a new role in his life, which he still couldn't quite believe he had taken on.

Rebecca continued to address Wilf as 'Uncle' and all the villagers were amazed how the unlikely friendship became a very close bond. It was as though they had always been together, and they developed a father and daughter relationship very naturally. While Rebecca had often visited Elizabeth when she had been playing in the area with her friends, Wilf had not really taken much notice of her or the other children. He knew that Elizabeth was very happy in the children's company, though he remembered being a little irritated if his tea was late because of the children distracting Elizabeth.

Rebecca maintained her studies and managed to get just above average marks in her end of year exams, which surprised the teachers, in view of all the traumas she had suffered. She became a bit of a loner, quiet and serious, turning down offers from school friends to join them at weekends. She enjoyed reading though, and always 'hed her nose in a book', as Wilf reported to everyone in the village, and she still liked to make up poems and stories.

Wilf did less work at the farm, so he could spend time with his new 'niece', though he was always happy to assist with the busier times when extra pairs of hands were needed to cart the hay and straw. He had seen these jobs get easier over the years since his childhood when he visited the farm estate with his father.

Bill Dobson usually milked the cows now. He still had a string of ailments to tell everyone about, whether they wanted to hear them or not. But he had had his hernia repaired a few months ago, so he was unable to complain about quite so many aches, pains or 'ruptures' now, although he had spun out his recovery time as long as he could. His tales of his hospital stay were told at the village pub with a fair bit of exaggerating along the way. Luckily the regulars knew that Bill was well-known for adding a bit of drama to his ordinary and fairly lonely life. Some wondered if the dairy herd ever got fed up with his tales and grumbling.

Michael had settled with his work and still lived in the family home. The council did not seem concerned that he had the big house to himself. In fact, he now had his girlfriend living with him and Rebecca could not get over how much he had changed. He had grown up, having had to mature very quickly. He had met Julie Shaw at a friend's party and had instantly hit it off with her. After seeing her for a few months, she moved in with him. This had been the talk in the local pub and village shop for a few days, but really the villagers were pleased he had also found happiness in his life again.

Rebecca hardly recognised her childhood home when she visited. Julie had transformed the house with fresh coats of paint, using lively bright colours and putting up new curtains. Rebecca's less happy memories of her home now seemed to have faded and been disguised beneath the new colour scheme.

Michael had tipped the contents of drawers into boxes

and put them in the loft. There was so much stuff belonging to their parents, which Michael delayed going through. He had told Rebecca that they would have to look through it all one day. There were diaries, boxes of photographs, clothing, some of Mum's wedding accessories and some 'treasures' from Michael and Rebecca's early childhood days. Little rhymes which Rebecca had written and some of Michael's early artwork. Rebecca was surprised that Mum had kept her scribbles. There were also scrapbooks, which had occupied Rebecca for hours as a young girl. She had pressed flowers and four-leafed clovers, which were meant to be lucky. Others were filled with pictures of ponies cut from magazines. She had also kept all her birthday cards from the age of four. Thankfully the loft could house all the scrapbooks and memories of her family's past until time could be found to sort through everything.

Michael had even put the famous Mason windbreak in the loft. He couldn't get rid of it as it had sheltered his family on their beach visits and triggered happy memories of their short family life together. Julie couldn't understand why he wanted to keep the fraying faded canvas item she had put out by the dustbin before Michael rescued it.

* * *

'Oh hello, Wilf! I wasn't expecting yew this morning. Whatever's the matter?'

'I don't know, Kathleen. I'm worried abowt Rebecca, that I am. She seems withdrawn. I don't know if she's sleeping properly. I think she might be having bad dreams an' all. I'm sure I've heard her calling out in her sleep. Do yew think I should take 'er to the doctor's?'

'Doctor's? That doesn't sound like talk from my brother-law! Oh Wilf, she's had a lot to cope with, hasn't she ... losing both parents. I was never really sure just how close she was to her mother... perhaps she's feeling a bit guilty... I don't know... yew know...missed opportunities perhaps... She was also very upset when she heard the news that the missing girl, Anna, had been found dead.'

'I thought she was. She had followed the story in the paper when she was off school, hadn't she? I also found this her' poem written in her English ex'cise book. It fair broke my heart, that it did... I copied it out to show yer. Here.' Wilf handed her a scrap of paper on which he had written in his untidy handwriting...

Happiness

I reached out my hand to you
But you escaped my grasp.
I now see you in the distance.
I know that you're there
So why can't I reach you?
Feel your warmth, your embrace
And let you lighten my load?
You must cross my path soon.
Let me join your radiance.
Teach me to laugh again,
A forgotten emotion
In my lonely empty world.

'Goodness, Wilf... that's a bit deep from a thirteen-year-old girl, isn't it? She's still mixed up, bound to be, plus she's thirteen... her body's changing... all those hormones stirred up... it's not easy for any child of her age, let alone an orphan. I tell yew what, I'll speak to her when I get the chance. I've always told her that she can speak to me anytime... about... yew know... girl's stuff... and we probably need to get her a few new clothes. I noticed her uniform is getting a bit small and she doesn't have that many clothes for out of school either. I could take her on the bus to Wexham to get what she needs.'

'Thanks, Kathleen, that's wholly decent of yer. That it is. It's occard for a mawther to talk to me abowt such matters. I'll be gettin' along then. Thought I'd mek her suffin nice for her tea tonight. Shepherd's pie maybe.'

'Elizabeth would be amazed, yew know, Wilf. Your cooking is something yew should be proud of.'

'Wull, yew tell her won't yer, next time yew visit her grave?'

'Of course; I talk to her all the time I'm at the graveyard, yew know.'

'So dew I… unless I think someone's watching me. There's two silly fewls in this village then!'

'Wull, I feel close to her somehow at her grave. Then I visit our mother's grave too and keep her up to date with what's going on.'

'Wull that's two of us that are certainly mad tergether. See you soon, Kathleen, and thank yer kindly. Hey, yew tell Tom he's married a good'un, won't yer, even if yew are as mad as me!'

'Oh I don't think he notices who he's married to sometimes! Do yew want to stay for a bit of dinner?'

'No, thank yer kindly. I've still got some drippin' from the Coddleton butcher's to finish off with some nice bread.'

'Alright. Bye, Wilf.'

The next Saturday, Kathleen took Rebecca into Wexham and they managed to find her some nice new clothes and replace her outgrown uniform. Rebecca was delighted with the new purchases and couldn't remember being able to choose clothes for herself. Mum used to show her the catalogue she used and she had a limited choice then, but was never able to try clothes on in a shop.

'Thank yew so much, Auntie Kathleen,' said Rebecca, 'for all these things.'

'This is the family allowance money we save for yew until yew need things, it's not my money. I must sew on your name tapes to your new school uniform when we git home, so don't let me forget.'

'No, alright but really, Auntie Kathleen, it's been great to go out with yew like this,' replied Rebecca, gazing in shop windows as they passed. 'Oh, can we go in this book shop? I'd love to buy Uncle Wilf a cookery book for Christmas… I know it's only November, but look, there's Margaret Butterworth's cookery book in the window… our cookery teacher was talking about it at school and says it's really good and has lots of simple recipes… Wilf says that Elizabeth carried so many of her recipes in her head and he would love to try and make some of her everyday meals.'

'Of course, that's a good idea. I never know what to buy him. I usually get him socks! Perhaps afterwards I will buy yew a milkshake and I can have a cup of tea in Miller's café opposite. I'm ready for a drink.'

'Oh, yes please.'

* * *

Christmas Day was spent at Kathleen's house and Wilf, Rebecca, Michael and Julie joined Kathleen, Tom, Leonard, Mary and John for a lovely dinner of roast turkey with all the trimmings. It was a squeeze to get everyone seated but Tom brought in an old table which had belonged to Aunt Agnes and, once covered with a cloth, it served well as an extension with chairs borrowed from Wilf. They all chatted together and enjoyed getting to know Julie, who was rather shy initially, being amongst several new faces. She had recently started work at the draper's shop in Coddleton. She was delighted to find the lucky sixpence in Kathleen's Christmas pudding.

'That was a delicious meal, Kathleen, thank yer kindly,'

said Leonard struggling to finish all of his Christmas pudding with rum sauce.

'Glad yew enjoyed it, Father. I put the turkey in the oven at half past five this morning and was at Holy Communion at eight! Mrs Coleman was asking after yew at church.'

'That was wholly nice of her. How is she?'

'Keeping well ... and busy helping to look after her granddaughter.'

'I haven't seen her husband recently, but then I haven't got down to the pub for a while.'

'Fabulous meal, I agree too, and thank you, Mrs Berry, for inviting me with all your family, you're very kind ... and very tired I should think, after your early start today.'

'Yew are very welcome her', Julie, and please call me Kathleen, dear. I am a bit tired. Mary helped me this morning though with all the vegetables and so on, but I think I might just sit down and listen to the Queen's speech this afternoon.'

'We'll sort the washing up, Auntie Kathleen,' said Rebecca.

'Yes, I'll help,' added Julie.

'I think yew should refuse, Julie, after Mother nearly broke your tooth with that sixpence!' Mary said.

'I am sorry I forgot to warn all of yew... I had forgotten I had put it in!'

'Your mother used to put a sixpence in the pudding, Kathleen.'

'Yes, I can remember that... this is the first time I've put one in and I thought I would use a pre-decimal coin to be more traditional.'

'I'll move this small table out now to make more room for us all to sit down.'

'Thanks, Tom. Dad, yew come and sit down in this more comfortable chair.'

'Thanks, Kathleen.'

'We need to leave about three o'clock, Kathleen, if yew don't mind. We need to be at Julie's parents' house at about five.'

'That's alright, Michael. I'm so glad yew could come today.'

'It's been great thanks, Kathleen... so much food... I hope your mum hasn't got a huge meal for us later, Julie!'

'Probably... you know what she's like!'

'So, Wilf, I guess yew might be cooking Christmas dinner next year... I hear you've got a cookery book for Christmas!' teased Michael.

'I don't think I will ever try to compete with Kathleen here and certainly not a Christmas dinner... but I will have to try out some of the recipes soon. I might surprise yew!'

'He makes a good shepherd's pie yew know, Michael!' added Rebecca from the kitchen.

It wasn't long before Leonard was dozing in the chair, a result of a large sherry and heavy meal perhaps.

* * *

Rebecca's fourteenth birthday was fast approaching. Wilf had been planning her present for months. She had continued to love horses and Wilf had managed to find one which would be just right for her. Jim Potter was happy to let him use one of the old stables at the farm, so Wilf had been busy smartening up the stable and making preparations for the pony's arrival. The pony needed a new home as its previous owner had outgrown it and was about to go away to college.

Eventually, Rebecca's birthday arrived, March 14th. Wilf had found it hard to contain his excitement over the past few weeks and had nearly given away the secret he had struggled to keep.

It was a Saturday and Rebecca got up and dressed and

joined Wilf for breakfast. Wilf's card had two ponies on it and wished her a happy birthday. She put the card on the mantelpiece next to the one from Michael, with a ginger cat on it. He had left it for her the day before and a crisp five-pound note had fallen out of the card when she had opened it. The card said 'To a dear sister' on the front; these were sentiments which she now believed could be true as they had grown very close.

The postman had not called yet. She expected a card from Auntie Ann and hopefully a letter inside with her news. She wondered if Wilf had got her a present, but said nothing as she knew he had spent a lot of money recently when he had traded in Elizabeth's old car for a nearly-new brown Vauxhall Viva which he had been very proud to show her. He hadn't really driven that much … well, cars at any rate. He was more comfortable behind the wheel of a tractor. He had been sad to let Elizabeth's Mini Traveller go, but it needed a lot of money spending on it, so he had finally decided to trade it in, after 'consulting' Elizabeth, of course!

'Thought we might go up to the farm today, Rebecca, if that's alright with yer? I promised I'd help Jim with some repairs to one of the buildings, but it shouldn't take long. It's a bit nippy out mind, so tek a jumper or your anorak with yew. Perhaps yew could help Janice with some baking whilst I'm there.'

'OK, then.'

'Sorry, it's not an exciting task for yer birthday, but…'

'No, no… that's fine, I understand,' replied Rebecca, a little hesitant. She sensed he was hiding something from her, but thought that perhaps Janice had made her a birthday cake or something.

They were about to set off when the postman arrived, whistling as he approached the open door. 'Hello Rebecca, all the post seems to be for yew today… it must be your birthday!'

'Yes it is… thanks,' replied Rebecca as she quickly opened the card addressed to her. It was from Auntie Ann and Uncle Bruce. Another pony card! There was a long letter inside and another five-pound note. Goodness, all this money!

'P'rhaps yew can lend me a fiver or two, Rebecca, as I'm cleaned out after that new car!' joked Wilf.

'I'm not sure about that! I'll read this letter later, if you want to be getting to the farm.'

'Yes, we'd better get off,' Wilf replied hastily.

They set off for the farm. When they got there, there was no sign of Jim and his truck was not parked in its usual spot.

Wilf led the way towards the stable. As they got to it, he turned and said, 'Happy birthday, my dear.'

Rebecca suddenly felt very odd and shaky… She peered over the stable door to see the beautiful rusty coloured pony who stopped munching hay to look at her.

'But, whose pony is it, she's bootiful…?'

'I told yew… she's yours…!'

'You're joking! Oh Uncle Wilf… I can't believe it! A pony of my own… I must be dreaming! Thank yew ever so much!'

'Yew deserve her, my dear… Let me introduce yer to Chestnut.'

'She's so bootiful!' Rebecca started to cry.

'Don't yew go gitting upset, enjoy yer new companion. Yer friend Clare'll cum and help yer git used to her and remind yer o' how to look after a pony.'

'Wull I haven't forgotten how to muck out! That looks like the first job to do! But first a huge cuddle...'

'Oh… and I thought yew meant with me!'

'Oh, yew can have one too! Yew are the best, Uncle Wilf! Can I… call yew… Dad?' Rebecca enquired hesitantly, surprised she had just posed the awkward question.

Wilf couldn't speak, choked by emotion. Eventually however he managed to get the words out. 'Yis, o'course yew can!'

Janice Potter appeared from the corner of the outbuildings with a box in her hand and saw their stunned faces. 'Hello, yew two! Happy birthday, Rebecca! Here... hope it fits.'

'Thanks,' Rebecca said, hurriedly opening the parcel, though thinking nothing would match the present that was munching before her eyes! 'Oh *thanks*, Mrs Potter, a riding hat is just what I needed!'

Wilf was discreetly wiping away a tear, still stunned at his new title, but he was happy to get used to it.

'Seems to fit yew a treat, my dear... I'm afraid it's not new, but Polly had quite a lot of riding equipment she's selling... so if there's anything else yew need, I'm sure she can help yew. Oh, and here's a card for yew too.'

'Thank yew, Mrs Potter... oh, that's a lovely card, but the horse is not quite as handsome as Chestnut here!'

'Of course not! Wull I'll let yew get on... I've left some baking in the oven, must get goin'. See yer, Wilf.'

'See yer, Janice, and thanks again for everything. This here stable'll dew just fine, won't it, Rebecca?'

'Oh yes. It's great. Someone has been busy. Did Auntie Ann know yew were getting me a pony?'

'Wull, yes she did... I was glad yew didn't get time to read her letter in case she mentioned it. I thought we would be out before Ivan arrived with the post.'

'That's why yew were hurryin' me!'

'It's been so hard keeping this beast secret!'

'I am such a lucky fourteen-year-old!'

'Oh and by the way, we are invited to Kathleen's tonight for a birthday tea for yew. Michael and Julie will be there an' all.'

'That will be lovely. The day can't get any better!'

* * *

'Oh, Auntie Kathleen, that cake is amazing!'

'I'm not sure the pony looks anything like Chestnut, let alone a pony come to that!'

'I think it's fantastic, thank yew. It must have taken yew ages.'

'I got so engrossed in the icing I forgot to go to the shop and buy some candles!'

'I don't mind, fourteen would have been a lot to blow out!'

'Yew old thing!' laughed Michael. 'Is it time for me to go and buy the "Nealopitan" ice cream yet?!'

'Ha ha, big brother! Oh look! It's a stripy cake!' remarked Rebecca, as Kathleen cut the tall sponge cake decorated with a horse's head created out of icing, complete with its liquorice 'shoelace' bridle. 'Thank yew, Auntie Kathleen!'

'I was careful not to tip in too much blue colouring for the middle layer! Poor Elizabeth was upset the time she made yew a brilliant blue sponge cake one year!'

'I always loved my cakes, whatever colour they were. What a shame to cut in to Chestnut's head!'

'These liquorice shoelaces bring back memories!' remarked Julie. 'I spent lots of pennies on these at our local shop. My mum is always reminding me how my teeth were always black from eating too many.'

'What party games are we playing, Kathleen?' asked Michael cheekily.

'Postman's Knock, if yew like! Or Pass the Parcel!'

'I remember Janet Jones always getting upset when yew played Pass the Parcel, Rebecca, as she wanted to win the prize. Mum once sent me to buy another pencil case and pens so you could play the game again and I'm sure she fixed it so Janet would win that time.'

'Poor Janet, she didn't have many friends. Mum always insisted I invite her to my party. I wonder what she's doing now. Her family moved away last year.'

'The cake is good, Kathleen.'

'Do yew want another piece, Wilf?'

'Oh, no thanks, that'll dew me nicely. I finished off the ham sandwiches, remember!'

'Wull, yew can take the cake that's left with yew for another day for yourself and birthday girl here and I'll wrap up some too, Michael, for yew and Julie!'

'Thanks, Auntie Kathleen, it's been a very special birthday. Thank yew all for my presents and a lovely day.'

'My pleasure, my dear.'

'Right then, Rebecca, shall we go home by the farm then?'

'Yes I must go and check Chestnut is alright. Are yew coming, Michael?'

'Yes, if that's alright with yew, Julie?'

'Of course, we need to meet Chestnut and see if she's as beautiful as you say she is!'

Chapter Ten

The Village Fête

Everyone in the village was busy preparing for the annual village fête, which was held in one of the Potters' large meadows. They hoped that the weather would be kind for the occasion, as two years ago it had been particularly wet and many of the usual activities had to be abandoned. However, two large marquees were erected to house the displays of homegrown produce and the baking and needlework displays by the Women's Institute.

The competitions were taken very seriously and, once a villager had won a particular section for the best cabbage or whatever, he or she would feel under pressure to win the same class again the following year. Bill Dobson was particularly proud of his leeks, which he hoped would get a 'first' again this year. He claimed his ancestors came from Wales, which was why he had inherited the knack of growing leeks! His friends who propped up the bar in the village pub would retort, 'It's a shame you didn't inherit the Welsh singing voice then, isn't it, Bill!'

Bill was known to start singing when he had drunk a few too many pints of ale.

June the 11th came and everyone breathed a sigh of relief when the sun began to shine. Michael was in charge of the swing boats, assisted by his girlfriend who was new to the great occasion but seemed happy to help. The more observant members of the community suspected that Julie might be pregnant. Her clothes were rather tight but she looked so happy and relaxed. She sat near to the swing boats, taking the money for the rides, appearing to be absorbing the atmosphere of the community and probably trying to imagine what future years might be like when she would bring her own child to this event.

Rebecca and Clare had organised pony rides and were enjoying each other's company again after quite a long break apart.

Michael found Wilf helping with the bowling. 'Wilf, can yew spare a minute?'

'Cors I can, Michael. What's wrong? Yew look worried.'

'Wull, I have something for yew… but I hope it doesn't upset yew… only… wull...'

'Wull, what is it?'

'Here, hev a look.'

'Thanks.'

Wilf tore open a brown paper parcel to reveal a beautiful sketch of Elizabeth. 'Oh Michael, have *yew* done this? It's… she's beautiful.' Wilf was stunned by the unexpected gift.

'Yes, I hev done it… but it's taken longer than I'd hoped. I just wanted to thank yew for all yew'd done for Rebecca… and me too over the last year or so. I was turning some things out of Mum's drawers and found a photo of your Elizabeth. I think it was when they had that photographer give a talk to the WI about his hobby. He developed his own prints. Well, he must have taken a picture of Elizabeth. There were photos of other WI members too. Mum must have forgotten to give them out when he sent the photos to her. She wasn't the most organised WI secretary. Anyway, I thought I would sketch Elizabeth from the photo. Do yew like it?'

'I don't know what t' say, it's wonderful. Yew are very

talented, Michael. Thank yew so much,' Wilf said, feeling a tear about to escape from his eye.

'Wull, as I said, we owe a lot to yew, Wilf. I'm glad yew like it.'

'Fancy 'lizabeth making an appearance at another village fête. She'd think that amusing!'

'That hadn't occurred to me, Wilf. Yes, I s'pose she has!'

The fête went well. The ice cream man had already gone home as he had sold out! He was another person who had been grateful for the good weather. The person running the hoopla was packing up as all prizes had now been 'captured'. The tombola table was also being packed up, as only a bar of soap had been left as a prize. Stall holders were counting up the takings to be presented to the treasurer of the village hall committee, who was adding up all the money to announce the fête's final takings, hoping it would be enough to fund the planned redecoration of the hall. Children could be heard laughing and screaming as they enjoyed the thrill of the swing boats. The pony rides were popular too.

Rebecca couldn't quite believe that she was providing one of the ponies for the rides. She had enjoyed the annual fêtes as a young child, especially when the rather large riding hat was placed on her head and she was led round the field for a shilling. She would wave to her mum proudly, concentrating so that the hat wouldn't cover her eyes. If only she could see her now. As soon as she was helped off the pony, she would plead with Mum for 'just one more ride… *please*'.

The chairman of the parish council declared that the competition winners would be announced, followed by the drawing of the grand raffle. There would also be an auction of any donated competition entries at the end. All auction funds would be split as usual between the church repair fund and the village hall maintenance fund. He was using the loudspeaker and the sound system kept emitting a high pitched squeak, which made the children giggle.

'Could all winners please come and collect their prizes from Peter, here at the tent. The winner of the best iced cake goes to ... Kathleen Berry. The winner of the best fruit cake is Janice Potter. The winner of the best marmalade goes to Christine Coleman. The winner of the best chutney goes to Millie Livingstone... I think she has just had to go home, but we'll get her prize to her... oh ... apparently she has won one of the tapestry section prizes too, which we will come to next....'

The winners were called out and there was a lot of cheering and clapping, together with some teasing between the regular competition entrants. Wilf won a prize for his dahlias and, to everyone's relief, Bill Dobson's leeks won the best vegetable section prize. The announcements took some time to read out. Mary took note of the winners as she was the local press correspondent, having taken over the job from her mum to give her a little more free time. At least the fête provided a little more exciting news than the usual weekly village events to report...

'And the winner of the open art competition goes to Michael Mason.'

'Michael, you've won a prize!' said Julie, still occupying the chair next to the swing boats where a few children were having a final swing before the boats were dismantled for another year.

'Don't be so darft, I didn't enter anything!'

'They've just called out your name... the art competition, I think they said.'

The small crowd was clapping and looking in the direction of the swing boats.

Wilf came up rather flustered and said, 'Sorry, Michael, I couldn't resist enterin' yer picture last minute. You're too modest to have entered any of your art works, I daresay! Everyone commented what a lovely picture it was and knew immediately who the subject was. Yew could take orders I'm sure. Go on, collect your prize. Well done!'

'Wilf, I'll get yew back! Looks like your Elizabeth has won a different competition at this fête!'

'She'd be really proud o' yew… and o'course yer parents would be tew.'

Michael swallowed hard; he now had tears in his eyes as he collected his prize, a voucher from a local art shop.

Peter Croft was presenting the prizes. He was really touched when he was invited to open the fête and present prizes to the villagers, many of whom he barely recognised. He shook hands with some whose last contact with him might have been in their christening robes! Many noticed that he must have given in to Esther's nagging as he was wearing a hearing aid. He had only just got it, but had been pleased with the difference it had made to his life. With the invitation to open the fête, he could hardly put off the inevitable need for an aid any longer. Esther had told villagers later that Peter could still turn it off or leave it in the drawer if she nagged him too much!

Peter was wearing a straw trilby hat, an open neck shirt, a cream blazer and cream trousers. The villagers remarked how strange it was not to see him in his dog collar and church robes. Although Esther had come too, they had been collected by Kathleen as both Peter and Esther had had to give up driving. Esther had cataracts and Peter had had a stroke the previous year, although he had made a remarkable recovery considering his deteriorating health. They lived in sheltered housing at Coddleton now.

* * *

Wilf later returned home and decided to hang the portrait of Elizabeth on the kitchen wall where she used to display her 'works of art' presented to her by the school children.

He realised he would have to redecorate the kitchen soon, as the wall still had evidence of the children's pictures having been there. There were faded and darker patches on the wallpaper where the treasured pictures had hung until recently.

Rebecca later came in, having put Chestnut to bed for a well-earned rest after his first fête duties. She felt proud that she was now the provider of the pony rides, but was quite exhausted. She sank in to one of the chairs in the kitchen and then noticed Elizabeth's picture smiling at her.

'Dad! Elizabeth's picture... it's stunning!'

'Michael did it for me,' beamed Wilf as he approached the picture. 'Hold yew hard a minute, my booty, you're a bit on the huh! Thass better,' he added as he adjusted the picture slightly so it now hung straight.

'Gosh, he didn't tell me. So that must be why everyone kept saying to me "What a talented brother yew hev", as I was leaving the fête. I couldn't hear what was going on during the competition announcements while I was walking Chestnut along the other side of the field. I can't believe it. He has become quite thoughtful these days... he never used to be.'

'Wull, I was really touched, I can tell ya.'

'I'm trying to remember a quote Miss Price once told us about art... it was something to do with Van Gogh. I think it meant seeing or remembering art helped loneliness. Anyway, seeing Elizabeth's picture just made me think of it... and it feels like she is here with us somehow... It's been a good day today, hasn't it?'

'Yis, it has, tha's for sure,' replied Wilf, suppressing the tears which were prickling his eyes.

'I hev so enjoyed helping with the pony rides. I just wish Mum could have seen me.'

'I know, my dear... maybe she did though, eh?'

'Yeh, maybe... Little Katie Fuller must have had six rides

on Chestnut today,' added Rebecca changing the subject before they both got too emotional.

'Does that beat your past record for the number of pony rides then?'

'Hardly! I remember running back and forth in to the hall refreshment area where Mum helped out and begging her for one more ride, then going to Dad helping on the skittles when she said she had no more money. I often forgot to ask for an ice cream as I was so besotted with the pony rides and yew know how much I like ice cream.'

'Yis, I dew!'

'So what cookery prizes did yew win then?'

'Wull, I didn't want to show up Kathleen, now did I! Thought I'd give the WI members a chance!'

'P'rhaps they'll ask yew to give a cookery demo at one of their meetings soon!'

'No doubt they will!'

'Talking of food, what shall we hev for tea tonight?'

'There's some boiled ham in the fridge. How about I go and dig some new taters from the garden and I'll find a nice lettuce. Will that dew?'

'That's fine. I'm too tired to cook. Oh dear, poor Mum used to always say that!'

'Wull, your old Dad can just about manage to dig a few taters up... yew just stay there and rest, my lady!'

'I've walked miles today, I'll have yew know...'

'Poor Chestnut I feel sorry for!'

'Thanks for your sympathy!'

'I'm only teasing ya!'

'I know.'

'Oh... and I bought a nice tea loaf at the fête sale... it's in the larder. We could hev som' of that, tew.'

'Lovely... who made it though?'

'Don't be fussy, your ladyship! I'm sure the good woman who med it hed washed her hands afore she med it!'

'…or the good *man* come to that!'

'Yis, o' course!'

'Did yew hear I won a box of Quality Street in the raffle?'

'No, wull lucky yew! I didn't win anything in the raffle. There were some decent prizes given this year. The butcher's at Coddleton had given a large joint of beef and did yew see the large fruit basket from the greengrocer's?'

'No. Oh and by the way… I'm afraid Clare and I have eaten most of the sweets!'

'Wull, I hope yew don't hev Kathleen's problem, losing a filling after eating a toffee!'

'Oh no! No, I don't want to go to the dentist. Thanks for the warning!'

They sat at the kitchen table and enjoyed the tea they had put out between them. Elizabeth's presence in the cottage seemed to have been reinforced by her portrait now hanging in pride of place in the 'gallery'.

'It was good to catch up with Clare again today. We're going to go riding along the beach next weekend, if that's alright with yew. Her cousins have a riding school at Holkham and have suggested she join them riding and said she could bring a friend if she likes. It would be nice to live nearer to the sea. Then Chestnut could be exercised on the beach. That would be such fun.'

'No, we're not gittin' a holiday hom' or even a beach hut, before yew suggest it, gal!'

'I know, I know… it would be nice to live near the sea though.'

'Stop yer day dreamin' and pass me the salad cream. Yew know I'm spent owt.'

'Here yew are then. Is there any hot water? I fancy a bath after tea.'

'Pro'bly not, but put the immersion on… it'll soon heat up. No wonder my 'lectricity bill is so big!' Wilf muttered.

'What was that?'

'Put the immersion on.'

'I heard that bit! I'll switch it on now then, and I'll ignore your mumbling.'

'I don't know how yew girls can spend so long in the bathroom. When I was your age, I had to hev a quick bath in a tin bath in front of the fire and I was lucky if I got in the water furst!'

'How awful that would be! I can't imagine sharing Michael's bath water… how revolting!'

'I used to fight with my brother to decide who would go furst. My poor mother used to git so cross with us an' all. Carbolic soap wasn't like the fancy sort yew like either!'

Rebecca lay in the warm bath later, thinking about the day. She was using the coal tar soap Wilf always bought. She had run out of her own supply of assorted soaps given to her by Kathleen for her last birthday, together with bubble bath and talcum powder. The distinctive smell of the coal tar reminded her of her grandad. She couldn't remember him very well at all, but he must have used this type of soap as she could vaguely remember being put on a potty in his damp bathroom, which smelt of coal tar soap.

Frank Mason had left his wife for a younger woman who had subsequently ditched him. He had then decided not to bother with women any longer and had lived alone in his council bungalow in Swaffham. He preferred the company of his friends at the pub at the end of the street, where he would also play darts. He also enjoyed watching horse racing and would place a bet most weeks. Rebecca tried hard now to recall other details about her grandad, but she couldn't picture him in her mind. He must have been at her parents' funeral, but she couldn't remember seeing him. However, much of that day seemed blurred in her memory. She would have to get Michael to get the old photos out of the tatty suitcase, which held so many pictures of her parents' past and of family members she had never known. Perhaps she could visit Grandad with Michael one day, though she wondered why he didn't keep in touch.

The water was getting cool, so she turned on the hot tap again till it regained a pleasant heat. She rubbed the soap on a pink fraying flannel and washed herself. The bath was wonderful after a hectic day. She gazed at the line of white tiles on the wall around the bath. Two or three tiles were loose and some of the plaster on the walls needed attention. Wilf would not want to spend money on it. He probably didn't notice that the work needed doing as he spent much less time in the bathroom than she did, as he constantly reminded her. The mirror on the bathroom cabinet was now steamed up.

Rebecca heard a peacock calling from the Hargreaves' estate, which she hadn't noticed for a while. They had several peacocks wandering around the grounds. She had been scared of them the first time she had visited to deliver a parcel for Elizabeth, who had altered some clothes for Angela Hargreaves. The peacocks seemed so big, but then she wasn't so big herself then. She remembered pedalling her bicycle as fast as she could to get past them, displaying their colourful fanned out tails.

Rebecca decided to wash her hair and reached for the jug ready to rinse away the lather. Perhaps it was time to have her hair short. Several of her friends had their hair cut in neat short styles. She couldn't ever remember having her hair short and it was a bit of an effort to wash it regularly. Wearing her riding hat made her hair rather greasy. As she used the shampoo, she thought of the time at primary school when all her class had nits. She could remember the foul smelling lotion Mum had applied and her own complaining when Mum had tried to comb out all the knots with a fine comb. Her hair hadn't been as long as it was now at least, but the experience had not been pleasant. Her brother had teased her terribly, until he found that he was also 'infested'.

* * *

A few weeks later, when Chestnut had been exercised, Rebecca was at a loose end and so called at the farm kitchen. The kitchen stable door was open and the usual good baking smells were wafting out.

'Hello, Mrs Potter!'

'Hello, Rebecca, how are yew?'

'Well, thank you.'

'Good. Come in dear. Oh I'm running late with my jobs today!'

'Anything I can do to help?'

'Well, could yew take the teas up to the forty-acre field for me?'

'Of course I can. You mean the big field near the woods?'

'Yes, that's right. I have a hair appointment and I need to go shortly. My cake took longer to cook today, I don't know why unless it's the size of eggs I used. Anyway, if yew can take this for me that will be a great help, thank yew.'

'What's on the farm workers' menu then?'

'Tell them these are ham with mustard sandwiches. There is a date and walnut cake cut up in this box. This large flask of tea should just go round them all. I've put sugar in the tea as they all take it. Will yew manage OK? Yew can take my bicycle.'

'Oh, alright, yes. Will it all fit in the basket?'

'Should do, let me help. There that's it... oh the wet cloths for them to wipe their hands, can't forget those else the bread won't be white for long! Thanks so much, Rebecca, yew've saved the day.'

'Yew are welcome, Mrs Potter, but don't be late now for that appointment.'

'I won't now, thanks to yew. Bye, dear.'

Rebecca set off cautiously on the bicycle, as it was a little difficult to steer with the basket laden with refreshments for the haymakers' tea and she hadn't ridden a bicycle for a long while, but didn't want to worry Mrs Potter. The workers were surprised to see her arrive on Mrs Potter's bicycle. They joked that she was still wearing her riding hat and Rebecca, blushing, found herself touching her head to check since Jim had said it so seriously. Certainly her riding hat had become very much a part of her that she could have believed she might have left it on.

The tea was soon eaten by the hungry workers and work resumed soon after. Rebecca collected up the enamel cups, shaking out any last drops of tea on to the ground and set off back to the farm, the bicycle much easier to control now. She much preferred Chestnut as a means of transport. She left the teacups and bag in the kitchen porch and left the bicycle propped against the wall nearby.

Chapter Eleven

Good News

'Hullo, Wilf. Watcha, little sis!'

'Michael! To what do we owe this pleasure?'

'I thought I should come and see yew both to tell you some good news… Julie and me, well… we are expecting a baby,' Michael announced awkwardly.

'Goodness, Michael!' exclaimed Rebecca, her jaw visibly dropping, 'but yew're not married!'

'Wull…'

'Congratulations, Michael!' Wilf added, rather surprised at the news.

'Oh, that means I'm going to be an auntie!' Rebecca shrieked.

'When is the baby due, Michael?'

'Early January… we think. We are going for Julie's antenatal appointment later at the surgery, to see the midwife. I just thought I'd come and see yer first because yew know what it's like down there… We're bound to see someone who'll put two and two tergether.'

'Wull, that's great news, Michael, that it is. You two seemed very happy tergether at the fête. I'm very pleased for the pair of ya. Shall we have a cup o' tea, Rebecca, to celebrate?'

'I'll put the kettle on.'

'Sorry, I can't stop, but thanks. I have to get back to work after the appointment. See you soon. Oh, Wilf! Yew haven't wasted any time getting that picture up, I see!'

'That I haven't, my boy! Not a minute too soon. I'm so pleased wi' it, I can't tell ya how pleased I am wi' it, Michael.'

Michael was quite taken aback and found himself patting Wilf's shoulder as he turned and left for the surgery. He could feel tears in his eyes again and didn't want to show himself up as an emotional young man. Tears weren't for men.

'Wull, what do you think of our Michael then? That's a turn up for the books!'

'He's a good'un, he'll mek' a good father, I'm sure o' that.'

'I'm not sure that would have been Mum's first comment if she had been given the news. She would probably have said he should have married Julie before making her pregnant.'

'That's as may be, but there's no denying they're both happy… and that's the main thing, eh?'

* * *

At the Coddleton doctor's surgery, June Fowler was coming out of the antenatal clinic with a string of young children in tow. It appeared she hadn't got round to the sterilisation she had promised herself after her last pregnancy! Perhaps after three children, childbirth really was like shelling peas, as some mothers of large families claimed.

'Julie Shaw, please.'

'Come on, Michael!'

'Dew I come in with yew?'

'Yes, of course.'

'Hello, come through please… I'm Maria Grant, the midwife and district nurse for this area. Sit down both of you. Now then, I believe you have already been informed that your pregnancy test was positive, Julie.'

'Yes.'

'OK. Well, congratulations. Are you pleased with the news?'

'Yes... of course, though it was a bit of a shock, I suppose.'

'Is this your boyfriend, Julie?'

'Yes, this is Michael.'

'Pleased to meet you, Michael. Are you pleased with the news too?'

'Yes I'm very pleased... we both are. We needed some good news.'

'How do you mean?'

'Well, I... um... my parents both died not so long ago and life has been kind o' rough really ... yew know.'

'Oh I see, I'm sorry to hear that Michael. OK, well let's get on with the blood tests and work out your expected date of delivery, shall we?'

'That's fine. I'm not sure I'm looking forward to the blood tests though. I'm not keen on needles. I fainted at school when we had our last jabs!'

'Don't worry, Julie, it won't take long. Let's have you lying down on this couch, then you shouldn't need to catch her, Michael!'

Michael and Julie left thirty minutes later and passed Bill Dobson coming in to the surgery.

'Cor, blast, Julie, hev yer got somethin' gorn abowt, yew look wholly pale!'

'No, I'm fine thanks, Mr Dobson, it's nothing to worry about... probably the sight of the nurse's needle just now!'

'I know what yer mean my dear... I'm just goin' for my blood test m'self. Hope she ha'nt blunted that there needle! Fare yer well tergether!'

'Old Bill doesn't change, does he? The antenatal clinic is one area of the health service that he can't claim he's needed to use!'

'The only medical service he's missed out on at the

surgery! He's no doubt tried to claim a reduced National Insurance rate though!' replied Julie. 'Glad he didn't see me coming out of the midwife's clinic. Though I expect our news will soon be round the village. Old May Smith, I think it was, kept smiling at me at the fête in a knowing way … do you think she knows?'

'No idea … but you know what the old village folk are like … read it in their tea leaves probably!'

'Oh, Michael! There's an idea for the fête next year… a fortune teller's tent!'

'I don't think you've quite got to know how this village operates yet! Come on, I must hurry up and get back to work and earn some money for our son's upkeep!'

'Oh, and how do you know it's not a beautiful daughter I have in here?'

'We'll see! Right… are you alright to drive back home and I'll get a lift back from work later or catch the bus?'

'Of course. I'm glad I got the day off at Harper's, I'm so excited I don't think I can keep our news secret for much longer… Michael, you are going to be a brilliant dad.'

'I'll do my best. It's a bit scary though, isn't it? I mean my son might turn out a difficult little sod like me!'

'Well, so long as he finally settles down with a beautiful girl of his dreams who will sort him out, he'll be OK!'

'So, it is a boy then!'

'Go to work! I love you Michael Mason.'

'You're not so bad yourself, even if yew are from Suffolk! See yew later,' said Michael gently kissing her on her cheek and handing her the car key to their second-hand Ford Escort. 'Go yew carefully.'

'Our heads are screwed on better in Suffolk than yours you know! Cheerio.'

* * *

'Mum, I haven't got a school blouse ironed for tomorrow.'

'Oh, Rebecca, I'm so tired this evening. Can yew do it, dear?'

'OK, Mum.' Rebecca found the blue plastic linen basket, which cradled a mountain of clean clothes waiting to be ironed.

Cynthia could not keep up with the family's ironing and seemed to just iron a few things off the top of the pile, as they were needed. Occasionally Rebecca would stand and iron as long as she could, but never quite reached the bottom of the linen basket. By the time this layer was reached, the clothes were either too small or had been forgotten about. She knew that she was rather slow at ironing, but felt she was helping her mother who was always tired from working at the pub or busy trying to keep some form of order in their chaotic household. On the occasions that she had a little energy to spare, she liked to meet up with Doreen, an old school friend.

Rebecca ironed her school blouse with difficulty, as the white cotton fabric was so dry. She sighed heavily, noticing that the cuff of one of the sleeves had a blue tint, which must have migrated from some clothing put in the whites wash by mistake. Possibly her navy PE knickers were to blame. Hopefully her teachers wouldn't notice. They were quite strict about school uniform looking neat and tidy at all times.

Rebecca knew that her school skirt was getting a bit tight, but daren't tell Mum that she needed a new one. The school uniform supplier was rather expensive. Perhaps she could ask one of her larger friends if they still had one of their outgrown school skirts that she could use, or she could continue to loosen the button fastening when she was sitting down behind her desk.

* * *

'Goodness, Rebecca, yew're mekin' a good job of that there ironing, gal,' remarked Wilf.

'I'm doing my best.'

'Yew know that Kathleen helps me with the ironing. Yew don't need to do it.'

'It's okay. I used to help Mum when I could… and practice makes perfect, though these blouses are still as difficult.'

'Yew've only just taken them off the washing line haven't yew?'

'Yes, I was trying to iron them before they got too dry. I was also trying to avoid the avalanche of crisp white cotton descending on your kitchen if I didn't keep up with my chores!'

'Well yew didn't need to iron these farm clothes. The cows won't mind how I look when I help out milking!'

Chapter Twelve

Shock And Despair

'Give us a pint of yer best ale, Kenneth, I've got a fair tharst on, that I hev'.'

'There yew go, my man.'

'Your good health, Kenneth... put it on the slate will yer?'

'Right yew are, Bill.'

'Hello, are yew a visitin' this fair part of the world?' enquired Bill of a well-built, ginger-haired man sitting at the bar, smoking a cigarette.

'Oh... hello... I'm just passing through. I'm on my way back to Appleby shortly. I've just been to a meeting at Coddleton.'

'Not a bad drop o'ale they giv' yer here, is it?'

'It's great, just what I need... Rather warm today, isn't it?'

'That it is, that it is. I've just bin to the surgery. The nurse ses I've got blood pressure... what does she know?'

'Oh dear, what's the treatment?'

'She wants me to lose weight and t'giv' up my pipe, beer, bacon, butter, cheese and God knows what else!'

'I see you're taking her advice then!'

'Wull, this beer won't kill me, tha's for sure. Anyway, I checked the obituaries this mornin' and I wasn't in it so... so far so good!'

'Ha, ha! Now I hadn't thought of doing that myself!

175

Actually, I've been told to stop smoking but you've got to have some pleasures in life, haven't you?'

'That yer have. Sorry what was yer name?'

'Charles... Charles Dewhurst... and yours?'

'Bill Dobson, pleased t' meet yer, my man. Cor, blast, thass better ... I needed that.'

'Can I get you another, Bill, though I don't want to get you into trouble with that nurse of yours!'

'Another pint'll dew me fine, thanks.'

Charles ordered more beer and he sat down again next to Bill at the bar in an otherwise empty pub.

'Cheers.'

'Cheers, yes good health! Not a bad day out there is it?'

'No it's a grand day and much better than yist'day. Think I might shoot some rabbits later, we're overrun with the damn things!'

'Oh. Do you work on the estate?'

'I dew an' all, yis, I work for Jim Potter and his father afore him an' all.'

'At least you don't have to travel up and down the country with your work, Bill. I seem to spend a lot of time driving to meetings and so on... This beer isn't bad, is it?'

'No, it's a good drop of ale, tha's for sure.'

'Bill, do you know... a woman who worked here, called Cynthia?' asked Charles, rather apprehensively, of his new acquaintance.

'Yer mean Cynthia Mason, that got killed?'

'What? I mean... it can't be who I'm thinking of ... quite a few years back, when I was passing... I got talking to a lady serving in the bar, she said she helped out here now and then...'

'That was Cynthia Mason alright... a good-looking woman an' all. Got killed in a car accident a few years back... wull... she lasted a bit after the accident but not for long, poor gal. Robert was killed an' all... her husband. The poor children though, it's not bin easy for 'em… thass for sure. It was a rum ole dew…that it was.'

'Goodness…' replied Charles. His colour seemed to have drained out of him.

'Are yew alright… yew look a bit peaky?'

'I'm fine, I'm fine thanks… I should be going… I'd quite forgotten the time. It's been good talking to you, Bill.'

'Likewise, Charles. Might see yew again in these parts. Fare yer well.'

When Charles got outside of the pub, he felt quite nauseated. He drove a little way from the pub down a narrow lane and stopped the car in a gateway. He got out and leaned on an old weathered gate that might not take his weight if he were to lean too far onto it. A rabbit darted out of the undergrowth and disappeared out of sight. He took some deep breaths of the wonderfully fresh air and tried to focus on the lush green landscape before him.

Cynthia… *dead*. He wondered what had happened. Had she been rowing with her husband perhaps? Might she have told Robert of the unexpected fling? Were other vehicles involved? He would never know… unless he looked at old newspaper reports at the local library… perhaps one day. He must have been mistaken; he thought Bill had said 'children' but there was only Michael. Charles tried to remember Bill's exact words but really couldn't be sure what he had said, only that Cynthia was dead.

The short affair with Cynthia had been passionate. She had been honest with him telling him that she was married, but she had said that she was not particularly happy. She said she didn't think she could ever leave her young son and that her marriage vows were important to her, even though she was too young to fully appreciate what marriage entailed when she had stood at the altar. Cynthia felt that she was just going through a rough patch and that things would get better. Money was not plentiful and most arguments in her household had been about financial problems.

Somehow Charles had kept a small part of him reserved for Cynthia, thinking that one day she might join him and they might settle down. Years had slipped by and they had not been in contact. Cynthia wrote letters to Charles soon after their affair on the understanding that he would never reply. She didn't want to risk being found out … not yet anyway. Charles read and reread the letters many times. He could have recalled every word of them, had he chosen to do so…

It was nearly fifteen years since their first meeting; he must have been naïve to think that she might still be waiting for him. No contact from him though, that was the agreement, not to reply to her wonderful letters through fear of someone finding out Cynthia's secret. She had telephoned him occasionally too, from the phone box near her home, usually ringing her sister afterwards so she wasn't actually lying when she said she had rung Ann if anyone asked where she had been.

Cynthia had acted quite out of character, when she was left in charge of Kenneth's pub, whilst he was soaking up the sun in Majorca. A young, good-looking man had walked in to the pub one quiet sunny afternoon looking for a pub lunch and a room for the night, ready for an early meeting locally the next day. What a wonderful two days of his life they had been.

A second passionate encounter had occurred when he booked in to a small inn just outside Coddleton a few weeks later. Cynthia had been so nervous of being discovered and had tried to disguise herself from local prying eyes when he had met her in Coddleton. Their secret meetings continued for several weeks but then Cynthia had stopped them abruptly, saying she needed time to think things through and perhaps they should wait a while before seeing each other again.

He had been patient for so long but as time went on, he realised that she had probably lost interest in him. What a fool he'd been to believe she would give up her family for him, but her passion was convincing... she had seemed so happy at the time...

He could almost smell her perfume as he stood in the gateway, remembering Cynthia's presence and the unexpected intimacy they had shared. He closed his eyes, tears were threatening. This was a strange emotion he was not used to feeling. The news had been shocking... all the plans he had made, lying in bed at night... wondering what Cynthia was doing... wondering whether she was happy now, or was she waiting for her opportunity to join him?

He took a cigarette out of its packet and lit it with his lighter, his hands shaking a little. He put the cigarette to his lips and inhaled deeply and felt a calming sensation as the nicotine kicked in. He continued smoking until the cigarette's length had been consumed and stubbed it out beneath his shoe on the road. Then he got back in to the car and continued down the lane.

He passed a farm gate, which had various items of produce for sale, out on an old wooden table. Charles had an idea. He stopped the car just past the stall and picked up a bunch of dahlias. He didn't have any change, so he left a pound note in the honesty box, an old toffee tin, and continued down the road as he remembered seeing the church in the distance.

He went into the churchyard and couldn't see anyone else around. He walked to the newer graves and soon found a gravestone belonging to Robert and Cynthia Mason. Cynthia died September 4th 1972, aged 36. Robert had died on September 3rd, aged 37. Charles repeated the dates to himself in case he wanted to find out more about the tragedy at a later date. He hurriedly put the flowers on the grave. Some fresh flowers were already in the vase on the headstone, but a second smaller vase was empty at the foot of the grave. It appeared to have some water in the base of the vase, probably from the recent rainfall, so he left the hurried arrangement of dahlias. Charles whispered, 'Dear Cynthia, goodbye, my love. How I dreamed you would come back to me.'

He returned to his car, a black Ford Capri and, still stunned, drove back to Appleby. He got home and wondered how he had got there. He couldn't remember the journey and thought later that it was a miracle he didn't have an accident.

So that was it. No Cynthia to dream of... only a few wonderful days to remember being in her passionate company, a box full of letters and fading memories of the phone conversations when they had giggled like teenagers sharing secrets, trying not to be discovered by prying parents. He had to be realistic... not even *full* days in her company.

Perhaps he had enhanced the memories of Cynthia over the years as he had not been out with anyone else since being with her. Well, at least no one of any significance. Had she used him at a low point in her marriage, perhaps? He wondered if he would ever find someone to settle down with.

At thirty-nine years old, he was beginning to tire of travelling up and down the country and living his bachelor's existence. He suddenly felt life had passed him by and he had not grasped his opportunity of real happiness when it had been within reach. He should have visited the pub when she might still have been working there. He could have kept his distance. He might have got the chance to talk to her, but the short relationship may have been one-sided after all...

'Children', Bill had said. 'Children'. He was sure of it now... He kept trying to recall the conversation... So she must have patched things up with Robert then... and they are buried together, so they can't have split up. Why had he tried to kid himself that she was waiting for him all these years?

What was it about Cynthia that had attracted him to her? He remembered her smile... a genuine smile... and a sparkle in her eye. She was an attractive woman, that was certain. If only he had plucked up the courage earlier to call in the pub his uncertainties could have been solved one way or another.

* * *

Rebecca decided to go for a ride on Chestnut when she got home from school. It was lovely to enjoy the fresh air after being in a classroom for most of the day.

As she passed the church, which was isolated from the main village, she thought she would go and visit her parents' grave. She tethered Chestnut to a secure post near the graveyard entrance. Many a dog had been connected to the post while its owner tended the grave of their loved ones. Chestnut was quite happy here for a while and started munching some long grass within reach. That was her contribution to the churchyard maintenance team!

Rebecca walked along the gravel pathway leading to the church, a Norman flint-covered building with a square bell tower. Only one bell remained, but no doubt more than one bell used to beckon the church worshippers to the services held here. Rebecca pushed open the heavy church door, which creaked and groaned as she did so. The few churches which Rebecca had attended all seemed to have creaky doors, as if to draw attention to latecomers who tried to creep in to a service rather late. She remembered hearing how little Esther Croft used to struggle to open this door whenever she went to the church.

A slightly musty smell greeted Rebecca and the air was cooler than outside. She took off her riding hat as an act of respect and sat down on one of the pews. She sat looking ahead at the altar. The flowers looked lovely. Some pink chrysanthemums had been arranged simply in the polished brass vases. She wondered if it was Kathleen's work, or perhaps it wasn't her turn on the church flower rota.

Rebecca sat staring at the cross. She prayed for her parents. She prayed that they had not suffered in their final moments of life and that they had found happiness together… in Heaven. She found herself now doubting the early teachings she had received from Sunday school at the age of six or seven. She could hear in her head the children at Sunday school, all singing, 'Jesus wants me for a sunbeam to shine for Him each day…' How could a just God allow all this suffering? What had she done to deserve all this?

The stillness was momentarily disturbed by a tiny mouse, which hastily disappeared out of view into a hole in the flooring. She smiled to herself and wondered if the mouse had a family waiting in their church home. It reminded her of a book about a church mouse called Montgomery; she had loved the book as a child and wondered whether it was in the loft at her old home where Michael now lived.

Rebecca eventually went outside again. Chestnut was still content, eating happily. She walked in to the graveyard. At her parent's grave, she noticed the fresh dahlias. No doubt one of Dad's work colleagues had visited recently and left the flowers.

Rebecca chatted for a while, looking down at the grave, hoping her parents might somehow know that she was saying that she loved them and hoped they had found peace. She said she was sorry if she had caused them any upset in the past and had never wanted to cause any hurt. A tear trickled down her face and she tasted its saltiness.

She looked at herself standing there in her second- hand jodhpurs and green quilted riding jacket. A pony had been out of the question when her parents had been alive …

and now… here she was in her riding gear. She felt a little uncomfortable now, wondering if she was somehow rubbing salt into old family wounds.

She was rescued from her thoughts, however, as Millie Livingstone appeared carrying flowers for her husband's grave.

'Hello, Rebecca,' she called.

'Oh, hello, Mrs Livingstone,' replied Rebecca as she walked towards her, quickly wiping her face with her sleeve. 'How are yew today?'

'Not too bad thank yew, my dear… not too bad. I miss him o' course, that I dew. But… Jack was getting very difficult to manage… yew know.'

'I believe so, Mrs Livingstone.'

'Now I've got Sam causing me a few problems again.'

'I'm sorry to hear that, Mrs Livingstone. Is there anything I can do to help?'

'Goodness no… thank yew, dear! He's got that sugar diabetes. They tried to control him on tablets but it wasn't enough. He won't listen to the doctor or the nurses' advice about his diet and his water is always loaded with sugar. He's always had a sweet to'th. He does like the pies I mek him, well he's got to have a little treat now and then, hasn't he? Apple pie or rubub pie with a bit of custard… oh, he loves that. Jack loved an apple pie and all, that he did. God rest his soul. The district nurses hev started cummin' at breakfast and teatime now to give Sam insulin injections.'

'*Poor* Sam… and poor yew… Yew have had more than your fair share, eh, Mrs Livingstone?'

'That I hev, my dear… but we all have our crosses t' bear… Sorry dear… yew had a rough time too… just listen to me running on! Your pony is a fine looking animal over there.'

'Thank yew, I think so too! That's Chestnut.'

'A real beauty she is. Oh dear! Just look at the time, I'd

best be off, it's nearly Sam's teatime now. Cheerio, dear.'

'Cheerio, Mrs Livingstone.'

Rebecca trotted home past the vicarage, which was less than a quarter of a mile from the church, and past old Amy's cottage, which was being renovated by her great nephews from London. She hardly recognised the building; it looked very smart. The windows had been replaced and she could hear builders at the back of the property and a cement mixer churning up some cement.

Rebecca decided to continue her ride through the wood on the bridle path. She had been here many times as a child with her mum and brother. She met Millicent Brown walking her dog; otherwise she had the peace and quiet of the wood to herself.

She decided to dismount and let Chestnut explore a little, as she gazed up at the oak trees and rubbed her hands over the thick bark. She remembered as a child bringing crayons and paper to do 'bark rubbing' here. Rebecca inhaled deeply, enjoying the wood's aroma. Chestnut glanced up at her briefly before checking out more of the wood's undergrowth. Rebecca loved this wood. It had probably witnessed her childhood secrets and many of her games.

* * *

The weekend came and Rebecca had a great time with Clare and her cousins, galloping along the beach at Holkham. When the tide went out there, the sand seemed to go on forever and it was a great place to exercise horses. Rebecca rode on a horse called Beauty, not the most original name, but a beauty she surely was and she was very happy for Rebecca to ride her.

All the girls chatted happily together when they arrived back at the stables and went to the farmhouse kitchen for a late dinner. Mrs Buckingham had put out some fresh bread bought at the local baker's with cheese and ham, pickles and apples. There was a box of jam tarts too. They soon devoured most of the food.

'I see the fresh sea air has given yew a fair appetite, girls!' said Mrs Buckingham as she returned to the kitchen. She put down a heavily-laden basket on the kitchen floor, full of dry linen brought off the washing line, which stretched the length of the garden. 'It's been great drying weather today. How was yer ride, girls?'

'Fantastic, Mrs Buckingham!' Rebecca eagerly replied. 'I just wish I was nearer to the beach, so I could bring my Chestnut here. It was wonderful on the sand... That tasty bloomer loaf we've just eaten looked rather like the rippled sand we've just been galloping on!'

'Yis, I think I know what yew mean, my dear... I wouldn't of ever thought of that, though.'

'Even down to the poppy seeds on top... the dark grains of sand speckled on the uneven surface of the beach... it could have been a giant bloomer loaf!'

'Oh, Rebecca! Yew daft girl... hope the bread tasted better than the beach!' said Clare.

'Of course it did! I loved it. Shame our village shop doesn't sell some just like it! Actually, on the beach holidays I had with my parents, we ate sand sandwiches often on the beach! Michael used to pretend the word sandwich originated from food eaten on a beach and I believed him, of course! He was always teasing me. I s'pose I was quite gullible.'

'Well, Rebecca, yew are welcome to come again if yew like. We hadn't seen Clare for a while, so yew both come back again afore so long. The horses have no doubt enjoyed having a break from all the beginners we get here at the stables. We dew get some rum sorts at times, that we dew... the parents are the wurst! So many littl'uns only come till they git their sustificates! Their parents are sat round watching 'em proudly perform and hoping their child is the best. Dear me… I wonder if all the children really want to come at times. I shouldn't complain though, it all keeps a roof over me head and the horses! Now who can eat this last jam tart… it's not worth putting that away now, is it? Rebecca?'

'Oh, well if no one else wants it, yes please! Mmmm! Lemon curd!'

'Wait for it… what will she liken the tart to, do you reckon?' teased Clare. 'A sweet pool from Heaven, perhaps?'

'Wull, I wish I could eat like yew do, Rebecca, and look as slim as yew! I think my horses will start complaining soon if I can't shed any weight,' remarked Mrs Buckingham as she cleared away their plates.

Chapter Thirteen

Visit To The North

Rebecca had decided to accept her Auntie Ann's invitation to visit her in Scotland. Ann was too disabled to travel now, but was anxious to keep in touch with her late sister's daughter. So at the start of the school holidays Rebecca caught the train to Glasgow with a feeling of adventure and excitement since the furthest she could remember travelling to was Appleby, when her Mother had been taken to hospital. She couldn't really recall the visits to Scotland, however hard she tried.

The journey to Scotland was long and tiring and she had to change trains three times. However there were no problems with the connections and the rail staff were very helpful to the young naïve traveller.

She telephoned Wilf, who was patiently waiting for her call at Kathleen's house, when she reached her final destination and he was relieved to hear she had arrived safely. Rebecca chatted enthusiastically about the journey and the unfolding landscape as she had ventured north. She was fascinated by the hills, having been brought up in Norfolk and had chuckled to herself remembering how Wilf cursed the 'hill' near the village shop which seemed mountainous according to him when he was carrying a bag of shopping on his bicycle's handle bars, whilst negotiating the 'uphill' return journey. Some of the hills she had glimpsed on her journey had sheep on them. At home, she was used to seeing cows grazing on the lush grass. Many of the fields had stone walls dividing them, which were a different sight to the hedges she was used to at home.

She saw the massive cooling towers of the power stations belching out their steam in the distance. She later described them to Wilf as giant cotton reels with their clouds of cotton wool. The slagheaps of the open cast coal mines were dark and dreary, but vaguely familiar from pictures in her geography books. She had hungrily devoured the details of her journey and tried to place them carefully in her memory so that she could recall the countryside and towns glimpsed from the dirty train window. If only someone could give her a commentary on all of the sights she was observing, to correct her if she wrongly made assumptions about the educational journey.

She had never seen blocks of flats and was amazed how people could live in the high-rise buildings with no garden and only a small balcony with washing hung on some of them. She wondered how many people had lost their underwear when a teasing breeze may have snatched their 'smalls' away! She remembered that was what one of her old great aunties had called her underwear, yet they had been anything but small! What happened when the lift didn't work in the flats? Perhaps the teachers accepted non-functioning lifts as a valid reason for being late for school in Glasgow. She wondered if the schools in Scotland were as strict as her grammar school was.

Wilf felt a little jealous that he hadn't joined her for the journey of discovery but felt Rebecca needed some time with her auntie. Their house hadn't much room for guests with so much equipment used to assist Ann with her daily activities. Simple daily tasks were now quite a challenge both for Ann and Bruce when he was trying to help her.

Whilst Rebecca was away, Wilf visited both his brothers; he had been intending to do this ever since Elizabeth's funeral. On another day he decided to catch the bus to Coddleton, rather than drive there, and look at a television set in Robinson's electrical shop, which would be a nice surprise for Rebecca on her return. It seemed all her friends had televisions. He didn't want her to be the only one without. Both his brothers had televisions and couldn't believe he didn't have one. Besides, the news and farming programmes might be interesting. Apparently Jim always watched *Farming Diary*.

Wilf had a good view of the farm land he passed in the bus, which he couldn't safely survey in the less elevated seat of his car. The bus was empty today until they reached Coddleton when three people got on as Wilf got off. Wilf decided to buy a television in the end though he had been tempted to just rent one rather than part with so much money in one go. Mr Robinson arranged to deliver the television set and install it before Rebecca returned home.

Wilf had just over twenty minutes to kill before the next bus home so decided to buy fish and chips at Our Plaice in the high street as he was feeling quite hungry. Two men wearing paint-splattered overalls were ahead of him in the queue. From their conversation with Val, who owned the shop and was working alone today, they appeared to be regular customers.

Wilf ordered cod and chips and shook the vinegar bottle liberally over the hot food, together with some salt and a splash of ketchup. He walked slowly up to the bus stop, eating his dinner and enjoying this unplanned treat. He rested against a low wall next to the bus stop and finished his meal. He screwed up the greasy paper and pushed it in to the litter bin which was rather full, emitting a loud belch as he did so. No one was around but Wilf said, 'Pardon me!' to excuse himself. He felt thirsty now, and looked forward to a cup of tea when he got home. He looked at his watch; the bus should be here by now. Ten minutes later, the bus arrived; Wilf produced his return ticket and showed the bus driver as he climbed the steep steps on to the bus.

* * *

Rebecca enjoyed her stay with Auntie Ann, but felt so helpless that she couldn't help her auntie more than she did during her stay. Rebecca wondered how her mum might have coped if she'd had multiple sclerosis instead of her sister. She couldn't imagine her having to rely on a wheelchair or Rebecca's father to get around. She also didn't think Mum would have wanted to survive the car accident if she had ended up being an invalid for the rest of her life.

Uncle Bruce looked tired and seemed to have aged considerably since Rebecca had seen him at Mum's funeral. He was devoted to Ann though, and didn't complain about the tasks he did for her. She had a catheter as she 'couldn't control her waterworks' and Bruce even attended to this, emptying the bag whenever it was full. A district nurse called twice a week to check on Ann generally and to dress a small bedsore. She also changed the catheter when necessary; apparently it blocked frequently and Ann often got urinary infections.

Ann couldn't write now because of the muscular spasms in her weak arms but she was happy for Rebecca to write some letters on her behalf to some of her friends whom she hadn't contacted in a while. Rebecca enjoyed doing this and pretended to be her auntie's personal secretary. She hoped her spelling was alright and insisted that Ann checked her letters thoroughly before she licked the envelope and carefully placed a second class stamp in the top right hand corner.

'Yuk, these envelopes and stamps should be flavoured,

don't yew think, Auntie Ann? The taste is revolting!' declared Rebecca.

'You're probably right there, Rebecca. I remember the last time I licked a stamp, I nearly swallowed it!'

'Goodness, that doesn't sound good.'

'Would you like to post the letters for me?'

'Of course.'

'The post box is only at the end of the street, near the garage.'

'Oh, I know where you mean. OK, I'll be back in a minute,' said Rebecca clutching the letters as she hurried out of the door, probably before the adhesive of envelopes and stamps had dried.

'OK, thanks, Rebecca. My friends will be surprised to hear from me. Hope they realise my next letter may be a long time coming.'

Rebecca became very grateful for her own good health, which she realised she had taken for granted prior to experiencing the visit to Appleby Hospital and now spending time with Auntie Ann. It was a shame she didn't live nearer, so she could help her auntie, or even keep her company if Bruce had to go out shopping. She did some baking for her, having found a cookery book on the kitchen shelves with recipes she was familiar with.

* * *

'Rebecca, be a dear and just get me a fresh handkerchief from my top drawer over there.'

'Of course… Oh look… it's that lavender bag I made for you when I was at primary school! I can't believe you've still got it!' Rebecca handed a handkerchief to Ann and then examined the lavender bag more closely, which she had spotted amongst the hankies and underwear in the chest of drawers.

'Of course I've still got it! I can remember opening the brown paper parcel you or your mum had wrapped it in … or *trying* to, it was covered in sticky tape I seem to remember! I don't suppose you can still smell the lavender now but you must have put a lot of effort in to that.'

'I suppose I did, but look at my stitching! I'm surprised it's held together this long!'

'Show me… och, that's not bad. You were only what… about six or seven at the time?'

'I guess so. I remember Elizabeth helping at school for a few afternoons when we made these. My needle kept coming unthreaded and she was so patient when I asked for her help. In fact, most of the class had problems threading their needles! I made one for Mum too… don't know where hers is now. It was meant to be an Edwardian lady. We made needle cases another time in the shape of a hat, with room for a thimble in the top of the hat! I don't think my sewing has improved a lot since primary school!'

'Even if it hasn't, you have many other talents, haven't you, dear? You can't be good at everything, you know.'

'I don't think I'm that good at much. I have struggled with lots of subjects at the grammar school. I see children in the village who go to Coddleton secondary school and they never seem to have homework… well not as much as I seem to get. Still, I suppose it's been good for me at the grammar and I don't get teased at the bus stop like I used to when I started.'

'Children can be so cruel, that's for sure, Rebecca. Shall we have a cup of tea?'

'Yes that would be good… I'll put the kettle on.'

'I wish I could make one for us both. I miss doing all these simple tasks you know. It's very frustrating.'

'It must be, Auntie Ann,' replied Rebecca sympathetically. She went and made the tea and brought back a feeder cup for her aunt as she had watched her uncle do. Rebecca helped Ann with the cup when the tea had cooled a little.

'I love your accent, Auntie.'

'Well I suppose I've adopted a slightly Scottish accent, haven't I?'

'Yes, it's lovely to listen to.'

'Thank you. What happened to your Norfolk accent, Rebecca?'

'I don't know really, but most of my friends don't seem to have a Norfolk accent… Wilf says they're posh! I suppose I've lost much of it, being with the girls at school, although Wilf will bring out the Norfolk in me when I'm with him!'

'Yes, he's wholly prowd of his accent!'

'That sounded very like him!' giggled Rebecca. 'He's so kind to me. It's as if I really am related to him, the way he takes care of me.'

'Well, you've become a very caring young lady and I'm sure you're a pleasure to have living in his home. I am so sorry Cynthia didn't get to see you become this beautiful young woman I see before me. You will make some young man very happy one day, that's for sure.'

'Oh Auntie, stop the silly squit,' replied Rebecca blushing.

'I'm just telling the truth. Now do you want to have a look at those photographs I was telling you about?'

'Oh yes, please. I can't really remember what Grandad Mason looked like now. And I want to see Mum in her school uniform. I bet she didn't have to wear clothes three sizes too big!'

'The box of photos is in the cupboard under the stairs, Rebecca. Just be careful of my hoist in the hallway; Bruce is always knocking his leg on it.'

'OK, I will… this must be it! It's rather heavy!'

'Be careful, Rebecca, there are lots of heavy memories in there!'

'There you are.'

'Thanks, dear. So tell me… how are you *really*, Rebecca?'

'I'm fine, thanks,' said Rebecca placing the box on the table near to Ann.

'Rebecca, I know it's been awful for you, dear... please tell me how you are... are you happy, dear? You know you can tell me.'

'I have been OK with Wilf, he's so kind like I said... but well... actually... I kept having nightmares after Mum and Dad's funeral... but it hasn't happened for ages now.'

'Can you tell me what happened in your nightmares?'

'It was often the same dream... Mum was not, well, you know... *dead*, and woke up in her coffin... and was banging on the coffin to let her out... she kept calling to me... I would wake up and the dream was so real every time... I'm sor-ry... I...' Rebecca broke down in tears.

'It's OK, Rebecca, come here, dear... There... you have a good cry now,' said Ann passing her the clean handkerchief, which she had requested in readiness for Rebecca's tears. She tried to comfort the girl while fighting back her own tears. 'Have you talked to Wilf about your nightmares?'

'No, I felt so foolish,' sniffed Rebecca.

'Not at all, he would have understood.'

'I didn't want to upset him. He might have blamed himself. He had offered to take me to the chapel of rest so I could say goodbye to Mum before the funeral, which I had wanted to do... but Auntie Kathleen put me off going. I kept imagining how Mum would have looked... I dreamt that I did go and it wasn't the Mum I knew that I saw there and yet it was as though she had gone for one of her "lie downs" like when she had a headache... And then her calling me in the dreams was just like she used to do... I kept waiting for her to ask me to peel the potatoes or something...'

'You must miss her, such a lot. It's not easy being without a mum, especially when you're growing up... and I know that she wasn't always the best mum in the world, but she was *your* mum nevertheless, wasn't she?'

'Yeah, p'raps I wasn't always the best daughter… I just felt that sometimes she was elsewhere, or her mind was… like she didn't care what I was doing… then I feel bad thinking that of her.'

'I think she was very proud of you, she just couldn't always express her feelings. Our poor old mum used to say she was "cold hearted" and she was quite critical of our mum, who always did her best for us and would go without herself, so that we always had enough to eat and decent clothes to wear, you know. I tell you what, let's look at these photos now… I'm sure you'll have a laugh at me when you see the clothes we used to wear… and Mum always dressed us the same. Even though I was older than your mum, she was bigger than me, so I ended up wearing all her cast offs, so that I wore some clothes for years with us having the same outfits. Imagine that!'

'Guess I was lucky having a brother then!'

'You probably were! I used to long for an older brother, you know. I suppose it was when I got teased at school, I thought an older brother might have stood up for me… but then again, he might have made matters worse. Talking of brothers… that plant pot over there was made by your brother when he was at primary school.'

'Goodness, it's lasted well!'

'Yes, and it's only made of paper maché.'

'The design is quite attractive; it shows he had artistic tendencies from an early age!'

'Indeed. I remember you coming to visit us and Michael proudly presented it to me… I can't remember how old you were, but I remember your mum trying to potty train you, so you were only a toddler. In fact, this old carpet was quite new then and, let's say, you "christened" it!'

'Oh dear, did I? How embarrassing!'

'Och, it didn't bother me, Rebecca, and the pattern has hidden many other stains since. It's about time we had a new one, especially as this living area is now also my bedroom, it is very worn. Perhaps you could drop a hint or two to Bruce to part with some of his money.'

'If he's like Wilf, he'll need more than hints!'

'Oh, be a dear and open the door, Rebecca. That sounds like the district nurse's knock!'

'Oh hello, I'm Betty McIntyre, district nurse… I've come to see Ann,' declared a middle-aged nurse standing on the doorstep, clutching a large black bag. She seemed a little out of breath.

'Come in, Nurse. I'm Rebecca, Ann's niece.'

'Of course! I had forgotten, she had told me that you were coming. How is she today… Oh, there you are, Ann.'

'I'm fine, nurse, thanks. You are late today. Have you been busy?'

'Oh yes, I have. I was planning to visit you earlier this morning, but Dr Yates caught me on the way out of the surgery with an urgent call which has made me late for my regulars.'

'Poor you. Have you had any lunch?'

'Oh, I managed a quick sandwich in the car just now. Don't worry about me.'

'Well, would you like a cup of tea? I'm sure Rebecca here will make one for you, won't you, Rebecca?'

'Of course.'

'That would be very nice, thanks. I'm always ready for a drink. My husband says it's because I talk too much!'

'What a cheek! Thanks, Rebecca. Nurse will be about twenty minutes sorting me out. Oh, and she has two sugars, don't you, nurse?'

'Yes, I do please. You have a good memory, Ann,' replied Betty, as she quickly washed her hands in the kitchen sink.

'Yet I can't remember phone numbers or family birthdays! Oh, Rebecca, cut a piece of your Victoria sponge cake. I'm sure nurse won't be able to say no to your delicious cake.'

'Cake, how nice! Now Bruce never offers me cake when he makes a brew. You should visit more often, Rebecca!'

'I think I would put on weight though, as she is really good at baking cakes.'

'Well a little extra weight wouldn't harm you, Ann, you know.'

'Och, I guess so.'

'You could have a little of my spare tyre I carry round my belly if you like!'

'Oh, but you have a nice figure, nurse.'

'I could do with losing a few pounds but offers of cake are hard to resist. Anyway, how's this wee sore doing?'

'Oh, that feels a bit sore!'

'Sorry, the dressing had stuck a little too well, I think. Oh, but it looks fine… and it is definitely smaller. The swab result was alright too, so those antibiotics seem to have sorted that infection you had.'

'Oh, good. I hated trying to swallow those pills. I think I will have to ask for liquid medicine another time.'

'Good idea. Yes, those antibiotics were rather big, weren't they? So have you been resting on your bed most afternoons?'

'Yes, I have done as you suggested and then I get up for tea. That new wheelchair cushion seems more comfortable, too.'

'Good, it was surprising how worn it was, but I guess you had used it for several years, hadn't you?'

'Yes, time flies, doesn't it? Probably six or seven years of my bottom squashing that foam square!'

'Well, let's say my bottom would have squashed it harder and worn it out long ago! How has this catheter been draining?'

'No problems really this week. Rebecca and I have drunk a lot of tea too, over the past few days, so you won't need to remind me to drink plenty!'

'That's good. OK, there you are, a new bag fitted. There, are you comfortable like that on your bed?'

'Not bad, if you could just prop me up a wee bit more, that will do fine.'

'How's that?'

'Great. Oh, that was this ripple mattress making that noise, not me!'

'I'll believe you, Ann! I will just go and wash my hands when I've got rid of this rubbish in your bin.'

'OK, thank you, nurse. My notes are ready for you on the sideboard over there.'

'Thanks.'

'Rebecca! Nurse is ready for her tea.'

Rebecca felt very close to her auntie, despite not having spent much time with her since her very early years, and she enjoyed their conversations. She was able to talk to Ann about all sorts of things and even discussed the embarrassing subject of periods with her. Luckily Kathleen had talked to her about the monthly problem and given her some Dr White's pads and sanitary belt, which took a while to get used to. Rebecca had also had some advice from some of her friends who had started their periods long before she did. She had begun to wonder if she would ever start her periods when out of the blue the unmistakable blood staining had occurred and she finally felt she was on the right road to growing up and becoming an adult.

* * *

'Tea's ready, Rebecca.'

'Thanks, Uncle Bruce. Great, I love shepherd's pie.'

'Och, is that what you call it? I call it cottage pie.'

'Well, it is delicious whether you've made it from cottages or shepherds!'

'Thank you. Your auntie had to teach me how to cook, as

she used to do it all.'

'I think you are a better cook than I ever was, Bruce,' added Ann.

'I helped Wilf with his cooking. He has surprised everyone in the village... no one would believe he cooks most things now,' said Rebecca between mouthfuls.

'Your mum didn't really enjoy cooking, did she, Rebecca?' asked Ann.

'Not really, but she was so busy working, I guess it was hard for her. Then Michael was often out late or forgot to tell her when he was going out, which made her mad when food was wasted.'

'Rebecca, I've made an Angel Delight for pudding. Do you like it?'

'Oh yes, I haven't had that for ages.'

'It's chocolate.'

'Yummy. My favourite.'

'You are easy to please.'

'Am I?'

'Yes you are.'

'Well I don't want to be a nuisance.'

'I don't think you are capable of being one of those!'

'Shall I make tea for you both tomorrow?'

'If you like; that would be a treat for me and your auntie, who must be fed up with my limited menu.'

'Och, Bruce, you know that's not true, dear. But, Rebecca, that would be lovely of you. Have a think what you would like to make and then we can check what we will need to get from the shop. The little supermarket in the street sells most things.'

'Well, how about toad-in-the-hole, gravy, mash, carrots and peas... and let me think... my speciality, lemon meringue pie?'

'Sounds lovely, dear. I can't wait till tomorrow.'

'I can watch the football on the telly in the afternoon,

then. Might even have a beer with my mate Matthew later. Rebecca, perhaps I can book you in to Bruce's "bed and breakfast" every six months or so!'

'I'm not sure Wilf would let her. He must be missing your help and company, dear.'

'He will probably be enjoying the peace, plenty of hot water and the bathroom always free!' replied Rebecca.

* * *

Rebecca enjoyed the time she spent with her auntie and uncle and was sad to leave. Auntie Ann was her closest relative apart from Michael. Bruce drove her to the station in his old Volvo estate car, which could carry Ann's wheelchair in the back, and she waved from the carriage window as the train slowly left the platform, heading south. Rebecca pretended she was a heroine in a novel waving goodbye to her fiancé as his figure was swallowed by the cloud of smoke from the imaginary steam train. She had no hatbox to place on the luggage rack above her head like her heroine might have done, only a tatty small suitcase on loan to her from Kathleen.

She thought of the evacuees who would have travelled by train to the relative safety of the countryside during the war. The children would have had to get used to different surroundings and new families. Kathleen had told her the stories of her experiences with Elizabeth when evacuees from London had stayed with them and their parents.

She knew she had a lot to be thankful for but still felt rather lonely at times. London … yes, perhaps that would be her next adventure. She would love to explore the sights of the capital city. Perhaps she could persuade Wilf to go with her, as the Underground sounded too much of a challenge to master alone. She didn't think he had ever been there, though. Or perhaps Kathleen would join them and she could meet up with Ann Catchpole, whom she still hadn't seen since Elizabeth's funeral. She kept saying she wanted to meet her and yet doing nothing about it. They would have loads to catch up with… a day trip wouldn't be enough. Once Kathleen got talking about the old days there was no stopping her. Rebecca was actually quite intrigued by the tales of the evacuees and wanted to hear for herself Ann's childhood memories of Watton.

Rebecca was still fascinated by the changing countryside speeding past her. Now she could examine it all again in reverse. For part of the journey she imagined again that she was an evacuee being sent from her city home to the countryside.

She had plenty of food to eat on the journey. Uncle Bruce had made some cheese sandwiches and had wrapped some fruitcake, which she had made, in foil for her and she had two glass bottles of lemonade. She wondered what it was like when food was rationed. Later she felt quite guilty as she devoured the last crumbs of the fruitcake before even half of her journey was complete. She had tried to pretend that she had no food, to feel what hunger was really like, and that her rations for the day were not to be touched till she reached Newark. It seemed her hunger pains were not to be ignored.

The time seemed to pass quickly with her role-play and soon she was watching the flatter landscape flash past her. The farmers were busy and many fields had combine harvesters methodically cutting grain with plenty of dust belching out in their wake. Some fields were bare, where the corn had already been cut and the straw bales collected.

Eventually she arrived at the local station, where Wilf was waiting for her as arranged. He gave her a hug and Rebecca felt pleased to be back home again. She talked non-stop as he drove the short distance from the station to their home. She was still telling Wilf about the trip when they walked in to the living room.

Rebecca stopped talking and gasped. 'A television!'

'I knew I'd need something to get a word in edgeways when yew got back! It's bin ever so quiet without yew, Rebecca. I've wholly missed yer, my dear.'

'Dad! I've missed yew too of course. Wow, a television, you'll be getting a telephone next! Let's warm it up shall we?'

'Yes in a minute, p'raps we can watch *Dad's Army* later, but finish telling me abowt Ann, poor soul. She sounds bad, that she does.'

* * *

Returning to school in September, Rebecca had to concentrate hard on her studies and work towards her O-levels the following summer. At least she had been to Scotland, which gave her some experiences to write about for her English essays and she hadn't had a chance to get bored with her remaining time at home, now she had Chestnut and a television. She had really missed her pony when she was away, and she knew Chestnut had missed her too by her reaction in the farm paddock on her return. She had galloped to the gate when Rebecca called her name quietly and enjoyed her rubbing her nose as she gratefully accepted the apple she presented to her.

Rebecca found it amusing to see Wilf watch all sorts of television programmes which she never imagined he would get hooked on, such as *Crossroads* and *Sale of the Century*, where lucky contestants had the chance to win exotic holidays or even a car. Sometimes he would intend to do a job in the garden and then totally forget about his task once he sat down with a cup of tea in front of the telly. He also watched the news and weather forecast regularly and soon his faithful wireless was rarely switched on.

Rebecca found herself watching *Blue Peter* and *Vision On*, even though they were aimed at children younger than she was. She finally knew what her friends had been talking about when they had mentioned these and other programmes they viewed regularly.

Chapter Fourteen

Speech Day

'…and now we present the literature prize. This year the winner has produced some excellent short stories and some very moving poetry. She has had more than her share of loss, losing both her parents in a tragic car accident when she was only twelve years old. Despite her grief, she has shown much courage and determination to succeed in all her chosen O-level subjects. Her literature, however, is a special talent and she is hoping to study A-level English in the sixth form next year. I understand she has recently become an auntie. Her niece or nephew will undoubtedly have lots of stories composed just for them… Could I have Rebecca Mason on stage please?' asked the headteacher, Mr Tomlinson.

Rebecca walked on to the stage, blushing crimson red, shook hands with the headteacher and received her book token as the hall applauded. She managed to say thank you and was relieved that she had not tripped over the microphone wire in front of the large hall packed with proud parents.

Mr Tomlinson handed her one of her poems and whispered to her. 'Do you think you can manage it?'

'I think so, sir…' she stuttered and cleared her throat. The whole hall fell silent. Wilf looked at the floor, urging

Rebecca to keep calm, hoping his thoughts would be conveyed to her.

Rebecca had written many poems in her English lessons. She had been thinking about grief and the anniversary of Elizabeth's death when she had written the piece she read to the expectant audience…

<u>Autumn leaves</u>

Autumn leaves me all alone,
Robbed of your love,
My heart is torn
Like the withered leaves.

This Autumn,
As the season arrives
With her gentle breath stirring the coloured leaves,
Scattering them around my feet,
I walk to the churchyard –
Black and white
To find another grave has appeared.
More flowers soften
The harsh mound of earth
Covering the slumbering body
Lying beneath.

Many tears are shed here,
Many 'if onlys' are said,
'If only…
I could have said goodbye to you
Or said sorry whenever it had been meant.'

The wound is deep within me –
No painkiller could ever relieve.
Nothing can extinguish the burning torment
Your departure has left in its wake

A year has gone
The season has returned
Without you;
Reminding us of your passing
Amongst the dancing leaves.

Yet we must be brave
And start to rebuild our world
Without your radiance,
Your smile
Your being.
The unique you.

We will not forget
Your colourful imprint left in our grey world.
Colours were erased
And emotions stolen
As Autumn left with you.

We search for new palettes of colour
New love
New buds of friendship
Watered by our shed tears.
Now tears announce
The arrival of a new baby.

New warmth and sunshine
Lightens the grey hue
Of the gravestones.
A father and new daughter
Visit their lost loved ones

Prayers and hope…
That they will not be cruelly wrenched apart.
Around them the leaves dance
Not ready to wreathe
This new beginning.

Autumn leaves them together,
The newborn baby
Blinking at Autumn's
Hazy new light
And clutching a fallen fragile leaf.

Rebecca's voice faltered as she finished the last line of her poem. Wilf had not heard this poem before and silent tears now moistened his stunned face. After what seemed an eternity, everyone was clapping again, all clearly moved by the emotional reading. The words felt most significant and very personal to Wilf and Michael. Wilf sat trying to recall the poem now in his head. Baby Elizabeth started to cry in her pram, parked at the back of the hall next to Julie, Michael and Wilf.

'Well done, Rebecca,' whispered Mr Tomlinson, as Rebecca returned to her seat. Strangely, she felt much of the grief that had burdened her over the past years had just been lifted from her. She didn't feel she should be congratulated for her written work, which often felt as though it was flowing from within… from her heart. Elizabeth, she was sure, was having an influence. She hoped that she was present somehow in this school hall, together with Mum and Dad. She felt a small smile now tickle her lips and felt an immense feeling of love for her family, past and present.

* * *

Rebecca gazed at the autumn sunshine through the rather smeared glass of her new classroom then roused herself from her thoughts.

'OK, girls… settle down please,' she said. 'I think the poor window cleaner can get on with his work better without your help. Now then… your homework for this weekend… Now don't groan! I want you to compose a short poem or verse about one of the seasons… or... *all* of them if you prefer. There are some books in the library whose titles I have written on the blackboard for you if you need some inspiration. Don't all rush in to the library this lunchtime together, though. Poor Miss Betts complained to me that, following your last assignment being set, she was nearly knocked over as you all barged in to the library. There are plenty of books in there. It is nice to know you are hungry to learn, but please be considerate to the staff and other users of the library!

'Or you might want to take a nice walk this weekend and keep your eyes and ears open for sights and sounds. And yes… even smells… which might inspire your poem. Thank you, Jenny… I heard that comment!'

'Sorry, Miss Mason,' Jenny apologised.

'OK, now. You all seem very excitable at the moment. The holiday projects I set for you can't have been too taxing for your young brains! Now let's all concentrate shall we please? The work should be your own… So, Pauline… tell your dad that if he wants to write a poem there are some new adult evening classes starting soon here at the grammar school, if he is feeling inspired! If you feel some of the well-known poets have influenced your piece, then please write their names somewhere at the end of your work. What do we call it girls if someone is accused of copying another's work and passing it off as their own?'

'Plagiarism, Miss?' suggested Pauline.

'Yes, well done. You won't forget that word will you? OK, girls. So, do your best for me. If any of you want to read your work to the class during Monday's lesson, that would be great, or I might chose some pieces of work if none of you feel brave on the day. I look forward to hearing your poems. Don't forget our work on metaphors and alliteration. Your work doesn't need to rhyme, it's entirely up to you what you write. I remember doing something similar to this assignment at your age… which *isn't* so long ago, before you start to work out my age! I would like you to hand in your work in your exercise books at the end of Monday's lesson. OK the bell is about to go, so off you go, *quietly* please, girls!'

* * *

'Hi, Ian!' how has your day been?' enquired Rebecca.

'Fine, darling, and yours?'

'Not bad really,' replied Rebecca, tugging at the wooden stick and leather band which were still neatly securing her long auburn hair in a bun. She shook her head and her hair cascaded over her shoulders. 'Is this tea fresh in the pot?'

'Yep.'

'I set my Class 2 a piece of work on the seasons. It reminded me of the poem which my headmaster made me read out at speech day, just after I had taken my O-levels!'

'Oh I remember you telling me about that!'

'Seems a lifetime ago. That poem was "a load o'ole squit," as old Bill would have said; I can't believe he's died. He's probably telling them all in Heaven he's got *suffin' gorn abowt,* right now. That's if he made it there!'

209

'Now, now, Rebecca! John was asking after you at school today. He seems to be coping with having three girls. He asked if you could reserve them all places at your grammar school!'

'I'll see what I can do! Mary has surprised us all having three children. Poor Kathleen is no doubt being kept busy. She seems to be pegging out nappies on the washing line whenever I've passed Mary's house!'

'When do you want to start pegging out nappies in our garden?'

'Ian!'

'Well I can just see you as the motherly sort! We could make a start now if you like!'

'I don't think you can work half as hard as us, at Coddleton, if you have the energy for that kind of thing! Anyway… what if Wilf calls round?'

'Who cares! Come here, Miss Mason!'

'You've just reminded me… I was called that by one of the pupils today. I will have to remind them I have been Mrs Matthews for a whole five weeks … and I am the happiest woman in the world… Oh! Please Sir! Alright, Mr Matthews! I hope your Great Auntie Amy isn't looking down on us!'

* * *

'Thank you, girls, for some really good work on your seasons' poetry and prose. Any volunteers to read their work? No? I've never known you all to be so quiet! Well then, I would like… let's see… Sharon, Jenny and Pauline to read your work to the class if you would please. Let's start with you, Sharon…'

'Oh Miss!'

'Come on, Sharon, it's a good piece of work.'

'I looked up at the barely dressed trees,
Which seemed to shudder in the autumn breeze.
Their ragged clothing had fallen at their roots;
I kicked the fading leaves with my boots.
The leaves twirled and scattered
Their dried curled edges torn and tattered.'

'Well done, that didn't hurt did it? Now, Jenny please; your work was also about autumn, I think…'
'Yes Miss….

I walked through the wood
And stoked up the fiery 'ashes' of leaves -
Once hot reds, burnt golds,
copper and brown.
Their heat and colour now almost gone.
My stick stirred up the faded hues
A gentle rustling and then it was still
I left the leaves to carpet the path
Until another like me disturbed their peace.'

'Thank you, that was also very good. Now, Pauline, what was your chosen season?'
'Winter, Miss.'
'OK, off you go.'

'Autumn left us and we shiver as
Winter now shrouds us in her mist,
Obscuring the view over the field.
Winter crops barely sown, a long wait for their yield.
The morning frosts have iced the brown leaves on the ground
Their icy patterns lie on the lace-like mound.
Our breath is seen as we gasp at the cold air.

Reddened ears yearn to be covered with our hair!
Our fingers wish we had remembered a glove.
Our toes are numb and stiff inside our boots, we so love.
Our spines tingle in the wind's chill
But we gather the wood still.
The bitter winter air bites at your face.
We hurry home, we quicken our pace.
An eerie silence descends with the fog.
We yearn to sit by the fire, each laden with a log.
Mother has prepared us a warm drink
She pours us the hot tea and returns to the sink.
She tuts at the discarded boots by the door
And the stray leaves and mud she's seen on the floor!
We sit and enjoy the warm glow
Of the crackling fire; it's dancing flames now quite a show!'

'Great. Thank you all. Any *volunteers* now to read their work? No? I don't know why you are all looking at the floor. Hoping I won't ask you to read your work, I suppose! Well, I am pleased with all of your poems. I think perhaps we should do a display of your work. The display board is looking a little tired and it will be parents' evening soon! So, tonight's homework will be to write out your poem on a piece of paper I'll give you, and you can draw a picture or colour around the edges of the paper if you wish. Or you can use the coloured card here to frame the poems. You can hand that in please for next week's lesson. Any problems? No? Good. You are unusually quiet today all of you! OK. Can anyone give me an example of a metaphor used in the pieces of work which you've just heard? A metaphor being what… Jill?'

'Is it something that you liken something to but it can't really be it… I can't explain it very well.'

'I think you're on the right lines. Anyone give me an example from their poems?'

'What about the "ashes" of leaves in my poem, Miss?'

'Yes, that's right Jenny; the leaves weren't literally ashes but you were using the word to describe the residue of the heat of the colours, I think. Is that what you were thinking?'

'Yes, Miss.'

Chapter Fifteen

Rites Of Passage

'Jonathan, is Bill ready now?'

'Yeah, he's sorted now. I've never known him so quiet!' replied Mark.

Jonathan and Mark had continued their uncle's funeral and joinery business very successfully since his death. Mark had married Clare Franks and they lived on the large estate of bungalows built on land sold by Jim Potter. Mark had done the joinery work for the new buildings and decided to buy one himself. The bungalows were all inhabited now and most of the occupants worked in Diss or Coddleton. A few retired people had moved from further afield and were still waiting to be accepted by the original village folk who were still trying to get used to all the new modern buildings which had scarred their village. The new dwellings had kept the parish council's agenda busy for months and discussions had never been so lively!

'Hey, Jonathan... I woke with a start last night. I had bin dreaming that I had bin buried alive! I fair banged my head on the headboard, that I did! Then as I lay awake, my head still ag'inst that there wooden headboard, I wondered if that was how it felt lying in a coffin!'

'Dun't yew be so bloomin' sorft, Mark!'

'Wull, just yew make sure I'm dead when my time comes!'

'I'll make sure you hev' a nice feather pillow in yer coffin too! Cor, blast, I could dew with suffin to eat … it must be dinner time. Shall we nip to the local for a bit o' somethin'?'

'Good idea.'

'Wull are yew now a' cummin? Yew look like your dreaming! I'm fair starving, that I am!'

'Oh right!'

* * *

On Monday morning, the exercise books were collected in. Rebecca sat nursing the stack of books in her holdall on the bus journey home. She had a lot of marking to do tonight, so Mr Matthews had better behave himself! She grinned as she gazed out of the bus window at the meadow of cows; some looked as though they were about to calf.

She wondered if she might be pregnant yet. She felt so in love with Ian. What a strange first meeting it had been too. She had been in the churchyard, putting flowers on her parents' grave when she became aware of a rather tall, dark-haired young man approaching her carrying flowers.

'Good morning,' he had said.

'Good morning,' Rebecca had replied, a little taken aback by the polite greeting.

'I wonder if you can help me?'

'I'll try.'

'Where do you get water for the flowers?'

'Oh… of course… sorry. There's a tank just behind the church, it catches all the rainwater. There's a jug there too.'

'Thanks. I'm Ian Matthews. I've bought the cottage next to the vicarage. I will be moving in soon. Thought I would just put some flowers on my great aunt's grave to thank her for bringing me to this lovely part of the world.'

'Pleased to meet you. I'm Rebecca. Dear old Amy… I can remember her. I had visited her with my mum years ago. Quite a bookworm, wasn't she?'

'Oh yes! So we discovered when her house was cleared. She had a few valuable books, mind, in her collection. A couple of them helped us with the builder's bills!'

'Well, they've done a good job. The cottage looks great.'

'Yes, I'm pleased with it. You're welcome to have a look, when I'm settled in. I've just got a job at Coddleton School in the science department. Can't believe my luck! I wanted to escape city life. It wasn't me, that's for sure.'

'Oh…Coddleton… you'll get to know John then, he's a teacher there.'

'I'll look out for him… John you said…?'

'Oh sorry, yes… John Sharples.'

'Nice speaking to you, Rebecca.'

'Yes… likewise. Bye.'

Rebecca felt a strange unfamiliar emotion within her as she left the churchyard. There was something about this newcomer to the village which she was attracted to.

In the weeks that followed, her visits to the churchyard became even more frequent than usual. She even made great efforts to ensure she looked her best, applying make-up which she normally rarely used. Wilf had remarked a few times, that she looked 'wholly pretty' and enquired where she was going. He had offered to accompany her to the churchyard but Rebecca made an excuse so that she could go alone. But there was no sign of the good-looking man bearing flowers whenever she had made her glamorous appearance amongst the headstones.

Her work at the girls' grammar school had continued, but she kept finding herself dreaming of Ian and trying to remember his features. He became more handsome every time she pictured him in her mind.

Ian had assumed that John was probably Rebecca's boyfriend and it had taken some time before he was put right by John in the staff room one day, when Ian had recalled the graveyard meeting of the pretty young woman.

Eventually their paths crossed again outside the village shop and Ian asked Rebecca out. He had surprised himself at his boldness but, on the spur of the moment, decided he must seize his opportunity in case he didn't bump into her again.

Rebecca had smiled to herself later, realising that when their paths had eventually crossed, she had been wearing some very old jodhpurs and an old sweater as she had been about to join a friend and exercise her horses. She had not been wearing a trace of any makeup. She was eager to accept the offer of a visit to the local cinema at Coddleton.

Their friendship blossomed and Rebecca and Ian fell in love. Rebecca accepted Ian's proposal of marriage after just six months of courting. The wedding date was set for July 17th so they would both be on holiday from their teaching jobs over the summer.

Kathleen had been delighted when Rebecca had asked her if she would help her find a wedding dress, which Wilf had insisted he would fund. They had spent hours in a large wedding dress shop in Wexham before eventually deciding that they had found the perfect dress. Kathleen was nearly as excited as Rebecca. Eva, the shop manager, had remembered Kathleen being in the shop with Mary when she had been shopping for her perfect dress several years earlier.

'That beats shopping for school uniform, Aunt Kathleen!' declared Rebecca, as they sat enjoying a snack in the café where they had shopped during Rebecca's school days.

'Oh wasn't it hard to decide … you looked stunning in so many dresses.'

'Thank yew! Well the price helped us decide with some of my final four choices!'

'Goodness yes!'

* * *

'Of course, I won't doze orf during the ceremony. That I won't!'

'Great… You look very smart, Dad,' smiled Rebecca, and she gave Wilf a quick kiss on his cheek.'

'Yew don't look so bad yerself, young lady. Oh I nearly forgot… I've got suffin for yer.' Wilf handed a thin box to Rebecca.

'Oh, they're lovely! Thanks, Dad!'

'They were Elizabeth's pearls… she wore them on her wedding day.'

'Thank yew so much, I will treasure them always. Can yew help me put them on?'

'If my old fingers will oblige, yes I will. There yew are. They look perfect.'

'Auntie Kathleen kept telling me I didn't need a necklace but I really wanted one… I s'pose she knew yew were giving me these, didn't she?'

'Yes, she did… and Elizabeth had been consulted too! Now let's git in this here cart or we'll be late tha'ss for sure,' said Wilf, sniffing a little as he became emotional.

Rebecca was dressed in a simple long ivory satin bridal gown with long sleeves trimmed with antique lace. A tight bodice showed off her slim figure and was buttoned at the back with tiny pearl buttons. Her long hair was swept up into a high knot. A few wispy curls had been trained to escape the secured mass of hair and some fresh pale cream roses were fastened to her hair in a comb. She wore only a little make-up.

Michael had found their Mother's wedding veil in the loft in a large box in amazingly good condition. Rebecca wore this as the 'something old', though felt it should be a 'something special'. She had looked at her parents' black and white wedding photograph many times as a young child, when life was like a fairy tale and many a little girl dreamed of being the princess in their bedtime story. Now she felt like a princess, that was for sure, and excitedly awaited the moment she would join her prince charming.

Jim Potter's friend, who farmed in Freckingham, was waiting outside Wilf's cottage for them with his horse and cart. Well, Wilf had said it would be a 'cart', but the cart before them was fit for any princess or even the Queen herself. Someone had adorned the edges of the carriage with white flowers and ribbons. Rebecca giggled nervously as she climbed into the little carriage and off they went to the church.

On the way, the older folk from the village were at their gates waiting to see the bridal party pass and give them a wave. Rebecca felt like royalty now. Wilf felt very proud and now wondered why he and Elizabeth hadn't decided to try and adopt any children. This was a very special moment in his life, which he had never imagined he would be a part of.

Walking down the aisle to the bridal march was very moving. The church had witnessed so much sadness and grief, but now the tears being shed were tears of happiness.

Kathleen and the ladies on the church flower rota had been in charge of decorating the church. There hadn't been a wedding for over a year in the church, so they really enjoyed ensuring the church looked its best for the happy occasion. It had been adorned with white carnations, pale cream roses, freesias, gypsophila and green foliage. The scent of the freesias welcomed the guests as they took their places in the pews. White ribbons had been tied at the end of the pews, which disguised the woodworms' work! The Women's Institute had kindly renewed the rather threadbare kneelers recently. Mrs Coleman played the old church organ, which was in great need of some money being spent on it since it threw off the occasional bad note, not that anyone cared today.

Elizabeth seemed totally bewildered by the occasion but held the little pageboy's hand as she had been instructed, and eventually had agreed to, during the wedding rehearsal. The pageboy was a nephew of Ian's and just a little older than Elizabeth. They almost stole the show.

Ian stood with his head bowed during the Bridal March, desperate to turn to catch a glimpse of his fiancée. When she reached him, he turned to her and audibly gasped at her breathtaking image. Her long veil was over her face but he could see the tears moistening her freckled cheeks. This beauty he had met in this very churchyard was to spend the rest of her life with him. How could his family say life would be dull in the country!

Meanwhile Charles sat in a pub with his closest friend, Adam, enjoying a few pints of beer. Adam, like most of his friends, was married. They had all tried hard to introduce him to their few single friends but Charles had not yet found the lady of his dreams.

He felt sad at times that he had not yet married or had children. Little did he know that he had a daughter and at this moment she was saying her wedding vows.

* * *

After the ceremony a wedding reception was held in the village hall, just a short distance in the wedding carriage. Rebecca had been tempted to ride the horse sidesaddle instead of travelling in the carriage, but said her frock prevented her bit of fun.

All the ladies in the village had got together and jointly organised a delicious wedding buffet under Janice Potter's direction. There was melon to start. There was cold roast beef and ham, a stunning dressed salmon, potato salad, green salad, tomato lilies, sausage rolls, pork pies, bread rolls and pickles. Kathleen had made sherry trifles, using legitimately sourced sherry, and Mary had made fruit salads and both were served with cream. Kathleen had made the wedding cakes. Janice Potter had iced them for her. Everything looked amazing to Rebecca and Ian. Lots of small tables had been set up and covered with white linen tablecloths. Each table had a small arrangement of flowers.

As Rebecca and Ian entered the hall, a small wispy trail of confetti followed them in. Guests advised them that they would continue to find this confetti 'for months yet' and they weren't far wrong!

The speeches followed after the meal. Wilf had struggled to write his but Michael had helped him and the short speech that he delivered was full of emotion and immense pride. The glass of sparkling wine had helped to calm his nerves and he forgot about his Norfolk accent, which he feared would sound foreign to Ian's family from further south.

The best man read out some telegrams. The most important one was from Ann and Bruce who were now unable to travel due to Ann's poor health. They sent their congratulations and love to Rebecca and Ian. They had very generously funded the honeymoon hotel in Bournemouth.

Then the tables were pushed aside. Some friends of Ian's provided some musical entertainment and the dancing began. Rebecca and Ian started the dancing. Later she crossed the hall to find Wilf and suggested he dance with her. He was quite taken aback and started making excuses that he might tread on her frock with his clumsy feet.

'So long as you haven't got your mucky rubber boots on, I'll take the chance!'

Wilf had been sitting listening to the dance music and remembering the first dance with Elizabeth he had had in this very hall. If only she had walked up to him first it wouldn't have taken so long on that first evening for him to gather courage and ask her to dance. 'It would be an honour o' cors, my dear, that it would.' Wilf felt very self-conscious at the thought of trying to dance to the modern music but the band suddenly changed pace and, at Ian's suggestion, played some more traditional music for the senior guests.

Michael and Julie were despairing of Elizabeth who had just spilt orange squash down her pink bridesmaid dress.

'Oh never mind, Lizzie, at least yew managed to keep clean for the church service, didn't yew?'

'Yes, Daddy, I did. Oh, listen to Robert, Daddy, he's crying again!'

'It's alright, Lizzie, I think he'll be hungry. I'll give him some baby rice in a moment. How about you go and dance with that handsome pageboy!' suggested Julie.

'Mummy, no! I don't want to!' Lizzie blushed. 'I want some more cake!'

Michael looked across at his sister, dancing with Wilf, and was so glad she too had found happiness. He was enjoying being a dad even if it meant disturbed sleep and chaos in his home. He would do anything for his children and wondered if his own dad had felt the same love towards him and Rebecca.

'What are you gazing at, Michael? Are you planning a wedding for us?' enquired Julie.

'I thought yew said yew didn't want any fuss like this?'

'Well I don't, but shall we arrange the registry office soon?'

'If yew like. Maybe when Robert is a bit more settled.'

'When will that be?'

'In six months or so, maybe.'

'OK, but let's set a date, else we will keep finding excuses.'

'Well, Robert came along, just as we were planning it last time, if you remember?'

'Yes, he did and he's a lovely excuse!'

'I couldn't be happier, Julie, yew know... that's what I was thinking before.'

'Me too. When Robert has finished this rice, perhaps you'll dance with me.'

'Certainly, Mrs Mason.'

'Hey don't jump the gun!'

'Michael, would you please put my bouquet on Mum and Dad's grave for me, later?' Rebecca asked her brother.

'Of course, little sis… They would be so proud o' yew today, yew know.'

'Well, I hope that they were here with us somehow today.'

'Hope so. Now if you'll excuse me I am going to have the next dance with my wi… I mean with Julie.'

'Of course. Do yew think everyone is having a good time?'

'Of course they are… just look around. No one has had a good wedding in ages around here!'

Sandwiches had been made up with the spare ham and also Janice and Kathleen had made egg sandwiches and several sponge cakes so that guests could eat again later after the dancing. They didn't want anyone to go hungry. Rebecca couldn't believe that the mountain of food had nearly all been eaten. Nobody wanted to leave the celebrations it seemed, apart from the tired children who were carried out asleep on their parents' shoulders. So the wedding celebrations had continued late into the evening before Ian and Rebecca had finally left for their new home together, which was only a short walk away from the village hall.

Kathleen and Wilf and many willing volunteers from the wedding party tidied up the hall and swept up the confetti.

Ian and Rebecca walked hand in hand up the road with Rebecca holding up the long skirt of her wedding dress and Ian carrying a bottle of wine his best man, Ralph, had just thrust at him as they left the hall. They would leave for Bournemouth two days later.

'You took my breath away, Rebecca, when I saw you coming up the aisle. You are beautiful. I am the luckiest man alive!'

'Yew mean *bootiful* if yew're living in this her' village now! Yew look wholly handsome and smart, darling. That's a very nice suit.'

'Come here a minute, Mrs Matthews,' demanded Ian as he gave Rebecca a passionate kiss; his free arm was now around her slim waist.

'Shall we continue this when we get home rather than on the side of the road?' Rebecca suggested, feeling her face flush.

'Sorry, I have wanted to do that all day.'

They got to their cottage and Ian asked Rebecca to hold the wine for a moment. He unlocked the door and then picked her up in his arms.

'I have to carry you over the threshold, Mrs Matthews!'

Rebecca shrieked as she was picked up. 'You are a romantic, my darling!'

Rebecca felt exhausted after the very emotional day, but also rather nervous spending her first night with Ian. When they got into their bedroom they guessed Ian's brother, Ralph, had been there earlier in the day as the newlyweds' bed had been adorned with horseshoes and ribbons, but more amusingly photos of Ian as a toddler with no clothes on had been attached to the headboard. Ralph's unmistakable untidy writing on a piece of paper wrote, 'Thought I should prepare you, Rebecca, to reduce the shock tonight!'

They laughed at the bed's decoration and Rebecca relaxed and succumbed to her husband's passionate advances, abandoning the newly opened bottle of sparkling wine Ian had brought with them from the wedding reception after only a few sips.

They had used cups for their wine as their wine glasses, if they had any, would be in one of the carefully wrapped parcels piled high in the small living room.

'Goodness, how do I get you out of this dress, Rebecca?'

'There's quite a few buttons at the back.'

'So I see!'

* * *

Rebecca woke early to find Ian gazing at her.

'Good morning, wife!'

'Good morning, husband! May I say *yew* took my breath away last night!'

'Can't guarantee I will every night, but wow, what a start to our honeymoon. I love you so much, Rebecca.'

'I love yew too. Wasn't yesterday just a perfect day?'

'It was. I have been lying here trying to relive the whole day and especially the wedding night!'

'Yes, that was rather special, as I said!'

'The hall was fantastic, wasn't it, and everyone had made such a great effort for us... well you, Rebecca. It seems everyone here adores you.'

'I have been fortunate to have so many people support me since Mum and Dad died.'

'I don't think I would have got the same help where I live... *lived,* that's for sure.'

'Just look at our bedroom!' gasped Rebecca as she surveyed the scene of discarded clothing and her beautiful wedding dress on the floor.

'I'm not usually that untidy but what a challenge your dress was! A hundred buttons to undo is not easy when your wedding night passion has been unleashed!'

'Yew do exaggerate!'

'OK, ninety-nine!'

'Shall I make us a cup o' tea?'

'You mean you don't want to finish this champagne for breakfast?'

'We hardly started it, if yew remember!'

'I know, darling. No, I'll make the tea as you won't know where everything is yet! Stay there, my sleeping beauty.'

'I'm not asleep and I'm your *booty* remember!'

'O'cors, my dear!' replied Ian in an attempt to say something with some Norfolk accent.

'No, sorry, your accent still needs some work yet!'

'I'll get Wilf to give me some lessons.'

'We are going to be busy opening all those presents today. I suppose Ralph brought those here for us.'

'Yes, he did. He asked for the cottage key earlier. I should have known he would do something *wholly darft* whilst he was here; those pictures of me were rather an embarrassment!'

'Thass gittin better but stop your squit and git me that there cup o' tea! I hev a fair thirst!'

'You really are sounding like Wilf now, Mrs Matthews!'

* * *

Wilf missed Rebecca when she had got married but it was lovely to know she was living in the village and since her home was near the church it was to become a frequent stop off after his visits to Elizabeth's grave. He was always happy to help Jim Potter whenever he needed an extra pair of hands at the farm and also kept himself busy in his garden, so that a weed was a rare sight, and he continued to produce cabbages, potatoes, carrots, runner beans and lettuces as well as plenty of apples from the small orchard. He dropped off his produce at Rebecca's cottage after trips to the graveyard so that she would often return from work to find a cabbage or a bag of beans on her doorstep. Kathleen also received regular deliveries.

Michael sat in his armchair at home, proudly feeding his son with a bottle of milk and gazing in to the open fire with its large fireguard around it. Some of Robert's clothes were airing on the clothes horse close to the guard; his own clothes would have been aired in front of the same fireplace. He also now had his own important documents stored in the handsome bureau his dad had been so proud to have passed on to him from his grandad.

'Michael, would you and Mark collect the milk crate in from the playground, please?'

'Yes, Miss,' chorused Michael and Mark and they went outside in to the cold playground, their breath visible in the cold air.

They soon reappeared carrying the crate of mini bottles of milk for the class.

'Thank yew, boys. Put it by the fire would yew.'

Michael could hear the teacher's voice as if it was yesterday. He remembered the glass bottles of milk, which were sometimes frozen at the top during the winter and in the summer sometimes tasted a bit off. They were all made to drink the milk, which had rarely been an enjoyable drink due to the ice topping or summer creaminess. Some of the class would sit a long time with a straw in the glass bottle sipping the milk. Samantha was often sick after being made to drink the milk. Only one boy called Stephen really enjoyed the milk, whatever the weather conditions it had been delivered in. He would happily finish off any spare bottles left in the crate or Samantha's milk, if she could discreetly swap bottles with his when the teacher was distracted. The open fires had long since been removed from the school and central heating put in. No doubt the school milk was now stored in a more suitable place and may even be quite drinkable now. Certainly Robert's milk was drinkable as he greedily sucked now at the empty bottle.

'Well done, Robert! Let's see if you have any wind shall we? Goodness, that burp didn't take long to surface! Let's see what Mummy has left for you to eat. She'll be back from her walk with Lizzie soon, I'm sure. I bet they've been picking primroses again.'

Michael felt very protective of his son and vowed to himself to always be there for him. He still felt guilty for his teenage years when he had rebelled against his parents and teachers at times. He knew he had mixed with the wrong crowd and he would make sure that his children didn't get led astray by any troublemakers.

'Daddy, look what we've got!' shouted Lizzie as she came

rushing in to the house still wearing her little blue muddy wellingtons, carrying a large bunch of primroses and a few straggly 'lambs tails'.

'It must be springtime, eh, Lizzie?'

'Yes, it is. What a mess, Robert!'

'You're a fine one to talk, Lizzie, look at your wellies!'

'Goodness, Michael, that telly is a bit loud!' said Julie as she came through the door and turned down the volume.

'Yew sound like my mother when my records were playing too loud! We were listening to the football results.'

'Are you turning our son into another football-crazy Mason?'

'Oh, he loves listening to the football, don't yew, Robert?'

'Bab ba!'

'I'm not convinced by that gurgle! Come on, Robert, come to Mummy and don't let Daddy brainwash you.'

'Daddy, can we do some drawing?'

'Goodness, Lizzie, where does all your energy come from?'

'Ple-ase, Daddy!'

'Alright, in a few minutes. How about I make us all a drink first?'

'Can I have a bun, Daddy?'

'If yew haven't eaten them all already! What is the magic word again?'

'Please.'

'I need to get a few things from the shop later, Michael, if you're OK with these two for a little while.'

'OK.'

'Have you heard Mrs Marsden is taking over the shop from Miss Brown when she retires at the end of the month?'

'Yes, I can't remember who told me now.'

'It'll be nice to see what she does with the shop. I think Mr Marsden is planning an extension so we might get a little supermarket in the village.'

'Do yew think the parish council will let that happen?'
'Why not? I think it's a great idea.'

* * *

Another meeting brought Charles to Coddleton. He wandered down the high street, stopping to look in some of the shop windows. At the local *Gazette*'s shop, he stopped to look at the black and white photographs of local events, which had been worthy of reporting. His attention was drawn to a wedding photograph of a very happy young couple. The girl, whose face was a little freckled, looked somehow familiar to him. He couldn't stop looking at her. What a lucky man next to her! Why couldn't he have found someone to share the rest of his life with? What had he got to show for his years of working? A nice car and a reasonably comfortable flat, but no one to spend time with in the evenings, or have a holiday with. Perhaps he should have allowed his friends to pair him off with someone after all.

He roused himself from his daydreaming and went inside to buy the local paper to read, whilst he later ate the ham roll and crisps he had just bought from the bakery in the high street.

The front page was full of the paper's lead story that the local chocolate factory was to close and production would be concentrated at Appleby. The local people were upset, however, that jobs would be lost as not many were willing to relocate to the bigger, more modern premises at Appleby. So no more meetings at Coddleton at least. Charles could forget this part of the world and try to move on. His job was secure, still travelling to the eight factories up and down the country, which would remain operational.

He was quite absorbed by the chocolate factory story and its effects on the local community, so it was some time before he reached the lesser news of local village events and the wedding reports, which he wouldn't have read had the picture of the pretty girl not caught his eye again. He read the short entry beneath the small photograph. A feeling of nausea returned, just as the last stunning news had hit him a few years earlier. Surely not… Cynthia would have told him…

He read that the beauty in the photograph was the daughter of the late Cynthia and Robert Mason. Her age, with a quick reckoning, tallied with the time he had had the fling with Cynthia. The familiar look of Rebecca was surely a replica of his unmistakable nose and colouring. Cynthia hadn't told him about a second child during their phone calls or in her letters, which had kept him going for several years after their short union. He couldn't believe the evidence which now explained a lot of Cynthia's behaviour. The baby he had heard on occasions during their conversations, crying outside the phone box, had always been a neighbour waiting to use the phone box with her baby in the pram, according to Cynthia. This had brought their conversations to an abrupt end. Could *he* have been a father all these years?

Chapter Sixteen

Autumn Returns

Rebecca walked through the woods, breathing the slightly damp air perfumed by the fallen autumn leaves. She was alone apart from the occasional pheasant which flew up clumsily in its panic to escape the solitary intruder in the otherwise peaceful haven.

Rebecca strode on, her step hasty though she had no reason to hurry. She had had a miscarriage three weeks ago and this was her first walk for several weeks. She could not face meeting the people from the village, exchanging small talk, when she hurt so deeply within. She could not pretend to be cheerful and knew that her drawn face would give away her body's torment, such a contrast to the feelings of happiness when she had learnt that she was pregnant.

She was fairly sure that no one would be out so early and walked on, feeling the dampness of the carpet of leaves through a growing hole in her old shoes. Her mother used to bring her and her brother here to this wood as children. Rebecca used to pretend the wood was magical and that fairies lived amongst the trees. Her mother always said her imagination worked overtime.

Michael liked to swing on the old tyre and rope which someone had tethered to one of the tree's branches. Her mother said the woods helped to clear her head when she was suffering from one of her headaches. The trees had grown considerably since her first walk here. She looked up and admired the sturdy oak trees standing so confidently next to the path and she yearned for their strength and stability. She wondered if they absorbed pain and sadness. Perhaps other people offloaded their emotional burdens amongst the stirring branches.

She had also come here at happier times, riding Chestnut through the woods. What a fantastic time she had had with her pony. Chestnut had been long outgrown and her spare time had soon been taken up with studying for A-levels before going to college to do her teacher training.

A blackbird was singing nearby, but Rebecca couldn't see the source of the beautiful voice. A dew-jewelled spider's web glistened in the hazy autumn sunshine.

Rebecca thought of her childhood and recalled the exhilarating roller-coaster ride at Yarmouth's fun fair. She could hear her own screaming in her head now as she felt the rather crude 'truck' plunge her down the steep slope. Her stomach had tugged and lurched and she had feared that she would not survive the ride. She remembered her tight grip on the safety bar in front of her and how she had tried so hard not to look scared in front of her brother. The feeling of nausea worsened, no doubt, by her greedy consumption of the sticky bright pink candyfloss.

She felt the nausea once more here in the woods. Her body felt so empty now, having anticipated the joy of feeling a new baby kick within her womb. She felt that she had once more been plunged to the very depths of despair and wondered whether she would ever climb back up to the giddy heights of happiness again. A poem she had written at secondary school came back into her head...

<u>Happiness</u>

I reached out to you
But you escaped my grasp.
I now see you in the distance…
I know that you're there.

So why can't I reach you,
Feel your warmth,
Your embrace
And let you lighten my load?

You must cross my path again soon.
Let me join your radiance
Teach me to laugh again–
A forgotten emotion
In my lonely empty world.

It seemed that whenever she found happiness, it was taken from her. First Elizabeth had died; she had always felt like a second mother to her, or at least a special auntie. Then both parents had tragically died, and now she mourned the loss of her first baby, a symbol of love and a new beginning she had found when Ian had entered her life. Strangely, all her losses had been in the autumn months.

Ian did not seem to understand how she was feeling. They would try for another baby, he had said. But Rebecca had wanted *this* one so badly. Ian's Mum had said that 'perhaps it was for the best' if the baby had been born severely handicapped, had it survived … it was nature's way. Nature was being particularly cruel, Rebecca believed.

She kicked the leaves in front of her and found herself shutting the wooden gate at the end of the wood rather forcefully. She hurried past the vicarage, not wanting to get involved with conversation with Reverend Patterson who might be out early clearing leaves from the path to the house. When she got back to the cottage, a little out of breath, she discarded the damp shoes in the doorway and left damp footprints as she walked in to the kitchen with her woolly socks still on. Ian was just making breakfast.

'Oh there you are. What's wrong, darling?'

'I couldn't sleep again. I got up early and decided to get some fresh air.'

'Have some tea, it's just made.'

'*Tea* ... yes, thanks,' she snapped. 'Tea solves lots of things, according to Kathleen,' Rebecca continued, rather more abruptly than she had intended.

'What was that?'

'Oh, nothing.'

'Darling, just have a quiet day today and rest. You'll bounce back soon. Shall I call back at lunchtime?'

'No I'll be alright; you won't have time anyway. I'm just feeling sorry for myself. I might sort out some of Mum's stuff, which Michael gave me, and I still haven't looked through. I have plenty of time now. I think I will try to get back to work next week though, to keep my mind occupied.'

'Well, if you change your mind, ring me at school. I'd better go. Love you, Mrs Matthews,' Ian said as he planted a kiss on Rebecca's forehead.

'Yew too. Have a good day at work. Bye.'

Rebecca finished her rather cold tea and then sat down in her armchair and opened up one of the large cardboard boxes containing her mother's things. Inside a brown case, she found a camera, which appeared to still have a film in it. Beneath the camera, she could see lots of mainly black and white photos and was soon absorbed in them. She had already seen some of them when she had visited Auntie Ann. Many were of people she didn't recognise.

Later she found some photos of her holidays in the

caravan. One photo showed her with Mum, Dad, and Michael. She couldn't remember who had taken the photo. Perhaps it had been someone else staying at the caravan park. She studied the photo carefully. Who did she take after? Michael had the unmistakable features of her father, his dark straight hair and pointed nose. She had freckles and curly auburn hair. She was perhaps a little like her mother but, however hard she stared at the picture, she somehow felt she didn't belong.

She had very few photos of the whole family, so she placed the picture carefully between the pages of her Bible, a gift from the Sunday school she used to attend as a child, and returned it to the bookcase. This piece of furniture had once held some of Ian's Great Aunt Amy's many books. It had a few scratches and woodworm marks but was still sturdy and a useful piece of furniture when they had set up home.

Rebecca's mood lightened when she found herself laughing at her own image in a ridiculous bathing suit and swimming cap. She also found a photo of Dad when he had bad sunburn one year. He looked extremely cross on the photo. Rebecca thought Mum had taken the photo to remind him on subsequent holidays of the importance of applying sun cream. Dad had claimed men didn't need sun cream until he had suffered. She found pictures taken on the beach and the spectacular sandcastles too.

Another box had photos of some of the village events and she found a picture of herself on a pony at the village fête. She found pictures of Elizabeth on a school trip. She looked so young. She was surrounded by school children laughing, some of whom Rebecca could recognise. One picture showed Elizabeth with a little girl holding what looked like a buttercup under Elizabeth's chin. She realised, on examining the picture more closely, that she was the little girl. She put the photo to one side, making a mental note to get a frame for the picture and to show it to Wilf. She couldn't remember the checked blue dress she was wearing in the picture, but she remembered the 'buttercup test'. If a yellow shade was visible on the skin when the buttercup was held beneath someone's chin, then they liked butter! A very scientific test! There were lots of animals in the background so it must have been the farm park trip.

There were also some dusty diaries in the box but Rebecca felt a little uneasy looking at them. She didn't know Mum kept a diary. She picked up one of them. Some pages had lots written on them, others were blank. She read odd remarks such as 'Rebecca's school fête' or 'evening shift at pub 6pm onwards'; nothing remarkable really. Then she noticed 'letter to C.D.' and 'happiest day of my life' and other comments which almost appeared in code.

Rebecca scanned through several diaries trying to piece together the odd clues, which seemed to be suggesting there was a part of her mother's life about which she knew nothing. 'Can't keep this up much longer' was written on one page, but nothing to explain it.

She glanced at the clock and realised it was already twelve noon. She would have another look at the jigsaw pieces of her mum's mystery life later. Perhaps Michael could make sense of it. It still didn't make sense to her. She felt quite tired now after the poor night's sleep and, pulling a rug over herself, soon fell asleep in the armchair, despite the many questions which were going through her head about her mother.

* * *

Charles eventually plucked up the courage to visit the Coddleton library and, with help from the librarian, finally had a copy of the edition of the local newspaper in front of him containing the report of Cynthia and husband Robert's car accident. There was a picture of a wrecked Mini. It was not surprising the couple had not survived the crash, looking at the mangled metal.

How ironic that Cynthia had been taken to the regional neurosurgery specialist centre at Appleby. If only he had known. She would have been lying in hospital, just a mile or so from his door... and he could have been with her, held her hand, seen her radiant face once more... Why hadn't he made contact with her, forced her to make a decision to leave her husband? Things could have been so different.

So that was it then. He had to forget Cynthia. But he kept thinking of the girl in the wedding photograph and wondering. Could she have been his child? He longed for a possible part of his love for Cynthia to have been preserved in a child with whom he could be reunited. However, even if the girl was his daughter, how could he cause her more hurt and anguish, entering her life now when it looked like she had found happiness? He felt so confused.

'Are you alright, sir?' asked Sandra, the librarian.

'Yes, thank you... and thank you for helping me find the article I was looking for.'

'You look wholly pale, if you don't mind me saying so.'

'I was a bit shocked reading about this family I met a while ago. I'm fine though, thanks.'

'OK. See you then.'

'Sorry, what do you mean?'

'Oh nothing, I'm just off for my lunch break.'

Charles checked the librarian's left hand as discreetly as he could and saw no evidence of a wedding ring. 'I don't suppose I could interest you in a coffee ... or snack for your lunch, could I? You've been so helpful to me today.'

'Well, I suppose I could... Yes, thank you.'

'That's great... sorry... um...'

'Sandra.'

'Pleased to meet you, Sandra. I'm Charles. Should we go

to the bakery in the street? I saw a small café there.'

'Yes that's fine, it's quite nice there,' agreed Sandra with a broad smile.

Charles couldn't quite believe his spontaneity in asking the young woman to spend her lunch break with him. He was glad he did though, and they enjoyed the hour chatting and arranged another meeting together at the weekend. Hopefully there would be something worth seeing at the cinema. Life might be looking up yet!

Sandra had enjoyed meeting the rather attractive man. He made a pleasant change from the little old ladies who were her usual customers asking for help to locate the latest sought after work of fiction, often a wartime romance.

* * *

Rebecca woke after about an hour and a half and forced herself to get up rather than give in to tiredness and doze for another hour or more. She wouldn't sleep tonight if she gave in to sleep now. She got up and made a cup of tea and a ham sandwich and cut a slice of tea bread, kindly brought for her by Kathleen a few days ago. She switched on the radio as it seemed so quiet on her own.

Rebecca picked up a black folder from the cardboard box and put it on the table next to her whilst she ate. She discovered some paperwork from the solicitor regarding her parents' deaths. There were copies of the death certificates. The first she looked at indicated her father died of multiple injuries sustained as a result of a road traffic accident. Her mother's listed a few contributory causes: head injury following road traffic accident, grade 2 astrocytoma causing probable seizure leading to RTA, secondary brain haemorrhage. Goodness, what did that all mean she wondered? She remembered being told her mother had a brain tumour... but Cynthia couldn't have known about it.

Rebecca tried to remember how her mother had been during the days prior to the accident. Nothing of any significance sprang to mind. She had complained of her usual headaches, that was all. Maybe now wasn't the right time to look at these boxes after all. Rebecca felt uneasy, images of her parents' coffins being lowered in to the deep graves came back to her. She needed to speak to Michael. Had he looked at these documents she wondered?

Rebecca felt she had more questions than answers about her parents' accident and deaths. She might look up 'astrocytoma' in the school library, but for now she placed the papers back in the folder and returned it to the box. The photos had been better to look at … the documents didn't seem to connect her to the life of her parents, and to think about their accident again was too traumatic just now. It magnified her feelings of loss.

So Rebecca got up and busied herself doing some hand washing, singing along to the songs she recognised on the radio. She knew she was singing out of tune but there was no music teacher reprimanding her here at home. She hadn't been accepted to join the school choir but was happy to have been rejected, as Miss Sharp was very strict with attendance at choir practice and her friends had been in trouble a few times when they had forgotten to attend lunchtime practice.

Rebecca wondered what Miss Sharp was doing now. Everyone thought she was aptly named due to her temperament and they were disappointed when she announced she was getting married and becoming Mrs Collins. She had left school and been replaced by a much quieter Miss Wood, who had made music a more popular subject again.

Rebecca had surprised herself going into teaching but gained a great deal of satisfaction from her work. She might have been influenced by Elizabeth, who always encouraged her to follow her dreams and praised her achievements, however small.

She had just finished removing the last of the washing from the spin drier and was hanging the woollen items on the airer when the door opened.

'I'm home, Rebecca.'

'So I see! How was work, Ian?'

'Fine. How are you feeling?' enquired Ian as he kissed her forehead.

'A bit better thanks, I managed to doze a little at lunchtime... well dozed probably too much.'

'That's good to hear, you need the rest, darling. I'm just going to get these books marked before teatime, if that's alright.'

'Of course.'

'What's for tea?'

'I thought I'd just make omelettes if that's alright. We've got plenty of eggs. I'm not feeling like anything too fancy. Goodness, I'm sounding like Wilf... nothing too fancy!'

'So long as you don't end up looking like him, I'll be OK! An omelette is fine by me. I must confess that I succumbed to school's hotpot and jam roly-poly with custard for pudding! Do you want a cup of tea?'

'Why not, if yew're making it, thanks, Ian. Yew'll be the one who looks like Wilf though, with a spare tyre around your middle, if yew keep eating school puddings!'

'I'll work it off when I play squash at the weekend. Clive from school challenged me to a game when we were in the staff room at break. What are all these things in this box?'

'Oh, some of Mum's things I've been looking through. I kept getting distracted by some old photographs.'

'Hope there are some embarrassing shots of you!'

'Of course, but yew're not seeing them now.'

'Later, when I've finished my work perhaps.'

'Perhaps. I was going to put these things away and tidy up.'

'Very secretive aren't you!'

* * *

Charles and Sandra had a lot in common and became very fond of one another. Sandra was quite shy and had found it hard to socialise, having moved to Coddleton quite recently with her parents. She was an only child and spent her spare time walking her dog, reading or sketching. She had considered joining the local art class advertised in the library, but couldn't pluck up the courage to join a big group of unfamiliar people. She had been engaged to her first boyfriend when she was only nineteen, but had called off their wedding plans, realising that she didn't really love Simon. He had later joined the Army and she hadn't seen him again.

Years had passed and she had never met anyone that she got on with but Charles was different. He was a little older than her but was a gentle caring sort and soon they fell in love. When he asked her to marry him she was a little taken aback but felt that this offer of marriage was definitely the right one. Her parents were delighted, after thinking they were going to have a spinster daughter at home till they were retired!

After the marriage and a wonderful honeymoon in Jersey, Sandra and Charles lived in Appleby in his flat till they moved to a bigger house locally, when Sandra announced that she was pregnant. A scan later revealed that she was expecting twins. Charles was so happy and couldn't help thinking that Cynthia had helped him find his 'Mrs Right' in the end.

He had decided not to pursue tracing Cynthia's daughter. Some things were best left alone and he couldn't be happier now. He had been promoted at work and was grateful that he only worked in Appleby. He was glad not to have to travel far and was able to spend time with his new family. His twin boys would ensure there was never a dull moment in the Dewhurst household!

His friends had been a great support to them both in the early days of parenthood and they took turns entertaining their friends and their families, which meant the house was often full of children of various ages. Having the twins, Sandra often felt it easier to offer to host the gathering of friends rather than get the boys ready and travel elsewhere. She was very happy with her new life and didn't miss her work in the library. Now she only had the children's many books to keep in order, which were invariably left on the floor or on a chair. Most of their friends' children were older so they were frequently given bags of toys and outgrown clothes to help them cope with the cost of raising two children. The passed-on play pen had proven particularly useful when Sandra needed to catch up on her chores and the boys usually were content to occupy themselves with the picture books and soft toys in the confines of the play area.

* * *

Wilf put a log on the fire and poured himself a cup of tea, having just got back from the graveyard. He had had a lot to tell Elizabeth today. He had told her about the lovely picture of her with Rebecca, now in a frame at Rebecca's cottage. He was going to have tea with Rebecca and Ian at the weekend. It was wonderful news that she was expecting a baby and all seemed to be going well this time.

Wilf had found himself in church one day when he had been down to the churchyard to check the flowers on Elizabeth's grave and update her with his news. He sat awkwardly in one of the pews and studied the large stained glass window in front of him depicting Christ suffering on the cross, and asked for a special request from God. He knew he wasn't good at attending church any more, now that he didn't have Elizabeth to encourage his attendance, but surely poor Rebecca had been through enough.

'Please God, watch over her and the baby and make sure all goes well an' all for them both. Yew took Elizabeth from me and that was hard, that it was… but losing both her parents at such a young age, that can't be right… and then to lose her first baby last year… Please Lord, see that all turns out well an' all… please.'

Wilf had lingered for over thirty minutes, sitting in the pew, taking in the details of the church he hadn't studied at such length before. This was probably one of the longest periods he had stayed awake in the church! He felt an air of calm and peacefulness around him and felt quite comforted by his moments of reflection alone.

He looked at the altar with the flowers in the polished brass vases and wondered if they received the same care and attention his late wife had given to them. Perhaps Elizabeth had felt the same comfort from her frequent time spent here.

He stood up finally, his limbs feeling a little stiff from sitting in the cold church, and knew he would come here again. Something… or someone would guide him back to his newly discovered sanctuary.

* * *

'We're getting there with this spare room. I'll put these boxes in the attic should I, Rebecca?'

'Yes please. I know we need the space in the nursery or will do soon! I didn't ever really sort anything out from Mum's boxes, but I suppose they will be there when I feel like taking a trip down memory lane.'

'You are a bit of a hoarder, aren't you?'

'I suppose I am. Some of my childhood is stored in those boxes and some of it I can't just remember or don't want to.

Oh by the way, I found my favourite story book – *Montgomery the Church Mouse*, in one of the boxes. I've put it on the bookshelf. It will be the first story we read to our baby!'

'She will grow up to be a bit of a bookworm then, will she?'

'Or *he*… Yes, of course. Well, with two teachers as parents, he or she will be born able to read!'

'Make way for the next child prodigy! Right, that's enough of your imagination running away with itself. Now go and get some rest. I'll clear away these other bits and pieces and then we can tell Michael we are ready to borrow the cot.'

'Great. I thought this day would never come.'

'Hey Rebecca, I love you so much, don't cry now. What's the matter?'

'I feel so tired and just want to get delivering this baby, so I can hold him and love him like I do yew. I've waited so long for this.'

'Or her.'

'What?'

'We might have a girl.'

'I know, I really don't mind, but come on baby, you need to come soon,' said Rebecca rubbing her tummy and then wiping her eyes with a handkerchief, one of her embroidered hankies she had used since her school days. 'It's funny, the ladies in the village keep predicting what sex our baby is by my shape! Elsie and Christine were still arguing the other day when I left them outside the shop. I think I will go and have a lie down now if yew don't mind. I am getting to be like my mum, after all, but at least I don't suffer with her headaches. I can't believe this boy of ours… or *girl* can make me so tired.'

'Of course I don't mind you having a lie down. The electric fire is still upstairs if you need some extra heat.'

'Thanks. I'd better start thinking of some girls' names then, since we've only decided on Philip if we have a boy.'

'Yes, and write your ideas down, so we can discuss it later. I think Amy would be nice… after my great aunt.'

'Maybe. We'll see.'

Finally, on October 1ˢᵗ, Rebecca went into labour and went in to the local hospital where she delivered a baby girl weighing 7lb 4oz. She was so delighted with the baby and felt she had finally found lasting happiness. Ian was delighted with their daughter and couldn't wait until Rebecca was allowed home after six days in the maternity ward.

Ian's mother, Marjorie, came to stay for a few days to help Rebecca with the new addition to the family. She tried to insist that her method of folding terry nappies was the correct one but eventually gave in to the 'new' way demonstrated at the hospital and by the visiting midwife.

Wilf came to visit Rebecca once she was home and was quite overcome with emotion.

'Hold her, Dad.'

'I can't, Rebecca, I'll drop her, she's so small an' all.'

'Yew'll be fine. Sit down in the armchair… here. Come on yew're a *grandad* now! One of your duties is to help me take care of her.'

'Oh, my word! Grandfather Wilf! Am I clean enough for the little mite?'

'Of course, you haven't been on the farm, have yew?'

'No, I s'pose not. Goodness… oh, how do I hold her?'

'That's fine, just support her little head.'

'She's bootiful that she is,' said Wilf, nervously cradling the little bundle wrapped in a soft pink blanket.

'She is the most beautiful baby I've ever seen! I still can't believe she's mine.'

'She has a bit of a frown on her; it must be me frightening her. Oh dear, she's crying, yew better have her back!'

'Probably hungry again!'

'There yew are, my booty, back to your mother. She's the best mother yew could hope for, that she is,' said Wilf as he passed his grandchild safely back to Rebecca and wiped his damp eyes.

'Cup of tea, Wilf?' called Marjorie from the kitchen.

'Oh yes, please. I'll come and keep yew company whilst Rebecca feeds this little mite.'

'Would you like a piece of my Victoria sponge cake too?'

'That I would… it looks good.'

'Well, from what Rebecca tells me you're a bit of a cook too, Wilf?'

'Oh what squit has she been running on abowt? Rebecca gave me a few cookery lessons when she was still at school. Let's just say some of my efforts were better than others!'

'He's being modest,' called Rebecca from the sitting room, feeding her daughter who sucked greedily at her breast.

'Well, there's nothing wrong with her hearing, that's for sure!'

'No you're right there Wilf. I'll just take this tea through for Rebecca; she needs plenty to drink. Won't be a minute. Sit down in this chair, it's a bit more comfortable than the dining chairs.'

'Thank yew kindly.'

'There you are, dear, I'll put the tea on this table so you can reach it when you are ready,' Marjorie said as she carefully placed a cup of tea near Rebecca.

'Oh thanks, Marjorie. Oh and you have found the best china!' remarked Rebecca as she took the cake and started to eat it.'

'Well, don't you think tea tastes so much nicer from a nice china teacup?'

'I suppose so… Mmmm, your cake is fantastic!'

'Looks like you need another piece!'

'Well, I am eating for two still really, with this little milk monster attached! I would love another piece please.'

'Just a minute then.'

'So Wilf, how are things with you?'

'Nicely thanks, Marjorie. This cake is good! I wholly miss Rebecca still… and of course my dear wife Elizabeth, that I dew. Life has had its ups and downs, but the last few years have been extr'ordinry. I never thought I would help take care of a young gal who would turn in to a capable young mother like Rebecca has done.'

'My Ian found a very special girl, that's for sure. You must be very proud Wilf.'

'That I am. Fancy them meeting in our village churchyard too!'

'Yes, it's not a place you would expect to meet your future husband or wife.'

'I met my Elizabeth in the village hall at a dance.'

'Oh yes, I remember you telling me at the wedding reception there.'

'I will never forget that evening, that I won't.'

'I met my Roger at work. It wasn't a romantic, "love at first sight" encounter like yours! Would you like another cuppa, Wilf?'

'Yes please, Marjorie. Yew mek a fine cup o'tea.'

'I'll just give this piece of cake to Rebecca.'

'She has always had a good appetite.'

'She's blaming our grandchild for it!'

'I hev been doing a bit of tricolating this week.'

'How do you mean, Wilf?'

'Decorating!' called Rebecca from the other room.

'Oh sorry, Wilf, I didn't know what you meant. Which room are you doing?'

'Our… *my* bedroom.'

'That's nice. What colour?'

'It's blue… nothing fancy, but it needed doing.'

'You do well to do it yourself. My Roger is not very good at decorating, so I usually get Walter Greenwood locally to help. He is very good, but always busy. You wait ages for him to fit you in, but he does a good job as I said. He has just decorated our spare room. Well, I thought the new baby might want to stay with Grandma soon!'

'Great... how about next weekend?'

'Gosh, she's soon learnt to talk!'

'Sounds like Rebecca needs a holiday, Marjorie!'

'Well, it will be lovely to have them all to stay. Perhaps you will all be able to join us for Christmas, Rebecca.'

'Goodness, well it will be here before we know it, won't it. You had better ask your son about that. Your first Christmas, Autumn, what about that,' said Rebecca gazing at her daughter's beautiful eyes which seemed to be fixed on hers. She then gently lifted her baby up and held her so she could rub her back until she eventually brought up some wind. 'Well done!'

'You didn't used to congratulate me if I belched after eating, Rebecca!'

'Of course not, but she will soon be taught her manners, Dad!'

'Right, Rebecca, I had better go. Nice to see yew and Autumn too, of course.'

'Bye, Dad. Call again soon. Don't forget your cap on the chair over there.'

'Righto. Don't forget I hev to take the car for its MOT tomorrow, hope it gets through alright. Malcolm Miles hed a look at it last week and done a bit of work on it.'

'Should be alright then, he's a good mechanic isn't he?'

'That he is. Bye, Marjorie, and thanks for the refreshment. I'll see yew again. Cheerio now.'

The next morning, Rebecca came downstairs looking rather weary.

'Morning, dear!'

'Morning... Mum,' Rebecca hesitated, still feeling uncomfortable addressing her mother-in-law as 'Mum'.

'You look rather tired, dear.'

'Yes, Autumn had several feeds last night and I can't

believe she has only just settled again to sleep now.'

'Poor you. I heard her a couple of times, but I soon got back to sleep. The camp bed is quite comfortable down here.'

'I'm glad we didn't disturb you too much.'

'Would you like me to run you a bath, dear?'

'Oh yes, please.'

'Here, there's a cup of tea for you. Sit down and drink that whilst I run that bath.'

'Thanks.'

'Perhaps we can wrap Autumn up well and take her for a walk later in the pram.'

'Oh, I'm not sure I have any energy left.'

'You look a little pale, Rebecca. Hope you are not anaemic. Shall I get some liver for your dinner today?'

'Oh liver! Um, well yes I suppose so. I haven't had liver for a long time.'

'Your iron stores are probably depleted, dear. Liver and onions it is then today! Perhaps you'll allow Grandma to take Autumn out in the pram then and you can have a rest this afternoon.'

'Of course.'

'I can't wait to show off my new granddaughter. The fresh air will do her good. Ian and his brother were always taken out in the pram, whatever the weather. Just wrap them up warm and they don't take any harm. She might sleep better at night too.'

'I hope so!' Rebecca was glad of the help she was getting from Ian's mum, but the cottage was rather small and she wasn't sure how long three adults and a baby would manage together. Ian was at work during the day, but space was a little cramped in the evenings. Wilf had told her many times that several families of six to eight whom he had known had grown up together in cottages of similar size. Luckily there was a small outbuilding where they kept logs for the fire and coal. Part of the building was just big enough to store the pram when not in use.

'Right, dear, the bath's run for you. I'll just nip to Coddleton to get the liver whilst Autumn is sleeping. She looks sound asleep when I just peeped in at her. The little darling.'

'Little darling aren't words I would have used last night!'

'Oh bless her, she's doing what all babies do! Anyway enjoy your bath. Is there anything else you need in Coddleton?'

'Another loaf of bread please. Oh, and would you mind getting some more sanitary towels for me, I am using plenty still.'

'Oh dear! Of course I will. I must say I'm glad that I don't need those anymore. Though the hot flushes were quite unpleasant whilst they lasted, it's still good to not need the Dr Whites!'

'There's some money in the pottery dish on the kitchen table.'

'Oh don't worry, we'll sort it out later. Now go and relax.'

'Don't go breaking the speed limit, we'll be fine for a little while!'

'I bet Ian has told you I got caught for speeding, has he?'

'Um, well yes, but I hadn't meant… well, what I was trying to say was don't rush, we'll be alright.'

'That's alright dear, but it won't take long will it? It's a shame everyone in the village has to go to Coddleton to get to a butcher's. I am so lucky having the supermarket within walking distance, though sometimes I forget and buy too much and curse carrying too many bags home. Anyway, see you later, dear.'

'Bye… Mum.'

Marjorie set off in her Ford Escort, which had a small dent at the rear, which she claimed someone did when she left the car in a car park a couple of months ago. She drove to Coddleton and called first at the pharmacy. Then she went to the butcher's. Arriving back at the cottage she found Rebecca dressed but asleep on her bed with the eiderdown over her. Marjorie tiptoed across to the nursery where Autumn was still asleep too. So she went back downstairs and unpacked the shopping and put the kettle on. Not long afterwards, Autumn could be heard murmuring and Rebecca woke from her dozing to attend to her.

'Oh you're back.'

'Only just dear. You managed a little nap?'

'Yes, after a nice bath. I am feeling a bit more human than earlier this morning. Look Autumn, Grandma's back.'

'Oh, come to Grandma!'

'Here you are.'

'Oh she's a beautiful baby, aren't you, darling? Yes you are.'

'Shall I make us some tea?'

'Oh yes, I put the kettle on just now and then started putting the shopping away.'

'Looks like you've been busy!'

'Well I passed the wool shop and thought I would knit Autumn some little woollies. She'll soon grow out of those two I brought you the way she's feeding! Look at this pattern, isn't it sweet?'

'Oh yes! I never got the hang of knitting, I'm afraid. It looks quite complicated.'

'Oh it's not too difficult and it will keep me occupied. These little cardies won't take long. I knitted an Arran sweater for Ian some years ago. Now that was hard work!'

'So long as he doesn't expect me to create one, I will be alright!'

'Shall I check this little bundle's bottom?'

'Please... if you don't mind.'

'Of course I don't mind. Come on Autumn, let's make you nice and comfy again then no doubt you'll want feeding won't you, my darling? Yes you will!'

'Shall we have a piece of cake too?'

'Not for me, Rebecca, but you carry on. Perhaps I had better do some baking for you later.'

'Thank yew. I'm sorry we've nearly finished this sponge cake already! I just can't stop nibbling and your cakes are very good.'

'Well, we are also feeding all of Autumn's admirers who come and visit her, aren't we?'

'Yes, that's true. Here's your tea. I'll just start my tea and cake whilst you finish nappy duty!'

'We're nearly done, aren't we, my darling? Oh I think Grandma just got a beautiful smile, didn't she?'

Rebecca smiled to herself, wondering if her mum had spoken to her like that when she had been a baby. She also wondered who might have helped her mum when she was a baby. She should have asked Auntie Ann all these things. She would have to write her a letter soon anyway to thank her for the baby clothes she had sent her when Autumn was born.

Everyone had been so kind, even people in the village whom she didn't know that well had arrived with little bootees and scratch mitts, bibs and rattles. Wilf must have spread the word that his 'granddaughter' had arrived. Elsie had delivered a pink bonnet and mittens which she had knitted, proudly declaring, 'Well, I knew it was a girl!'

Christine had to admit her prediction of a boy was wrong and had to hide the blue cardigan which she had knitted in advance and hurriedly started a white shawl! No doubt someone else in the village would produce a boy before long!

Rebecca soon established a routine with her baby and was very content living in her little cottage with a husband she adored and a beautiful baby. She felt her life had finally settled into near perfection and she was very thankful for all those who had helped her reach this experience. She might return to teaching once Autumn was older, but was in no hurry. She missed her work at times but was kept too busy at home to get bored.

Wilf regularly had meals with her and occasionally would cook for her too. His favourite meal he produced was his hearty stew complete with 'taters' from his garden and perhaps a spring cabbage. Sometimes he would add some dumplings too. The smell of his stews would greet Rebecca, Ian and young Autumn at his door over the coming years. Wilf was not adventurous with his cooking, but always had apples to 'stew', pears or rhubarb from the garden depending on what was in season. Rebecca would sometimes make some pastry for a fruit pie, or sponge mixture for an Eve's pudding, whilst Wilf finished preparing the vegetables, to add some variation to the pudding on offer.

It was strange being back in the kitchen where she had learnt to cook with Elizabeth, had later discussed cooking with Wilf, had lived for a few years and now was back as a visitor with a family of her own. Maybe Autumn would soon have her first cookery lessons here!

Wilf had sometimes found himself daydreaming when Rebecca was laying the table for dinner. She would be spreading the same red gingham tablecloth which Elizabeth had used for many years, now fraying at the edges. How he wished Elizabeth was here to enjoy the company of Rebecca and her family.

Ian and Rebecca had helped Wilf decorate and tile his bathroom, which was a great improvement. Wilf even agreed to get new lino and curtains. He had to agree when the work was complete that his new green bathroom was a vast improvement, though he wondered if Elizabeth would have chosen that colour.

Wilf seemed to age slowly and was determined to continue riding his old bicycle. He spent lots of time in his garden still and also in front of his companion, the television. He eventually got a telephone, but much preferred to visit

Rebecca rather than speak in to the 'contraption'.

* * *

'Dad, hello, it's Rebecca!'

'Hullo, is anything wrong?'

'No, not at all. I just thought I would ring and tell you that Michael and Julie have finally set a date for their wedding. It's June 14th at Coddleton registry office.

'Oh I see, that's good.'

'Put it on your calendar.'

'I will right away! What time will it be?'

'Twelve noon. Afterwards we are all going back to the pub in the village where there'll be a buffet.'

'Am I invited then?'

'Of course you are! There won't be too many there, just the close family and a few of Michael and Julie's friends. Mrs Potter has offered to make the wedding cake, which is kind of her.'

'Talking of weddings, hev yew heard that Doctor Stimpson is getting married?'

'No, I hadn't. That's nice. I've met his fiancée Sharon a few times. She's a midwife at the hospital.'

'Tha's right. Oh, and did yew see *Opportunity Knocks* last night?'

'No, why?'

'There was a young gal on who sang bootifully that she did and she was only twelve. She went on to win! Oh she was good.'

'I don't know what yew would do without your telly now! Anyway, I had better go, Autumn wants to go outside to play. She's just watching *Playschool* at the moment.'

'Alright then and I'm glad Michael finally got round to it! Cheerio.'

'Cheerio, Dad. Autumn is saying bye-bye here too!'

'Cheerio, my booty.'

* * *

'What's for tea, Mum, I'm starving?'

'Shepherd's pie, Rebecca. The mince is in the oven. Can you just help me finish peeling these potatoes and cut them up small so they cook quickly? I must get this electricity bill paid. I've had a reminder today that it's overdue. I'll just quickly go to the post office and get a postal order and I should catch the post if I hurry.'

'Alright, Mum. Oh I'm tired! I have just had double history, it was so boring!'

'History was never my favourite either. Now where's my bag?'

'It's under your jacket there isn't it?'

'Oh, yes, thanks. See yew soon.'

'Yeah, I'll just have to nibble a biscuit or two to keep me going till tea. Can you buy some more biscuits, there's only two left in the tin?'

'Oh, Rebecca! You'll look like a biscuit, the amount yew get through.'

'A garibaldi, I guess, with these spots!'

'Are yew a daydreamin', Rebecca?'

'What?'

'You've been mashing those potatoes for ages! What's for tea?'

'Shepherd's pie. I was just thinking of my mum making this. It was a regular fixture on the Masons' menu!'

'Same on the Matthews' menu too!'

'By the way, yew are starting to get a Norfolk accent, the way yew said "yew a daydreaming" before!'

'It's difficult not to when I'm teaching classfulls of you Norfolk dumplings!'

'Cheeky!'

'Daddy!' cried Autumn as she rushed in to the kitchen.

'Hello, Autumn, that's a lovely hug! How's Daddy's special little girl?'

'Good... Mummy says I've been good!'

'Are you looking forward to tomorrow?'

'Yes, yes, yes! Mummy, I'm hungry.'

'Well go and wash your hands dear and how about yew look at *Montgomery the Church Mouse* with Daddy whilst I finish cooking your tea.'

'Alright. Where did we leave Montgomewi, Daddy?'

'Montgome*ry*, dear. Is it in your bedroom still?'

'Not sure.'

'Try and find it whilst I just finish my cup of tea.'

'OK Daddy,' Autumn replied as she rushed off to find the book.

'I'll miss her when she's at school,' sighed Rebecca.

'Well I'm sure the day will fly past... and you could always sort those things of your Mum's you keep putting off doing. I can get the boxes down from the attic if you like.'

'Oh yes, I could... but I will probably get sidetracked with the photos again.'

'Shame Michael didn't supply some of those for me for our wedding night! I bet there are some embarrassing ones of you.'

'Yes plenty!'

* * *

Wilf put the last of Elizabeth's clothes from the drawers in the bags. It still felt wrong to get rid of them but he had finally done it and Kathleen would take them for the jumble sale at Coddleton Secondary School at the weekend. She had asked Wilf a few times if he had any old clothes for the sale, suspecting her sister's clothes were still in the drawers several years after her death. He also put her handbag in the bag, having emptied it of the personal effects which he had put in a box and then placed it in the cupboard under the stairs.

Wilf then put some of his own clothing in the newly emptied drawers, trying to mask his own feelings of emptiness he now felt again. He decided to put two old shirts of his in the jumble bag as he didn't wear them anymore and it felt right to put some of his own things with Elizabeth's.

He sighed heavily and decided to make a cup of tea and see what was on the telly. As he turned on the kettle, he looked around the kitchen and decided he ought to paint it soon. Cream coloured paint would be alright again, although no doubt Rebecca might have other ideas. Soon Autumn might tell him what she thought too of his home. Bless her, she was such a lovely little girl and already reminded him of the little girl who had spent time with Elizabeth baking or following her round the garden, holding pegs to help with the washing being pegged out on the line, or trying to help with some of the other housework.

Autumn had loved starting school and had started just half days initially for the first week. Wilf had bought her some sweets as a treat after her first morning when she had rushed in later to see him with Rebecca and told him all about her school and teacher. She had brought Wilf a picture she had drawn at school and Wilf immediately said, 'Wull that's very good, that it is, my dear. Let's put it on the wall here next to Elizabeth. This is where your Mummy had her pictures when she was a little girl!'

Autumn beamed with pride at her picture. She said it was her outside the school but it was hard to tell what it depicted without her explanation.

* * *

'Autumn, dear, dry your eyes darling, yew'll be alright now.

Let's clean up that graze and find yew a plaster for your knee… There now, that's better.'

'Yes, Mummy.'

'Right then, will yew be alright for your second full day at school?' asked Rebecca of her beautiful daughter, Autumn, who had curly auburn hair, and dark brown eyes moistened by the recent tears.

'Think so, Mummy.'

'Great, yew are a brave girl. Now be careful this time on the path; those damp leaves have made it slippery.'

'I need to take some leaves for Miss Price. We have to find lots of coloured leaves.'

'For the nature table?'

'Yes.'

'Well that shouldn't be difficult in our garden at the moment. Here, take this paper bag to collect some. Grandad Ford's wife used to help with the nature table when I was at school. Don't be long, we need to set off for school soon. We could collect some more in the wood later if you like but yew may be tired after school so we'll see. Ooooh, Autumn, that baby in Mummy's tummy has just given me a big kick! Bet it's a baby brother with a kick like that!'

'I don't want a brother… I hate boys! I want a sister.'

'Now then, young lady! We'll love whatever we're given. Don't forget Uncle Michael is my brother. I can't complain about him being my brother, even if I did when I was younger! Those leaves are lovely, look at the colours. Come on we must get to school now. Here, let's zip up that coat for yew, There's a chill in the air this morning.'

…and from the ashes
a sapling grew,
another fragile new life
cautiously pushed through the earth
reaching for the light;
unsure who had firmed its roots
clinging on to its existence
and searching for those
who would sustain it.

Lightning Source UK Ltd.
Milton Keynes UK
UKOW06f2258230315

248363UK00007B/178/P

9 781908 098443